BURN

RUTH CLAMPETT

L.A. Untamed Series Book 2

To Christine,

Thank you for your
support :) keep the fire of
passion burning

♥ Ruth Clampett

Cover Design:
Jada D'Lee
www.jadadleedesigns.com
Cover Photograph: Luis Rafael
Cover Model: Jay Amato

Content Editor:
Angela Borda

Copy Editor:
Melissa of There For You Editing
www.thereforyoumelissa.wix.com/there-for-you

Interior formatting:
Christine Borgford of Perfectly Publishable
www.perfectlypublishable.com

My Grandma Dossie was

the toughest woman I've ever known.

This story is dedicated to her

and all the badass women in my life.

Women of strength and courage

leave their mark in many ways.

They've inspired this story.

Chapter 1: The Reign of T. Rex

The truth will set you free, but first it will piss you off.

~ Gloria Steinem

Cutting the crotches out of my husband's pants is harder than you'd think. The dress slacks were okay after I'd sharpened the scissors, but now that I've worked my way to his jeans, my hands are getting numb.

Rage can do funny things to you. It can tear you apart, or if you take control of it, it can calm you down and give you an unfiltered, laser focus. Now as I sit on the floor of my bedroom surrounded by the contents of my husband's side of the closet, I'm eerily serene.

I have given myself a task, the first of undoubtedly many which will extricate Mikey out of my heart and home. I set the scissors I've been gripping down for a minute to rub the cramp out of my hand.

The irritating thing is that the bastard always looked exactly the same no matter what he wore. *Why the hell did he need so many pairs of pants?*

"Lying asshole," I repeat under my breath with each snip of the scissors. I toss his favorite jeans, now crotchless, to the other side of the room.

The sage green walls of our bedroom suddenly take on the sickly pallor of a hospital ward. My gaze scans the room full of trendy furniture that Mikey dragged me up and down hip Beverly Boulevard in West Hollywood to find.

What a colossal waste of time those weekends were as he tried teaching me about mid-century design versus regency style, which he haughtily claimed to prefer.

At this moment I sorely wish I had an ax in the garage so I could re-style all this pretentious crap too.

I hear a door open and close, but refusing to get distracted, I unfold the next pair of jeans in the pile.

"Trisha?"

I brush my hair off my sweaty forehead with one hand as my fingers from the other hand tighten over the scissors. Then I hear a woman's voice echo the man's.

"Trish!"

Elle and my brother, Paul. I let out my breath with a huff.

"In here," I call out.

They tumble into the bedroom with my other brother, Patrick right behind them. I'm strangely relieved to see them. It's like a mod squad's here to save me . . . well, a squad with two mods and a well-meaning geek.

"You got here fast," I say.

"Well, you were screaming in the phone . . . we were freaked out," Patrick explains.

"I'm still freaked out," Paul says, gesturing to the ravaged pants all over the floor.

Elle studies the fabric wreckage and looks up with an expression brimming with intrigue. "Whatcha doing?" she asks with a lilt to her voice, apparently trying to keep things light.

Good luck with that one, sister.

"Altering my soon-to-be-ex-husband's clothes. And for the record, he's now going to be referred to as dickwad or asshole, not Mikey."

Paul nods at my response, his eyes widening as he takes in the spoils of my fury.

"You call that altering?"

"Paul," Elle whispers as she gestures toward me. "She's got sharp scissors."

He takes a step back.

I nod as I wave my scissors at him. "Yeah, watch out for the crazy, enraged woman."

Patrick steps forward and drops down to his knees, so we're eye to eye. "What happened, Trisha?" he asks in a gentle voice like he's addressing a toddler on the verge of a meltdown.

My gaze shifts to Paul, who is dragging his fingers through his hair, and Elle who's tapping her finger on her chin as she watches me.

It's all so humiliating but there's no point beating around the bush. The truth will have to come out eventually. I clear my throat. "I dropped by the shop after dinner and became an unwilling witness to Mike being violated by Sasquatch."

"Oh my God!" exclaims Elle.

Brave Patrick crawls several feet toward me. "Trisha, you know Sasquatch is a fictional creature, right? Did you forget to wear your contacts today or something?"

"I know what I saw!" I yell at the top of my lungs. The trio leans back like a fierce wind is about to topple them.

"And you saw Sasquatch?" Paul asks, clearly playing along to placate me. "What was said Sasquatch wearing?"

"Sasquatch doesn't wear clothes," Patrick says in his accountant voice.

"You guys are idiots. I don't mean literally Sasquatch! It was the flower shop manager, Stanley. You've met him. He's the tall, husky one who's sporting what I'd consider a fur coat of body hair."

"That big dude with the black curly hair and beard?" Paul asks.

I nod with a grimace. "He even has that fur covering his ass."

"How do you know?" Patrick's eyes are wide with

shock.

I wave my scissors in the air dramatically and snap them open and closed. "I know because his jeans were around his ankles while he had Mike pinned down over the work table in the back room!"

The color drains from Paul's face and the room goes silent so I snap my scissors again. "I thought he was being violated. I mean, he was yelling out foul words and pounding his fists on the table."

"Oh good God," exclaims Elle. "What did you do?"

"What any good wife would . . . I grabbed the nearest weapon, which in this case was a heavy oversized crystal vase, and lifted it to smash it down over Stanley's head."

"Did you split his head open?" Patrick asks.

"I wish. No, as I charged forward I heard something that stopped me in my tracks."

They wait silently for me to continue and I take a deep breath.

"Mike was begging . . . well, I can't repeat it, but it was clear the violation was consensual."

"Oh, Trisha, I can't even imagine . . ." Elle sinks down to her knees next to Patrick.

"Don't even try to imagine it. It was horrible, and now I can't unsee what I saw."

"What happened then?" Patrick asks.

"I lost my grip on the vase and it exploded when it hit the cement floor. That sure slowed them down."

Paul lifts his hands up in the air and takes a step back. "Wait a minute . . . wait a minute. Dickwad Mike is gay?"

Elle turns toward him. "Bi, you mean."

He ignores her attempt at being politically correct. "Imagine that . . . holy stereotyping! Your florist husband who loves to decorate, and is a gourmet cook, is gay?"

"Ironic, isn't it?" Patrick chimes in.

Paul slaps the doorjamb and curses. "I've defended that fucker a thousand times from being called gay. Oh holy hell, wait 'til Dad hears about this."

"The issue here isn't just his being gay, it's that he's a low-life cheater," Elle points out.

I look down and jab the scissors into the crotch of a pair of dress slacks as I blink back the tears stinging my eyes. I may be a badass, but even I have my limits. My heart feels like it's hollowed out and will never be full again. Mike had been my savior at one point in my life, and now he's a complete traitor.

I was a wife and a lover, and now I'm a statistic. I feel like I've been discarded, my insides dusted with the blackest soot.

"Did you see this coming . . . any signs?" Patrick inquires.

I shake my head and return my focus to stabbing the pants over and over and over as my vision blurs with tears.

I have a vague sense of Elle crawling closer to me and I feel her hand lower over mine to still me. When I let out a wail, she gently wiggles the scissors out of my grip and hands them to Paul. Next thing I know she's pulled me into her arms.

"I'm sorry, Trisha," she murmurs over and over. "I'm so sorry."

As she rocks me I allow myself to be comforted and the thought passes through my head that who knows when I'll be held again. The tears start flowing faster and I bury my head into her shoulder.

In this haze, I hear Paul swear, "Oh hell no!" and stomp out of the room.

"Darn," Patrick curses as he gets up off the floor and follows him.

"What?" I pull away from Elle and study her. Her head

is tilted toward the hall like she's trying to hear something in the distance.

She holds her index finger across her lips to quiet me. "He's here."

"Mike?" I say between gritted teeth. My inner battle begins whether to go after him with something more threatening than a crystal vase, or to hide and trust that my brothers will make sure he leaves less gracefully than he entered.

"Paul has the scissors?" I ask, a spark of evil surging through me.

Elle nods. She leans toward the door and then turns back to me. "He's telling him to leave."

"I hope he kicks his ass," I whisper.

"Me too," she agrees.

There's a flurry of sounds from the hallway. My stomach tightens as I cross my arms across my chest protectively.

"Trish!" Mike yells out as he lunges out of Paul's grip and into our bedroom—or what used to be *our* bedroom. Now it's the tomb of shame.

"Get the hell out of here," I growl, not even recognizing my own voice. I can't help but notice that his face is red as a beet and his eyes are bugging out like a crazy man.

Patrick starts jabbing his finger at Dickwad, and his eyes narrow and his jaw locks. "Do you have any idea how punitive cheating is in divorce proceedings? Before you dropped your drawers did you even consider the tax implications and lifestyle adjustments that will occur when your assets are split?"

Dickwad looks at Patrick like he's crazy and then focuses back on me.

"Trish, we need to talk!" His voice is raspy and breathless, possibly due to the fact that Paul is trying to drag him out of the room by the back of his shirt, and the collar is hiked so high on his throat that it's choking him.

"Talk about what? That our entire marriage is a sham and you're a cheating bastard?"

"It's not a sham, Trish. You know I love you."

"Do you know what I know? I know the look on your face when you were taking it up the ass."

Elle gasps, and Patrick sputters something between a cough and a gag. I can't blame him, I want to gag too.

"Can we please talk privately?" His begging tone is pissing me off. He finally looks down at the pile of pants strewn all around me, and his mouth drops open. "Hey, what are you doing to my pants?"

"I'm altering them." I hold up the pair of jeans I just hacked up with the scissors. "Look, they're chaps! I hear you gay guys like to wear chaps."

"Oh for the love of God, Trisha," he moans. "Please, can we just talk privately?"

"Anything you have to say, my family can hear."

"What you saw was a mistake. A horrible mistake."

Paul eye's narrow, his hands clenched into fists. "So you're saying that was the first and only time you and Stanley—"

"No, I'm not saying that. I'm saying it's a mistake!"

"Well infidelity is more than a mistake, it's a violation," Patrick states.

I shake a fist at Mike. "Yes, I've been violated!"

"And your vague statements are making me think you've done this repeatedly," Elle says to him, her fists pressed down on her hips.

It's a good thing I'm not still holding the scissors because as soon as I see the sheepish look on Mike's face, I know the truth and the truth makes me want to cut more than the crotches out of his pants.

The calm serene stage of my rage is over. As I scramble to get up to find another weapon, I let out a feral howl the likes of which I've never heard. It scares everyone including me, and my legs get tangled in the web of ravaged pants. I fall back down on my ass, but before I hit the floor my head clips the corner of the dresser.

"Get out . . . Out . . . *Out!*" I scream. The last thing I see before the room goes black is Paul and Patrick dragging Mike down the hall.

Chapter 2: Thin Walls & Swedish Meatballs

When you have no problems, you're dead.

~ Zelda Werner

Three weeks later . . .

The muffled moans from down the hall are killing me. I'm pretty sure Elle and Paul have no idea how the paper thin walls and shared heating vents provide stereo sound for their impressive marathons between the sheets. I flip over in bed and pull the pillow up on the sides to cover my ears. *Do these two ever stop fucking? They're like a couple of amped up rabbits.*

When they brought me to their place to stay the night my marriage ended, I should've realized that a sex-addict and nymphomaniac wouldn't make ideal housemates. All I knew was that I couldn't stay another moment in the house I had shared with my cheating husband.

I hear a squeal that even the pillow can't muffle. What the hell? Sitting up, I glance at the clock—4 a.m. And to think I heard them going at midnight when I slipped into bed.

One time Paul told me that he steadfastly refused to sleep with Elle for months, until he knew they were in a committed relationship. I didn't honestly think the former man-whore had that kind of restraint in him, but he proved me wrong. So apparently now they will forever be making up for lost time between the sheets.

The next morning I'm slow getting up. I rub my eyes, wander into the kitchen to grab some coffee, and search out Elle. I know Paul's at work already, but I find Elle typing away in her office. She's dressed up like she's going to work, with her long hair pulled back with a fancy barrette and make-up on.

"Hey, sleepyhead," she says, then waves to the chair. "Have a seat, I'm almost done with this email."

I settle down and sip my coffee as my gaze wanders across the walls of the den. There's a striking framed black-and-white print of Elle and Paul on a bridge I hadn't noticed before. "Where's that?"

Elle glances up to where I'm pointing. "Huntington Garden in Pasadena. Paul had it done for Valentine's Day."

I shake my head. "Who knew that the big lug was such a romantic?'

She smiles. "He's pretty great."

"Can I ask you something personal?"

"Sure, anything," Elle replies, scooting her desk chair closer to me.

"How important do you think sex is in a relationship?"

"Sex?" she asks with wide eyes.

I guess she wasn't expecting that from me first thing in the morning.

"Yeah, sex . . . well like great sex. After sleeping in the room down the hall from you guys for three weeks, it's apparent to me that it's pretty important to the two of you."

"Oh God," she moans, slapping her hand over her eyes.

"But do you think it's critical to a relationship working?"

She sits up straight like she's at a business meeting. "Are you asking because of what happened with Mike?"

"That's part of it. He left me a message last night begging me to give him another chance. It broke my heart, and on the third listen I almost caved and called him, but all I could think of was why would he want that if he desires men? And why would I want that? I don't want a cheater. As it is, I'd never want to sleep with him again."

"I understand. It's hard for me to imagine you taking him back, honestly."

"I don't even trust my instincts anymore. Do you know that I've only slept with two guys, and the experiences with both of them were messed up?"

"Paul told me about your college boyfriend, Sam. He said he turned out to be an asshole."

I nod. "He did. But Paul only knows the half of it. Sam was abusive."

Elle's expression falls. "Oh, Trisha, I had no idea."

"He was a real hot-head and so am I, so we used to argue a lot. As time went on, when we'd fight, if it got heated enough, he'd shove me against a wall, or pin me down. He even hit me a few times."

"Asshole," Elle snaps with gritted teeth.

"Oh believe me, I hit him back but that only made things worse. It was crazy. Three times I broke up with him, and he promised he'd change. It was my first real relationship, and I thought maybe I was doing something wrong . . . I know I'm not the easiest person to deal with. So I'd give him another chance."

"Paul said that he also left you when you thought you were pregnant. Is that right?"

"Yes, and the asshole asked me to take him back after he found out I wasn't pregnant after all, but I'd finally come to my senses and was completely done."

"Good for you," Elle says.

"But then one night he showed up on my doorstep to pick up something he'd left at my place. I was an idiot to let him in. He'd been drinking and he kept trying to pick a fight and I refused to take the bait. So then he . . ." Pausing, I fold my arms over my chest and look down.

"Oh no," Elle whispers.

I nod and when the memory hits me I close my eyes for a moment to regain my focus. "He didn't just hit me that time. . . ."

"He raped you?" Elle says. Even though I'm not looking at her I can hear the rage in her voice.

"He did. And I didn't think that could happen with someone you had once loved. It wrecked me. It took me a long time to get back on my feet."

"Of course."

"At the end of that year I met Mike and he ended up being my savior—he made me feel protected. It was healing for me at first after what Sam did to me, but then after a while having a passive sex partner, who wanted me to take the lead in the bedroom, got old. It was so confusing to me. Truth be told, I'd like a man to be a man. Is that too much to ask?"

Elle leans forward with a determined look. "No it's not too much to ask. You deserve that kind of passion."

"So you can see that in my only two relationships, sex was a failure. How can I help but think it's me? What if it never gets better? Maybe I just bring out the worst in men."

"That's not it, Trisha. It's about finding the right person. For most of my first marriage, the sex with my ex-husband wasn't good at all. So it makes me appreciate what Paul and I have all the more."

"I guess, but how will I meet the right guy? I've been told that I'm attractive, but I've never dated much. I think I scare a lot of guys. And frankly if they can't handle a strong woman, what would I want with them?"

"You need a real man, Trish. You've gotten through two wrong relationships and now you know what you need.

So what I want is for you to start believing you deserve it. Okay?"

I study Elle and it hits me that she genuinely wants what's best for me. And although she and I are pretty different, she's become the sister I never had.

I give her a confident nod. "I promise I'll try."

The next morning at breakfast, I let Paul and Elle know I'm feeling more grounded and I'm ready to move back home.

"Are you sure?" Paul asks, trying to hide the relief he must be feeling. Watching his sister crying into her soup every night is probably getting old.

"I can stay there with you tonight, if it'd help," Elle offers.

I shake my head. "That's really nice of you, Elle, but I've got to face it and move on. I already told Mike to take his crap out of the house, so being there is going to feel different anyway, and that's probably good."

Paul scratches the back of his neck. "Wasn't *all* that fancy furniture and stuff Mike's?"

I nod. "And good riddance to it. I never liked his stuff. I don't really need much furniture. Just a bed, and maybe a table and chair."

Elle glances over at Paul alarmed.

She puts her hands on her hips. "I'm coming by after my morning meeting. Will you be there?"

"Yeah, I'm not scheduled back at the station until Thursday."

The minute I walk into the house, I realize that Mike took my direction to get his stuff out of the house, and apparently he ran with it. I know I threatened to drag all his stuff out to the driveway for a deeply discounted yard sale, but this is ridiculous.

Asshole. Maybe he was afraid I'd cut holes in everything.

The place is cleaned out. The living room is empty other than a side table, desk chair without the desk, and a small landscape painting on the far wall that belonged to my namesake, Nanna Pat.

The fragmented room is so ridiculous looking that I laugh out loud.

The rest of the house isn't much better. The dining room is empty and all that's left in the bedroom is the new firm mattress I bought last year when I couldn't take his old soft one any more. I peek in the closet to see if he altered my clothes but everything appears untouched and sad. Seeing his side of the closet and his bathroom drawers empty stings.

For some reason that's what makes me feel more empty than anything. I used to smell his aftershave if I got home while he was still at work, and it made me long for him. Now there's no aftershave, and no Mikey. I realize that I long for the man I thought Mike was, not the disappointment he turned out to be.

Sinking down on the corner of the mattress in the bedroom, I cry fat tears so full of anger and loss that they feel heavy on my cheeks.

"Mikey," I whisper in between my heaving and gasps for breath, folded over like a broken toy.

I'm finally starting to get tired of listening to myself sob when I hear Elle calling out for me.

I hear her footsteps pause in the living room. "What the hell!" she howls.

Next thing I know she storms into the bedroom and gasps when her gaze scans the room, finally landing on my sorry face.

She gestures to the empty walls and then points to the living room. "Are you fucking serious? Where's the bastard? I'm going to kill him."

"Go ahead," I mutter.

"What was he thinking?" she yells, and then steps back with an alarmed expression. She continues on with a much softer tone. "Sorry, I'm just so pissed off! He's left you nothing."

"I told him to take it. I don't want his stuff, Elle. I never liked it anyway. It was a big deal to him, so I let him do what he wanted in the house."

She stares at me like I'm an alien, or that I've got horns growing out of my head. I guess I shouldn't be surprised. Judging from her place, she really likes home design. Folding her arms over her chest, she regards the room like she's making a list in her head.

"Besides, I'm glad it's gone. I needed it to be gone."

"Okay, but I'm taking you shopping tomorrow," she says with such command, that I'm hesitant to disagree with her.

"It's really not necessary—"

She juts her hand out like a traffic cop. "This isn't up for debate. We'll start at Restoration Hardware, their new home store is very chic."

I shake my head.

"Pottery Barn?" she asks, with a hopeful look.

"Ikea," I reply, sitting up straighter. "And only if we can have lunch there. I love those Swedish meatballs."

She rolls her eyes. "Okay, but we'll have to take your truck since they don't deliver."

I nod. "Deal."

Chapter 3: The Gentle Giant

The most courageous act is still to think for yourself... Aloud.
~Coco Chanel

I'm at the station with the guys trying to wind down from our last call. We thought it was a straight-forward kitchen fire, but it ended up something much messier. When our truck pulled up a couple was screaming at each other and the woman was holding a frying pan like a weapon.

Fires or accidents caused by domestic disputes are my least favorite response. We can put out a fire but we can't fix what's broken inside. No one ever wins in a domestic dispute.

I'm drained from the call but for some reason, our dramatic evening creates fodder for this group of goofballs.

"I was kind of hoping she'd nail that dude with the frying plan," Scott says.

Bradley, also known as Bobo, shakes his head. "Someone needed to gag that woman. She didn't shut up the whole time we were there."

"Really? Gag her? Shut your trap, Bobo," I snap.

He turns to me with narrow eyes. "Screw you, T. Rex."

Glaring at him, I stand up and step away from the table. The guys think I hate my nickname, and as a result they'll never stop using it. What they don't know is that I think T. Rex is a lot more badass than Trisha, and badass is my middle name.

"Where you going?" Bobo asks.

"The bathroom. Got a problem with that?" I stalk out the door before he can reply.

"I'm halfway down the hall when I hear Joe's deep voice, and I stop in my tracks and edge back toward the door. Our work schedules are rarely in sync, so I'm not around him that much. I'm curious what he's going to say.

"Why don't you lay off her, man," he says.

"T. Rex?" Bobo asks.

"Her name's Trisha."

My breath hitches. I never thought Joe paid much attention to me. Why is he defending me?

"Yeah, give her a break, Bobo. Her marriage just fell apart," Scott states.

"Is it true that she walked in on him with a dude?" Jim asks.

I hear several groans, and my head drops with the sting of humiliation. I press my back into the wall I'm leaning against.

"That's some fucked-up shit," Bobo mutters.

"So give her a break." Joe's commanding tone gives me comfort. From what I've heard, no one ever challenges him. There's something about him that demands respect, and not just because he's lieutenant.

"Yeah, sure, Joe. Whatever."

Taking a deep breath, I continue down the hall. The rest of the night I keep thinking about Joe defending me.

I'm keeping to myself the next day when Joe calls me into the office. I follow behind him into the room feeling not just nervous, but small in every way. The man is well over six feet and standing next to him makes me feel like a miniature person.

Once I'm seated, he shuts the door so quietly I don't even hear the latch catch. He's a gentle giant and I can't help but study his every gesture. It's a relief to be focused on anything other than the endless empty ache inside of me.

"How tall are you anyway?" I ask as he slowly lowers himself into the desk chair.

He runs his thumb around his angular jaw. "Six-five. Why?"

I shrug. "Just wondering."

His gaze scans over me like he's sizing me up. "How tall are you?"

"Five seven. Not like I'm short or anything."

One of his eyebrows arcs up. "No, nothing small about you, Trisha."

"Thanks . . . I guess." I give him a weak smile as I twist my hands together. "So what's up? Am I in trouble or something?"

He slowly drags his large fingertips across the surface of the desk. "No, you're not in trouble. It's just Chief and I were talking and wondering if you could use some time off."

I fold my arms over my chest. "Because?"

He looks me straight in the eyes, with unwavering focus. "Because as I understand it you've just been through rough stuff at home, and—"

I cut him off. "Rough stuff?"

He clears his throat and his gaze makes me squirm.

"Why are you talking to me about this and not Chief?" I ask.

"Because he knows that I've been through something . . . well, let's just say that I can relate to what you're going through."

"Oh," I say quietly.

I study my surroundings in more detail while I wait for him to speak again. There's a faint smell of lemon furniture polish. The vibe in the office is type-A all the way—every paper, manual, and pencil in its place.

The silence is making me twitchy so I speak up. "Am I not doing my job? Am I causing problems around here?"

"You're doing your job fine. As for problems, no more than usual." He smiles, and it's such a small smile for a big man that I can't help but smile back.

"I know, I know. My parents always told me I was a handful."

His smile gets a little bigger. "Well, I think you're all right."

"Thanks."

"So what do you think? Do you want some time off?"

"No way. Actually, can I get more hours? It's really lonely at home, and it helps being here, having stuff to do. I helped wash the trucks this morning and it wasn't even my turn."

"Okay then. I'll tell the Chief you want to be put on double duty."

"Hey, can I retract that offer? On second thought I don't think I could take that much of Bobo."

He presses his lips together. "Me neither."

And then he winks at me, and even though it's not a flirty wink, but more of a 'I get you' wink, I feel a flutter inside. For despite the fact that I feel like a complete loser, like the biggest failure in the marital world, this giant of a man is being kind to me. He's showing me care when I probably don't deserve it.

I want to drink all the attention in until I'm drunk with it. He better stop with this stuff or I'll have the most epic crush in history on him that will destroy me when it undoubtedly goes unrequited. He already sports my favorite look in a man: strong, masculine features, dark blue eyes, thick black hair, and a built, solid body.

I sigh inwardly. I'm not exactly a man magnet, and there's not a single reason to think that Joe Murphy, the giant, would be any different. Before I get up to leave I stare at his hands as he spreads his fingers over the desktop. It's like watching porn, those strong, rough fingers spreading apart and closing. Holy hell. If rebounding is a religion, I'm ready to be baptized in the church of Joe, just to have those big manly hands on me.

That Thursday I start dreading our weekly family dinner from the minute my eyes open in the morning. Although we've talked on the phone since my marriage's untimely demise, I've managed to avoid our Thursday nights. Now it's time to suck it up and finally face my parents.

Depending on the nutso L.A. traffic, there are several routes I take to their place, and tonight I feel like the slow, scenic route. I start out on Moorpark heading east so I can pass the Saint Charles church. I'd always liked the look of the architecture and Paul told me that it was built almost a hundred years ago in this cool Spanish Colonial style. That surprised me since I'd always figured it was built for a film set or something and then just left there. Either way now it's our little bit of Europe in North friggin' Hollywood.

In the early part of the twentieth century this area was mainly orange groves, so I bet this church has seen a lot of crazy as the L.A. metropolis sprung up around it.

Next I cut through Toluca Lake, driving right past Bob Hope's former estate. I saw an overhead shot of the property once and holy hell, for an entertainer who became famous in the forties, that guy had some serious bank. I wonder if he paid to have the Burbank airport named after him? Whenever I pass his estate I wave and call out, "Thanks for the memories, Bob!" and then chuckle to myself.

Toluca Lake ends where the Warner Bros. Studio Lot begins, so I turn right there and head up the hill toward the

Lake Hollywood turn. My favorite part of the drive is slowly driving the winding road around the tree-lined reservoir that's pretending to be a lake nestled in the hills. You feel like you're at a manufactured mountain retreat but it's only minutes from crazy town also known as Hollyweird.

Back up the hill from the lake, I dodge the groups of amped-up tourists taking pictures on the plateau facing the Hollywood Sign like they've reached fanboy Mecca. From there I wind down into freaky-deak, bohemian Beachwood Canyon before turning onto shit-show Franklin near my folks.

By the time I pull in front of their house I'm glad I pushed myself to come. Elle suggested that she and Paul could pick me up on their way over, but I passed on the offer. I just needed to pull on my big girl panties and get on with it.

"Hey," I call out once I'm in the front door.

Ma comes rushing down the hallway, twisting a dishtowel in her hands. "My baby," she wails while extending her hands in a wide sweep. She grabs me and holds on so tight that I feel smothered.

I slowly unpeel from her embrace. "It's okay. I'm okay, Ma."

She places a hand on each of my shoulders and pushes me back far enough for her gaze to run from the top of my head to my toes. "You don't look okay," she says with pursed lips. Her Irish brogue is thick tonight.

"Gee thanks." I roll my eyes.

Her soft hand cups my cheek. "I can see, my girl, you're broken." She taps her fingers on my chest. "You're broken in here."

I resent my instant tears, and I blink them back furiously as I nod. "Yeah, I guess I am. I loved him, Ma."

She smooths my hair down like she did when I was a

child and it comforts me. "Yes, of course you did, sweet girl. You married him and loved him with your whole heart, and you know what that makes you?"

"An idiot?" I ask, trying to push the picture of Mike bent over the worktable, out of my head.

She shakes her head furiously. "No! It makes you brave, Trisha. You're not like all those shallow girls who are putting on a show—out there just looking for someone to spoil them. You are true-blue. No games, just you, the rough edges and all."

Rough? All I can picture is sandpaper and more rough edges than anyone has time to smooth down.

"Maybe I don't deserve a good man," I say, trying to monitor the level of pathetic pandering in my voice.

"Maybe most of these soft men don't deserve you. You have to find the strong one who does."

"Hopefully while I'm still able to breed. I'll be too old before I know it."

"Oh good Lord! First things first, my girl."

"Right." I shrug.

"And you'll get through this. You're tough! Remember what they voted you in your senior year?"

I let out a long-suffering sigh. "Most likely to survive the apocalypse."

"Yes!" she exclaims.

Just then my dad approaches us. We fall silent as he wraps an arm around each of us and pulls us into a three-way hug. After we step apart, Dad leans in close to me.

"You know I want to kill him, right?" he whispers in my ear. "Yer Ma hid my rifle."

"No!" I exclaim.

"She did!" he insists.

"What are you two going on about?" she asks, with a frown.

"None of yer business, woman," he says with a pretend stern expression.

An idea occurs to me and I turn to my father. "Hey, can we go to the shooting range this weekend?"

If he's worried by my request, he hides it well. "Sure, lass, let's go Saturday. Twenty bucks my score beats yours," he taunts.

"Oh yeah?" I tease.

"Yeah."

"Well, never underestimate an angry woman with a gun."

The tone at the dinner table is subdued. Patrick is explaining the new tax laws, and if he keeps going on like this I'll want to stab him with my steak knife. When he goes into the pros and cons of IRA restrictions, I slap my hand over my forehead.

"What?" he asks.

"Oh nothing. Nothing at all. Pay no attention to me, I'm positively riveted to your every word."

He huffs and folds his arms over his chest. "No need to be rude, T. Rex. What would you like to talk about?"

I narrow my eyes as I give him the death stare. "How do you know about that?" I hiss.

"Your nickname?" he asks. "Did you forget that Bradley is one of my clients?"

"Bradley, as in Bobo?" I ask, horrified.

He nods with a goofy grin.

"And what else did he tell you about me?"

"That most of the guys are scared of you."

Elle looks at him and shakes her head abruptly but he doesn't seem to notice.

"Is that so?" I ask.

He nods. "And that's why they call you T. Rex."

I roll my eyes. "And all this time I thought it was because my arms are really short for my body."

Paul laughs at my joke, and Patrick seems confused.

"Your arms aren't short, Trisha."

Dad slaps his forehead.

"Paddie, she's teasing you," Ma says gently.

"Oh." His cheeks turn red. "Well you could try being nicer to them, Trisha."

I sigh. "But what fun would that be?"

Later when Paul and I are doing the dishes, he nudges me.

"Hey, you doing okay?"

"Not really."

He sighs. "It sucks. I'm really sorry, Sis. Have you talked to him?"

I shake my head. "Other than leaving messages for him to come get his stuff? No. I just can't. I think I'm still in shock. It's a lot to process when you find out your marriage was a lie."

"I know . . . but I do believe that he loved you."

"Yet I wasn't enough." I blink back the tears.

"Don't say that," Paul responds with sad eyes.

"Am I ever going to stop hurting?"

He takes the soapy dish out of my hand and sets it down, then pulls me into a hug. I rest my head on his shoulder as the tears slide sideways down my face.

"Shhh," he whispers and he gently rocks me. "It's going to take time but it'll fade and then one day you'll realize you aren't hurting anymore. You're strong. I know you're going to be okay."

Chapter 4: Big Man in a Tiny House

The question isn't who's going to let me; it's who's going to stop me.

~ Ayn Rand

My next day working at the station, I sit off on my own at lunch and eat silently. The guys glance over at me once in a while with wary expressions but otherwise they leave me alone.

T. Rex is not coming out to play today, boys.

I'm almost done with my Mexican casserole when Joe storms through the door. It takes me aback because I've never seen him seem so openly agitated. He slams his keys down on the table and then walks over to the kitchen so he can grab a bottle of water. Sinking down into his chair with a huff, he grumbles as he unscrews the cap and takes a swig.

"Hey, dude, what's wrong?" Peter asks.

Joe growls and tips his head back.

I notice Bobo and Peter give each other nervous looks.

I fixate on the veins protruding along Joe's neck. If I were a vampire I'd be all over that man, sinking my teeth into his warm, thick neck until I got my fill of him.

That wasn't weird at all.

I pinch myself in the arm. *Get a grip girl.*

"I'm so angry," Joe finally offers.

"We can see that," Bobo says. "Wanna tell us what's going on?"

"It's my house."

"In Calabasas?" Peter asks.

"Yeah. Well, it *was* in Calabasas. I've been informed that I have to vacate the premises in five days."

"I thought you had another couple of months to find a space for your rig?" Bobo asks.

"Apparently not," he grumbles. "The developers changed their plans."

"Where are you going to move it to? I remember you were researching it a few weeks ago."

Joe gives him a hard look. "That's the thing . . . I have no friggin' idea. The place I had been looking at in Woodland Hills is no longer available. The tenant decided not to leave."

"Damn, that sucks," Peter says.

The table goes silent as Joe downs half the bottle of water. I try not to stare at him as he drinks, but suddenly everything about him fascinates me.

How are his teeth so white?

Where does he buy shoes big enough to fit his supersized feet?

Does he notice that I'm sitting over here obsessing over him?

I guess being rejected by your husband for another man makes you want to immediately attract someone else, just to prove you can.

I force myself to turn away and keep my focus on my own lunch.

After I'm done eating the restlessness gets to me. It's messed up, but I'm kind of hoping for a big call so I can get my ass in gear and think about nothing other than putting out a fire or extricating a victim safely out of a freeway pile-up.

I pace the day room and when I pause to look out the window, I notice Joe in the back patio doing chin-ups on the outdoor equipment. I watch, fascinated. For a big guy he moves in smooth sweeps, his body arcing up as he lifts himself up and juts his chin over the bar.

I should know better, but my legs have a mind of their own and they start moving toward the staircase. Before you know it I'm in the back patio, close enough to Joe to see the fine sheen on his face.

He jerks five more chin-ups before releasing his grip and landing back on his feet.

I can't help but stare as he moves to the gym mat and starts doing squats, every thigh muscle rippling under his shorts. He still hasn't acknowledged me. It's like I'm not even here. I'm not sure if I should walk away or take my chances.

What the hell? What do I have to lose?

He's deep in a squat when I finally pipe up. "So what's this about you having to move your house?"

He doesn't reply to me, but continues with his count and after what feels like forever he rises to his full standing height. He finally looks at me with a steady gaze.

"Why?"

I shrug. "I'm curious."

"The owners of the land sold it to developers, after telling me they weren't going to sell it for a couple of years."

"That blows."

He nods, then lowers himself to the mat and starts doing sit-ups. I wait patiently for him to finish but damn, he does a lot of them. No wonder his stomach is flat as a board. I imagine he thinks I should leave him alone to work out, but he doesn't say anything, just keeps at it and I'm pretty persistent when I want something.

"So what kind of house is it that you can move it around? Like one of those mobile homes with metal siding?"

"You sure have a lot of questions. Why aren't you working out? We have a training meeting after this."

I shrug. "Couldn't sleep, so I hit the gym before breakfast."

Falling silent, he starts up with the sit-ups again.

"So don't those mobile homes have to be taken apart to move?"

He groans and rolls over and rises up on his knees. I suspect I'm irritating him.

"No, mine is built on a trailer bed so it can be towed. It's a wood structure."

I try to picture what such a house would look like while he drops and does push-ups. *Jesus, his arms are so cut.* I imagine running my fingers over the hard curves of his shoulders. It's hypnotizing watching the muscles in his arms bulge and flex. His face is starting to get flushed but he doesn't appear to be sweating.

Before I start thinking inappropriate thoughts I try to focus back on his house. Suddenly, I remember a HGTV show I saw at my parents'. "Wait a minute! You have a tiny house?" I ask excitedly.

He scowls. "I hate that term. Don't call it that."

I can feel my eyes grow wide . . . a giant man in a tiny house. I have to bite my lip to keep from laughing or saying something snarky. The situation makes me think of the Hans Christian Andersen fairy tales Ma used to read to us when we were little. They were full of tiny people, giants, fairies, and witches. They freaked me out, but the idea of tall Joe in a tiny house makes me happy.

He stretches his arms over his head, which gives me a peek of a sliver of skin from his washboard stomach. "Anything else you want to know?"

I'm sitting on the edge of the picnic bench, swinging my legs.

"Nope, that's about it."

He shakes his head, picks up his towel, and wipes his face down.

"The thing is . . . I was just thinking that I could help you out. It's not a long term solution but it would buy you some time."

He pulls the towel down, his expression somewhere between confused and curious.

"My house is on a double lot in Valley Village, just north of Studio City."

He stares at me without saying a word. It makes me nervous so I just continue on; for all I know I'm babbling like a crazy person. This man unnerves me.

"Mike, also known as Dickwad, my soon-to-be-ex-husband, had the idea of building rental units to the side the property but the zoning wouldn't allow it."

He narrows his eyes and scrunches up his face. I guess this is too much information about my ex.

"So I was thinking you could park your tiny house on the empty part of the lot. Of course, just as long as you need it before you find where you really want to be. You wouldn't owe me anything . . . I mean, you wouldn't have to pay me or do stuff."

"Do stuff?" he mumbles with a wary look.

"Nope. I promise," I say, raising my hands to make my point.

"Why?"

"Why what?" I ask.

"Why would you offer that to me?"

"Out of the goodness of my heart?" I squint noting how ridiculous that sounds coming out of my mouth. I'm no angel, and I'm sure he knows that.

He folds his arms over his chest and waits.

"Maybe I'm not used to being alone there. It's a big

place. It would make me feel better knowing someone I can trust is nearby."

"And I'm someone you trust?"

I think about the firefighter's oath, and the band of brothers. The trust between us is paramount—it can make the difference in surviving a crisis, or not. But there's something about Joe which makes me feel extra safe. I don't even know him that well. Not really. But it's a feeling I have, and I trust that feeling.

"You are."

He looks down, deep in thought and I know he's considering my offer.

"Don't make up your mind now. Why don't you come by after our shift ends in the morning and look at it? No hard feelings if you pass on it . . . I promise."

There's a long pause and then he clears his throat. "Let me think about it. Okay? As you know, I'm in a bad position right now . . . so a temporary move would be really helpful."

I smile realizing that there's a chance he may say yes. "Okay, just let me know if you want to see it in the morning."

Late that evening I'm holed up in my room watching a training video on my iPad about new procedures for handling brushfires. I missed the formal presentation this afternoon because we got a call when some asshat teen T-boned a minivan, before wrapping his car around a fire hydrant.

I'm just about to shut the video off when there's a rumble downstairs as the wide doors roll up and the trucks pull in. Glancing at my alarm clock next to my bed, I realize how long the guys were out on that call. I wonder how bad it was.

I lie still and listen to the familiar pounding of footsteps up the stairs. A minute later the plumbing rattles with too many showers getting turned on at once. My stomach sinks. It must have been a rough situation with a lot of soot and smoke.

As I wait for the plumbing to quiet, I let my gaze settle on my sparse surroundings. Besides my cot and side table, there's a set of drawers, a plain desk and a matching maple wood chair. It's a purely utilitarian space.

Because I was living in an over-decorated house that my husband filled with too much stuff for my liking, I always found comfort in the simplicity of this room. Some guys put more personal stuff in their space, but not me.

The one thing I used to have on display was a framed picture of me and Mikey on my nightstand. It was taken in Monterey on our first anniversary.

I remember when that picture was shot vividly. That was the day we went to see the Monterey Aquarium. Afterwards, we took a long walk in the brisk sea breeze, and while stopping at a lookout point to take in the view, we asked a passing woman to take our picture.

In the photo our cheeks are pink and my dark brown hair windswept with wisps wrapped around my neck and fingers as I hold it off my face for the shot. We're grinning like fools and I've loved that photo as a reminder of one of our happiest times.

There's now an empty spot on my nightstand where the picture once stood. You'd think I would've taken it down right after I threw him out of the house, but for some reason I couldn't do it.

But that damn dream I had a few weeks ago was my snapping point, the moment that made me hurl the framed picture in the trash. In the dream Mikey and I were walking hand-in-hand through our neighborhood, but it was that weird dream-thing in that it wasn't actually our neighborhood, yet I seemed to think it was. The sky was strangely hazy with the thick L.A. smog of my childhood days before all the emission laws went into effect.

I remember feeling perfectly content as we strolled along until a tall man with dark hair and a leather jacket came walking toward us. He passed us without a word or gesture but a moment later Mikey let go of my hand and lengthened his stride forward. As he moved farther and farther ahead of me my world started crumbling, the sidewalk breaking apart under my feet.

I woke up with my face wet with tears. In the quiet darkness my heart was aching for what I'd lost and how much I was still missing the man Mike used to be to me. For a while I held the framed picture to my chest and cried but then when the tears stopped the anger set in, and in the trash it went.

The next afternoon Bobo caught me in the station's dumpster digging through the garbage for the picture. My regret of tossing it had gotten the better of me.

"What are you up to, T. Rex? Disposing of a body . . . one of your victims?" he asked.

"Yeah, right," I snapped. "Watch it or you could be next."

Unfortunately my threat didn't dissuade him—instead it apparently intrigued him. He walked right up to the dumpster and peered inside. "You did a good job. I don't see the carnage."

"I've got skills," I replied with a shrug.

"What are you really looking for?" he asked.

"A framed picture I didn't mean to throw away."

"Huh," he said, his gaze moving over the mess. "Is that it?"

On the other side of the dumpster from where I'd been digging around, I saw the corner of the black frame rising up out of the garbage where he was pointing. I reached over and lifted it out only to see that the glass was shattered and the picture badly scratched.

"Hey, that's you. Is that your—"

"Yeah," I cut him off. "It's my ex."

His expression fell and he looked down. "Oh. And now it's busted. Sorry, McNeill."

"Me too," I responded as I held it for a moment and then dropped it back down onto the pile of crap that was no use to anyone.

I suddenly snap out of my memory and realize that the plumbing has quieted so that means that the showers must be over. Swinging my legs over the side of my bunk, I stand up and stretch, then head out my door. Hopefully someone will be in the dayroom to tell me what went down.

I find Alberto and Scott sitting at a table nursing bottles of water. Scott is hunched over, resting his head in his hands, and Alberto is leaning back with his legs stretched out wide. They look beat.

"Hey, McNeill, be glad you missed that call. What a bitch that job was," says Alberto.

"That bad?" I ask, feeling remorse I wasn't there to help despite the fact that I wasn't on the call list.

Scott nods. "Abandoned warehouse in Sun Valley. Someone said it was a porn studio back in the day when the Valley was our nation's porn capital. Now it's just a shithole."

"Three stations were called. At least there was no chemical crap to deal with," Alberto says.

"Standard stuff, if it weren't for Murphy and his damn heroic stuff."

I frantically look around hoping to see Joe. "What do

you mean? Is he okay?"

"Yeah, but no bullshit, there was a few minutes where we thought we lost him," Alberto replies.

I feel a surge of fear. Even though they say Joe is okay, it's as if I can feel myself at the scene and that the horror of knowing one of our men is at high risk, especially Joe.

"What happened?" I ask.

"Murphy was working a line and a homeless guy came out of nowhere and grabbed him to say that his buddy was still inside."

"It was dangerously late, and Murphy knew it. The ceiling could've collapsed at any minute, and he went in anyway. That heroic stuff only works when you come out alive," Scott grumbles.

"And he did," I state defensively.

"He was lucky," Alberto says, shaking his head.

"Where is he?" I ask.

"After the shower he said he needed some air. I think he's down in the yard."

I stand up and look out the window. Joe's sitting facing out on the picnic table bench, still as a statue.

"I'm going to go check on him." Grabbing a bottle of water, I thank the guys for the update.

I'm sure he sees me approach from the corner of his eyes but he remains silent and still. Sitting down on the bench a few feet from him, I offer him the bottle of water. He accepts it, unscrews the cap, and downs half without pausing.

"I heard you saved a man. You okay?"

He nods. "Yeah, I'm fine."

"You don't look fine. They say you shouldn't have gone in. It was too late and the risk, Joe—"

He holds up his hand to silence me.

He has the haunted look about him that I've seen in

guys who took big risks on the job, challenging the Grim Reaper head on. As firefighters we can never be sure of the outcome. I think of all those firefighters who charged up the stairwells of the Twin Towers and my heart twists for the millionth time.

Challenging death changes us, and we can sense the shift in our psyche like we've just shed a layer of who we used to be.

I know how private a guy Joe is, but I think it would help if he could talk about it. I wait patiently to see if he will.

After what feels like a minute he clears his throat. "It sounds reckless, but I felt pretty sure I could get back out. And what was I going to do, let him suffocate on the smoke and then burn to death? He was homeless, Trisha."

I nod. "Yeah, they told me."

We sit silently, processing all that we aren't saying. We occasionally have to deal with the homeless at fire scenes. Sometimes they start the fires, sometimes they just get trapped in them. Either way I've at times sensed an attitude like they aren't worth the risk to save. Obviously Joe doesn't feel that way.

"I think you were very brave. I admire what you did."

He glances over at me. "Really? The other guys thought I was an idiot."

"Screw the other guys," I huff.

I watch his face as his expression reflects appreciation for a moment before slowly darkening again.

"What?" I ask with a gentle tone. I'd like him to feel like he can confide in me.

He takes a deep breath, which sets off a coughing fit. He probably got too much smoke despite the mask. I pat him hard on the back until he nods that I can stop.

"The guy's friend, the one who told me where to find

him, kept saying, *'He's a good man, he's a good man,'* and that got to me. So I masked up fast knowing there may only be a few minutes left. Luckily, despite the fact that parts of the ceiling and beams were falling, there was enough of an open path in for me to find the storage room he'd been living in."

He pulls his fingers through his hair and sighs. "I can't even tell you the feeling I had when I found him. The first thing I see is that this guy did his best to make this place his home. Everything was neat and seemed to have an order, when his life must have been chaos."

I blink at him, trying to imagine the scene he's describing.

"So I get to the guy and he's unconscious but still hanging on. He's so thin that it's not hard to lift and hoist him over my shoulder. But right before I rushed us out the door I had the strongest feeling hit me . . ."

"What's that?" I ask.

"There but for the grace of God go I," he says with a faraway look.

I have to stifle my gasp. How could Joe possibly compare himself to this homeless man barely surviving in an abandoned warehouse?

"I've been knocked down hard, but at least I'm employed and I have my rig as my refuge. When I was at my lowest, my home gave me hope that things could get better. What if in a matter of minutes it was destroyed and I didn't have the resources to rebuild? What would I do?"

"Well, you *do* have a good job, *and* friends. We would all help you get by and rebuild."

He nods. "I'm blessed. Despite my disappointments, I can never forget how lucky I am."

I nod. "As am I."

"Tomorrow I'm going to check on the guy and see if I

can help in some way. They took him to county."

My heart swells. Lieutenant Joseph Murphy is a good man. I'm taken aback by his compassion. I've never known anyone quite like him and it only makes me want to know him more.

"Let me know if I can do anything . . . anything at all," I say.

He looks over at me, his gaze intense and searching. "Thank you, Trisha. I will."

I'm glad we've had this talk. It's like it's given us a foundation to our friendship . . . something that feels real.

I stand up. "You ready to come inside? Don't forget that in the morning you get to see my homestead for your rig."

He smiles. "Right. Another thing to be grateful for."

He stands up and we silently head back inside.

Chapter 5: Landing his Rig

Do not bite at the bait of pleasure, till you know there is no hook beneath it.

~Thomas Jefferson

Early the next morning I see Joe in the day room having breakfast with several of the guys and smiling as they joke around. Thank goodness he woke up in a lighter mood. Maybe our talk last night helped.

When it's time to leave I load up my truck and fire up the ignition. I have the radio on really loud, playing the oldie station as I truck down Magnolia Blvd. from Van Nuys to Valley Village. I sing along with Tina Turner as she howls, *'What's love got to do with it?'* I bob my head as I sing. Tina knows her shit—she's been through it, too.

Joe trails me on his motorcycle and it takes everything I have to keep my eyes focused forward. What in the hell is wrong with me? When we were leaving the station and he pulled on his helmet and straddled the seat of his bike, I had a strong urge to get out of my car and ride with him. I can picture it vividly. I'd be pressed up behind him with my arms wound tight around his waist.

Of course then I immediately feel guilty to have these thoughts when just last night I was thinking about the lost picture of Mikey and I.

Hell, I'm a spinning top, a flickering of light from dark to bright, then dark again. I really need to slow down and get my head on straight.

When we get to Addison Street, I make a sharp turn into the

driveway and he pulls up alongside me. I try to look away as he swings his leg over the bike and lifts off his helmet. This bad-boy, motorcycle-riding side of him is unexpected. I swear, I thought he drove a truck. *What do you bet he has tribal tattoos on his back?*

It occurs to me that I'm becoming obsessed with Joe because he's everything Mike wasn't. And maybe that's ridiculous or maybe it's okay for now.

He stands tall in the driveway taking it all in. I try to imagine how the house looks to him.

"This is yours?" he asks.

"For now it is," I answer.

He nods his head.

"Come on, let me show you what I was thinking."

He follows me down the driveway and through the side gate.

I point to the wide patch of land bordered by fruit trees. "This is where you could park. The water and electrical lines are over there, the only thing I'm not sure about is sewage."

"I have a composting toilet," he responds.

I turn to watch his gaze take it all in.

"What do you think?"

He nods, seeming to be calculating something. "This could work."

I try to sound lighter about it than I feel. "Well, it's yours if you want it."

We start walking back to where we parked.

"Let me talk to the chief about it."

Surprised, I turn to him not trying to hide the confusion I'm feeling. "Why do you need to talk to him about this?"

He lifts his helmet off his bike and sorts the straps, preparing to put it on.

"Well, just to make sure it's not inappropriate."

"Why would it be?" I ask, not hiding the irritation in my voice.

"You know . . . like if I'm taking you up on your offer so that I can do inappropriate things with you whenever I want."

My breath catches and I have to fight to stay composed. "But you aren't," I insist.

He swings his leg over his bike and pulls his helmet on, then fires up the engine. I'm frozen in place, waiting for his reply. Right before he tears out of the driveway our gazes lock together. "No I'm not," he states. "But that doesn't mean I wouldn't want to."

I've gone to visit Elle for advice when Paul comes rambling in to where we're sitting. I look at him and point toward the door. "You need to leave."

"Is that so? Did you forget that you're in our house, visiting us, not the other way around?"

I purse my lips at him. "I need to talk to Elle."

"What do you need to talk to Elle about that you can't talk to me about?"

"Sex."

"Did you forget that I'm an expert on that subject?"

Elle nods. "He is, you know. He knows everything."

Grinning, Paul thumps his chest. "That's my woman!" he says, winking at Elle. *God these two are so annoying together.*

"Expert or not, you're my brother and there's no way I'm having this discussion with you here. That's just gross."

He holds his hands up in the air. "Okay, okay. Your loss," he grumbles as he walks away and closes the hall door behind him.

"So what's up?" Elle asks as she pours wine in my glass.

I shake my head. "I just don't understand what's happening to me. You know I met Mike right after I got hired by our Battalion Chief. At that time I was completely focused on Mike, and had less than zero interest in any of the guys in my squad. Sure, most of them are good looking, in top shape with bodies that any woman would appreciate. But I never looked at them that way, especially once I got to know them well. But something weird is happening to me. I'm thinking inappropriate thoughts a lot, even at work, and it's making me crazy."

Elle sits down and scoots her chair closer to the table. "So is this about feeling more sexual in general, or is there one guy in particular you're fixated on?"

My cheeks get hot and I turn away.

"It's one guy," Elle says without waiting for my answer. It must be her female instinct. "What's his name?"

"His name is Joe. He's the lieutenant for our squad."

"Is he hot?" Elle asks with a grin.

"Oh yeah." I fan my face with my hand. He's scorching."

"Whoa, I've never seen you like this."

"I know, right? I never even came close to feeling this physically drawn to Mike . . . like I want to climb his tree. This is why I'm pretty sure I'm losing it."

"Maybe this is just what you need. He's not in a relationship or anything, is he?" she asks.

"Not that I know of."

"Okay, so that's good."

"And it's not just his looks . . . not by a long-shot. We had a talk last night after he'd been on a tough call, and he was really shook up. He genuinely cares about helping people. He's a good man, Elle, and that's what makes him really stand out."

"He sounds pretty great," she responds with a gentle smile.

"And you know how I've talked about the guys at the station always giving each other shit, and cutting each other down? Well, Joe's been so nice to me lately . . . like extra nice. Those guys are never very nice to me, usually riding me harder than the others. His kindness makes me want to . . . you know, get closer to him."

"Has he made the moves?" Elle asks.

"Oh, he's not interested in me that way."

"How do you know?"

"I'm not the kind of woman guys like him want."

"How do you know that?" Elle asks in a stern voice.

"I just know," I answer defensively.

Elle folds her arms over her chest. "I swear, Trisha, where do you get these hang ups? Paul said his friends still ask about you."

I roll my eyes at her.

"That face of yours with those blue eyes and full lips. To top it off you have a great body."

"No I don't."

"Just quit arguing with me and take the compliments."

"Honestly, Joe doesn't say much so it'd be hard to tell even if he did like me that way."

Elle taps her fingers on the tabletop. "Hmmm."

"Although there was one thing . . ." I say.

"Yes?"

"When he came to my place to see about parking his tiny house there, he said something about being inappropriate with me . . . or maybe it was *not* being inappropriate with me. I was so flustered that I may have it all mixed up."

"Well, either way, that's promising . . . just the idea that he's thinking along those lines," Elle says with a big smile.

The hall door opens and Paul strolls back into the kitchen to pull a beer out of the fridge.

"Wait, did you say he has a tiny house?" Elle asks.

"Why is he parking it at your place?"

"Who's parking what at your place?" Paul asks as he pops the cap off the bottle.

"The lieutenant from her station may be parking his tiny house on her property," Elle explains.

Paul scowls.

"Don't worry. It's just temporary. The land he was on was sold and they're rushing him to move. I'm just helping him out, and I like the idea of having someone around."

Paul sits up taller. "Well, I want to meet him."

"You mean like check him out?"

He nods.

I roll my eyes. "He's the lieutenant at my station, not a drug dealer, dude."

Elle leans over and strokes Paul's cheek. "That's so sweet that you're looking out for your little sister, baby."

"Will you two stop it before I vomit?" I push back my chair. "I'm heading out, but before I leave you've got to tell me. Do you think something's wrong with me . . . you know, because I'm suddenly thinking about this guy all the time?"

"Is she talking about the lieutenant guy?" Paul asks Elle. I love that he's asking her like I'm not here.

"Yes, his name is Joe and he's hot," she replies with a wink before she turns back to me. "I don't think anything's wrong with you being worked up and liking this guy, Trish. It may be just what you need to get over what happened with Mike."

"But isn't it wrong for me to be attracted to another man while I'm grieving the end of my marriage?" I ask.

Paul shrugs like it's the most natural thing in the world. "It means you're alive."

My eyebrows knit together. "Alive? Like what? I was dead before?"

"Maybe," he says with an earnest look like I should figure out what the hell that means.

Elle glances at Paul, and then at me, and the fact that she doesn't disagree makes me think she thought I was dead too.

I feel a deep anger stir up deep in my gut. It would've been handy if they'd pointed this out before my whole life blew apart. Was I that detached to not realize my life should have been more?

And how exactly do I resurrect myself? I need a manual to teach me how to live again . . . or perhaps I need a strapping firefighter who's willing to give me some hands-on lessons.

Late that night I get another call from Mike. As I let it ring to voicemail something comes over me. Maybe it's exhaustion, or just my curiosity getting the best of me, but I pick up the call. I don't say anything, just sit silently and wait for the cheater to talk.

"Trish?" he says. "Are you there?"

"I picked up the call, didn't I?"

"Finally," he sighs. "How are you doing?"

"Just peachy. Thanks for asking." To say my tone is sarcastic would be an understatement. My bad mood is in full swing.

There's a long pause. "Please don't be this way. I'm hurting Trish, it's bad. Don't you miss me at all?"

I bite my tongue. I want to go off on him, but judging from his bleak tone, I don't have it in me to be that mean. Something else occurs to me.

"Hey, when we were still together did you happen to notice that I was dead inside?"

"What are you talking about?" he asks, sounding

frustrated.

"You know, dead—lifeless, without life."

"I know what dead means, Trish. I'm just not sure how it pertains to you."

"I just have all these crazy feelings now and I don't understand what's happening to me, and Paul and Elle implied that it's because I'm not dead inside anymore."

"That's just awesome. Can you thank the happy couple for me? It feels great to know they think I enhanced your life so profoundly while we were together."

"Sure thing," I say.

"Trish, are you serious with this stuff. Did you really feel dead in our marriage?"

"I don't know. I went to work, I came home, I did yard-work and got the groceries, and waited for you to come home from the flower shop. I can't say I felt particularly alive."

"There's a lot of mundane tasks in all of our lives, but what about the other times, like when we had fun?"

"When was that?"

"Like when we'd go to Greenblatt's deli and have pastrami sandwiches and then see the acts at the Comedy Store on Sunset. That was great."

"We haven't done that in at least two years, Mike. You were always working at the shop."

"Well, how about we go next weekend?"

"You aren't getting what I'm saying."

He lets out a long sigh. "I get it. Believe me, I do. What makes you think I'm not dead inside, too? Especially now that you kicked me out. I think we won't really feel alive again until we get back together and work things out."

He was always so fucking stubborn. He always has to get his way.

He clears his throat. "I know! Let's go to Italy. You've

always wanted to go there."

Really? He's the one that wants to go to Italy. My head suddenly feels hot and I'm fired up. Am I transforming like the Hulk or something? Because I'm pretty sure T. Rex is in the building.

"Will Stanley be joining us in Italy?" I ask between gritted teeth.

"No Stanley won't be joining us," he says with a gruff voice. "You aren't going to make this easy, are you Patricia?"

"Why should I? You don't deserve easy. I think my disdain for you is well deserved. On top of it, you knew I was dead in our marriage and you didn't even mention it."

"Mention it?" he says, his voice an octave higher.

"Yeah, fuck you for not mentioning that I was dying a slow death right before your eyes. But oh yeah, I forgot you were never home enough to notice."

"Says the firefighter who spent over half her life living with a bunch of hot men who wear suspenders with no shirts and slide down poles."

What the hell with the suspenders with no shirts?

My fingers grip the phone so tight my fingertips turn white. He must have a secret stash of those sexy firemen calendars. What do you bet he gets off looking at them?

"Says the cheater who'd gladly trade spots with his wife to be around all the hot men."

"Oh Jesus, would you just stop? For God's sake. I bet you'd be happy if I were dead. Not this bullshit pretend-dead, but really dead. Wouldn't you?"

"I'm not playing into your emotional blackmail. Screw you, Michael Irving Castallani the third. Screw you and the Sasquatch you screw!"

I poke my finger at my phone's screen to end the call when I desperately want the satisfaction of slamming the receiver of an old-school phone down so the sound is like a gunshot in his ears.

Stupid fucking smart phones.

I spend the next hour storming through the house ranting and throwing things until I have nothing left in me. I head to the bedroom, strip naked—too drained to care about my pj's—and crawl into bed. Why I start crying like a baby when my head hits the pillow, who the hell knows? I guess it's just one more sign that, like it or not, I'm finally alive.

I'm trying my best to focus the next day, and I'm doing pretty good through the morning's equipment check, and gym time. But we're filing into the training room when Joe steps up close behind me, and leans in to whisper in my ear, "I need to talk to you. Meet me in the office after."

I don't turn around, just silently nod as I try to maintain my composure. But damn, his breath on my neck and the whiff of his aftershave have sparked a throb between my legs and I squeeze my knees together tightly. Suddenly I'm feeling extra alive.

Needless to say, the training session on disabling hybrid cars in an emergency becomes a hopeless cause due to Joe distracting me. It's all blah, blah, blah . . . propulsion system . . . blah blah blah . . . live ignition recognition.

Considering how many hybrids we have in L.A. with all these do-gooder *'anything to help the environment'* folks, I really should learn how to extricate one of these kale munchers out of their toy cars in the case of a pile-up.

Sorry environment, but give me a beefy pick-up truck any day, so when one of those do-gooders rear-ends me while texting on the 101, it'll be their car folding up like an accordion while their battery explodes, and I'll have a few scratches on my bumper.

I look over at Joe and he's taking notes and asking per-
tinent questions. It pisses me off. I'm squirming in my seat
imaging sitting on his lap and kissing him, and he hasn't
glanced my way once. I remind myself it's likely that all I
am to him is a piece of land he can park on until he's ready
for greener pastures.

Yes indeed, I'm a piece of land . . . and a drought
parched, barren one at that.

When I let out a long, sorry sigh, Scott looks over at me
and gives me a stern look. I narrow my eyes at him until he
turns back around.

I practice a pretend conversation with Joe in my head a few
times so that by the time I follow him into the office, I'm as
cool and contained as an unskinned cucumber.

"What's up?" I ask, plopping down into the chair facing him.

"Chief gave me the A-okay," he says.

"A-okay for what exactly?" I reply with an arched brow.

"To park at your place until I can find something else."

"And he's not worried about us being inappropriate?"

He shrugs. "It never even came up. He must not be
worried about it."

My eyebrows furrow together. "Should I be offended?"

"Why would you be?" he asks with a confused
expression.

"That I'm not appealing enough for someone to be inappropriate with?"

He shakes his head. "You're over thinking this. Damn it
must be exhausting to be you."

"You have no idea," I grumble.

"So you're still okay with this?"

I nod. "Sure."

He lets out a deep breath. "Good. We're both off tomorrow, can I land my rig late morning?"

Land my rig?

It takes everything I have to keep my voice light. "Sure thing. I'll be around if you need anything."

"Thanks." He gives me a big smile like he's genuinely happy, and I realize it's the first time in a long time, maybe ever, that I've seen him smile like that.

I did that. I made him smile like the sun had just broken through the clouds, and not to be a softie or anything, but I feel pretty awesome about it.

Chapter 6: The Muffin Lady

She looked as if she had been poured into her clothes and had forgotten to say 'when'.

~ P.G. Wodenhouse

Late the next morning, I've settled back into my home routine after two days at the station. I'm rolling the full trashcans out to the street when Joe and his tiny house come slowly roaring down my street. My heart starts thumping wildly. This is really going to happen. All of a sudden my life feels wild and out of control, and I like it.

I've already opened the wide gate on the right side of the property when he pulls up in his truck with his house, and motorcycle hitched to the back. His tiny house is a grand sight, all wood and rustic looking, and as soon as he notices me I wave widely.

He rolls down his window.

"Hey! You ready for me?"

"Ready as I'll ever be," I reply. "I've got the gate open. Do you want me to help direct you in?"

Maneuvering rigs is a particular skill of mine, and it's frequently put to good use at the station when the guys have to back the truck into the apparatus bay.

He points at me, and we signal each other as his home slowly slides alongside mine.

I give him a thumbs-up when the position looks good to me. "You want to get out and make sure it's how you want it?" I ask.

He nods, throws the door open and jumps down before

surveying where his rig is positioned. He rubs his chin as he walks front to back, finally turning to me. "Looks good."

I stand awkwardly in the yard while he shuts everything down and starts to prepare for the water and electrical hook-ups.

"Can I help with anything?" I ask.

"No, I'm good, thanks," he responds.

"I'll be in the house then. Just let me know if you need anything."

"Will do," he says.

I've probably spied on him through my kitchen window over a dozen times and it's not even lunchtime yet. I'm going to have to get a grip, but those long legs clad in worn jeans, work boots, and his bright white T-shirt are like a shining beacon in my otherwise dull day.

I'm digging up the flowerbed in the front yard to prepare for a new planting, when he rolls his bike out to the driveway.

"Where you off to?" I call out.

He slings a bag over his shoulder so that it crosses over his chest. "I'm going to go check on Bernie, the homeless guy from the fire. Then on the way home I'll go to the gym," he calls out.

I give him a nod before he pulls on his helmet and takes off. I watch his bike turn the corner and keep staring even after he's out of sight. I really better get a grip. It's day one and I'm already coming undone.

Joe hasn't been gone that long when my doorbell rings. I peer through the peephole and when I confirm it's not a mass murderer or a cookie-pushing Girl Scout, I open the door. Standing before me is a full-figured woman in one of those wrap dresses wrapped just a little too tight. Her face is pretty enough but she should really tone down the tomato red lipstick. It's just a few steps short of clownish.

She gestures toward Joe's rig. "Do you happen to know if Joe's around? I knocked on the door but he didn't answer."

"He's at the gym."

She sighs. "That's Joe all right. No wonder he has such a great body. Will you tell him Nicole dropped by?"

I lean on the door jam and size her up. She looks like she wants to butter his biscuit and I don't like it. Not one bit.

I shrug like I couldn't care less. "Sure thing."

"Is this your place?" she asks.

"Yup."

"Well it's really nice you're letting him stay here."

"Happy to do it," I respond with a big fake smile. Can she fucking move on and get out of my face?

"I baked him some muffins. Will you do me a favor and give them to him for me? They're his favorite."

As she hands them to me I picture pitching them in the trash as soon as she's waddling her fat ass back down my driveway. I probably won't, but the idea of it makes me happy.

I also realize that I'm done with our Joe bonding session. I point inside. "I've got something to take care of."

"Oh sure!" she says brightly. "Nice to meet you . . ." She waits for me to say my name.

"Tricia, but the boys at the station call me T. Rex." I give her a teeth-baring smile that's more of a snarl, and get exactly the reaction I hoped for. She backs away from the door with a startled expression and gives a quick wave, before speed-walking down to the street where she's parked her compact car complete with flower decals on the door panels.

"Don't hurry back," I whisper as I firmly shut my front door and lock it.

It's late evening before I return home. Once I made up my mind to get out of the house and away from my kitchen window, I ran every errand I could think of. After that I visited Patrick and the folks, and even stopped by Elle and Paul's for dinner.

I'm disappointed when I look through my kitchen window and see that the tiny house is dark. Joe must have gone out. I fold my arms over my chest. How nice for him that he has a night-life.

I busy myself by cleaning up the kitchen and taking out the trash. I'm only a few steps into the backyard when a voice startles me.

"Where are my muffins?"

My mouth drops open as I scan the yard. "Joe! Where are you?" I yell.

"Up here!"

I look up and see that he's sitting on his roof. It appears like he's attached railings around the rig's edges to create an outdoor deck, or a landing pad for a really tiny helicopter.

What the ever-loving hell? Dude is yelling about muffins from the top of his tiny house? He's looking smug and sitting in one of those folding beach chairs like it's the most natural thing in the world. Is this a side of Joe I've never seen? It occurs to me that I'm glad I didn't follow through with my compulsion to throw the muffins out.

I put my hands on my hips. "You want the muffins now? Should I throw them up there?"

"No just climb the ladder and bring them up. You're a firefighter, you can handle a ladder with a basket of muffins."

"So demanding!" I huff before marching inside. After pulling on my hoodie, I grab the muffins and march back outside.

He gestures toward where the ladder is attached to the backside of the rig. "Grab a chair while you're at it."

"Anything else? A pitcher of margaritas? My iPad so we can stream a movie? A lap blanket?"

"Alright, alright . . . you made your point. Shut up and get up here."

I take several steps back and wind up my arm before hurling a muffin at him. My softball years pay off when I nail him right in the back of his head.

"Was that a muffin?" he yells.

"Yup. Tell me to shut up again, and you'll have another chance to see how good my pitching arm is."

"Hey, I meant it affectionately. My mom tells my dad to shut up all the time."

"That's friggin' weird, but I'll keep that in mind."

He falls silent and I take the ladder slow and steady, since I'm hauling his crap. When I get to the top he reaches over and takes the chair from me, unfolds it, and sets it down across from his chair. I plop the basket of muffins down as I step onto the roof.

It's fascinating to see not just my house and yard, but the entire neighborhood from this viewpoint. "This is cool," I remark since he seems to be watching me intently for my reaction. "Do you sit up here a lot?"

"Almost every night that I'm home.

"And what do you do when you're up here."

"Look at the stars and think."

"What do you think about?"

"Everything. Nothing."

"Ah, so you're a deep kind of guy."

He huffs, and then reaches into what looks like a back-pack. "Want a beer?"

That explains why he's been acting differently. This must be Joe with a beer buzz. "Sure," I answer before I settle into the second lawn-chair.

He hands me the beer and when I crack it open I notice a book lying next to his backpack. "What's that?"

"A book I'm reading. I like to read up here until there isn't enough light."

"That's cool. So what are you reading?"

He lifts up the book and shows me the cover. "I like biographies. This one is about Thomas Jefferson."

I grin. "Wow . . . old school!"

He shrugs. "He was fascinating. Did you know that he invented the swivel chair?"

"Really?" I try to picture the old guy with knickers and a ponytail turning circles in his new contraption, the swivel chair.

"Yeah. Somehow he fit that in between writing the Declaration of Independence and running the country."

"A multi-tasker, apparently," I say.

"And he spoke six languages."

"Show off."

"No, it came in handy for his skillful handling of international relations."

"I barely remember much Spanish even though I took three years in high school."

"He was passionate about so many things. I think what I like best about him is his belief in personal rights."

"Very cool, I'm with Thomas on that. Maybe you'll let me read it when you're done."

"Sure."

He gazes off in the distance. "So where were you this afternoon?" he asks.

"Ah, you know . . . errands and stuff. Also I went to see my family."

"They live nearby?"

I nod. "Sometimes it's too close. Plus, we all have dinner together every Thursday. But they're good people."

He doesn't say anything but stays focused on the view.

"Where's your family?" I ask.

"Eugene, Oregon." He reaches down into basket, pulls out a muffin and takes a healthy bite.

I guess we're done talking about his family.

"So Nicole, the muffin lady . . . is she your girlfriend?"

"No, why?"

"I don't know. She just acted like she wanted to butter your biscuit."

He chuckles into his beer. "Yeah, there's a bit of that."

"So *does* she butter your biscuit?"

He arches his eyebrows. "We used to get together once in a while."

"I thought so," I say with a frown.

"You're pretty forward, you know."

"It's part of my charm." I sigh inwardly.

It's crazy but I'm feeling kind-of heartbroken, without having any right to feel that way. I should be heartbroken over my husband betraying me, not over a co-worker who I didn't really start becoming friendly with until a week or so ago.

Joe had overnight become my fantasy gentle giant, intriguing because he was such a mystery. Now knowing that he has nailed the muffin lady takes the intrigue away. Is that fair? No. But life isn't fair, so why should I be?

He clears his throat. "For the record, she hasn't buttered my biscuit for a long time . . . not since college, actually."

I fight back a smile. I like that he wants me to be clear on his status. Maybe this woman isn't anyone to worry about after all.

He holds the basket up toward me. "Want a muffin?"

"How about a bite of yours?" He grins and hands me his half-eaten muffin. His eyes grow wide as I take a huge bite and then hand him back the remnants.

Take that, muffin lady.

I'm three beers in when I ask him to show me the inside of his tiny house.

"Please," I beg when he gives a deadpan look at my request.

"Not tonight. Besides, it shows better in the day."

I huff. "I don't care about how it shows. I want to see your bed. Is it one of those dealies where you have to climb a ladder and then flop flat on the mattress because there's no room to sit up?"

"I don't have a loft bed. So no ladders, no flopping."

"Where do you sleep then?"

He takes a long drag of his beer. I wonder how many he's had. "Why do you care where I sleep?" he asks.

"Maybe I want my very own tiny house. And once I have it I'll park it next to yours and never leave you alone."

"Is that so?"

"I know, hot, right?" I wink at him, just to kick it home.

He narrows his eyes at me. "Are you flirting? It seems like *you* want to butter my biscuit."

"Ha! I don't even know how to flirt, but if I did, maybe I'd flirt with you."

He smiles against the mouth of his beer bottle. "Yeah, what would you do?"

It occurs to me that maybe I should stop drinking but then the thought slips right back out of my head. "I don't know—press against you and whisper dirty things in your ear? By the time I was done you wouldn't be able to resist me."

"I can only imagine," he says with a long sigh. "I can barely resist you now."

"You're teasing me, aren't you?" I'm a little fuzzy from the beer, but I'm pretty sure he isn't serious. Just to be safe I give him a warning. "Be careful with teasing me—I can be fierce."

He stands up and holds out his hand to me. *Damn, he's tall.*

"Come on, fierce Ms. T. Rex. It's way past your bedtime, and we have to be at the station bright and early."

He starts down the ladder and then waits for me to get on right after him. It only takes a few steps down the rung for me to realize that he's created a body shield so I can't fall off.

We work our way down, rung by rung, and I'm almost sorry when I'm finally down on the ground.

I have a weird compulsion not to let the evening end. I turn to Joe.

"Hey, I have an idea. Why don't we do a friend's sleepover in your tiny house? That'd be fun, don't you think?"

"I'm sure it would be, Trisha, but no, I think you should sleep in your own bed tonight."

"All right, but now you'll never know what an awesome cuddler I am."

"True, but my guess is that you'd never stop talking."

"Oh, shut up!" I say with a laugh.

He grins. "There you go . . . now we're even."

Chapter 7: Happy Betty

If you obey all the rules you miss all the fun. ~Katharine Hepburn

The next day at work, Joe, the guys, and I are on grocery shopping duty so we drive one of the fire trucks to the grocery store. We always take the trucks for errands in case we get a call.

Turns out Joe can cook. *Holy hell.* Just watching him pick out produce, the focused way he squeezes the tomatoes and breathes in the scent of fresh herbs, is enough to fire up more inappropriate thoughts about him.

"What's for dinner?" I ask.

"I'm thinking lasagna. Can you get the lettuce for the salad? Romaine would be good."

Scott wanders off to get the ingredients for garlic cheese bread. Alberto is scouting out other items. I realize their exit gives me a chance to talk to Joe.

"Hey, can I ask you something?"

"Sure, what?"

"For as far back as I can remember we were on opposite schedules. I've been around you less than any of the other guys, and now we not only have the same schedule but we're assigned to do chores together."

He just silently stares at me with a box of pasta in each hand.

"What's that all about?"

"Maybe Chief wants me to watch out for you?" He responds with a tone like he isn't sure of the answer but is willing to guess.

ont "Really?"

He nods. "Sure. You've been through a lot lately. Maybe having a friend in the squad helps."

I blink several times. "So I'm like your buddy? Like when you go into a new school and you get teamed up with someone who can show you the ropes?"

"Yeah . . . like that I guess," he agrees, yet seems unsure. He rubs the back of his neck and scrunches up his eyebrows.

"Oh for fucks sake," I growl. I toss the heads of lettuce in the cart and storm off. Do they really think I'm that pathetic? I know I'm not at my best lately, but it's feeling like every time I think I'm moving forward in my life, I discover I'm not getting anywhere.

Still in a huff, I wander out the exit and sit on a bench right next to the Buzz Lightyear Rocket Adventure rocking ride. I'm half-tempted to dig through my pockets for some quarters to ride Buzz to *infinity and beyond*.

See that, even my innocent thoughts sound perverted these days.

A few minutes later Joe and the guys roll the cart out of the store. They scan the parking lot, and Scott spots me and points me out.

Joe pushes the cart over to Scott and tells him something, before slowly walking over to me.

He jams his hands down into his pockets. "You ready to go?"

I look up at him with wary eyes. "I don't need a babysitter you know."

He studies me for a minute silently, and then nods. "Okay."

Rising, I brush off my ass. Who knows what was on that bench. "Good, as long as we're clear on that." I pull my shoulders back and start walking to the truck, while he follows close behind.

I steer clear from Joe the rest of the day, and the following afternoon I'm at home, finally facing the bills that have piled up since my marital Armageddon. When I threw Dickwad out I wasn't thinking about how the bills would still be coming but now it may be just me covering them. As I start adding things up it becomes clear that I'm in a shitshow of epic proportion.

It occurs to me that since Dickwad cheated, he should pay up. He should've thought of the financial ramifications before he dropped his drawers and bent over the flower shop worktable.

I pick up my phone to call Jeanine and remember that she's heading to Boston today. Why not go straight to the source? I find a letter that I'd gotten from Mike's law firm and dial the number printed on the bottom of the page.

I have to go through a few people to get the guy, but when I do it becomes clear that this ass is a great example of why people hate lawyers.

I clear my throat. "Hi Steve, I'm Mike Castallani's ex, Trisha and I need to check on something."

"You do realize, Ms. McNeill, that your lawyer should be the one contacting me, correct?"

"Well, she's traveling today and I can't wait for an answer. I'm paying bills right now and I need Mike to pay his half of the mortgage. The bills already late so he needs to get right on it."

"Is that so?"

"Yup."

"Well Mike isn't paying half of the mortgage unless he's living there, and my understanding is that you threw him out on the street and threatened to give away his collection of regency furniture."

"Oh he's such a drama queen. I didn't throw him into the street even though I probably could, and I said I was selling his furniture, not giving it away."

"You acted with hostile intent, and we are considering approaching the judge assigned to our case to allow Mike his rights to live there with you until you decide to sell it and split the equity."

"Over my dead body," I growl.

"I'll make note that you said that," he replies in a creepy calm voice. "You need to understand that it's his right."

I slap my hand down on the table and the bills go flying. "What about my rights? Huh? We made a promise to each other when we got married, and I kept my promise and your client didn't. Shouldn't he have to pay for that?"

"It doesn't work that way, Ms. McNeill."

"Well it should! That asshole should pay me for every time he bent over and took it up the ass while I was at home doing his laundry. And you know what else? I should get extra for the time I walked into his place of business while he was going at it! Do you know what kind of noises he was making? I can't unhear that, and I sure as hell can't unsee it either—"

"Ms. McNeill," he says loudly, interrupting me. "You really need to talk to your lawyer about this. I have a meeting and this conversation can't continue."

I'm working up for my next rant when I realize he's not there. I look down and my phone screen is blank.

"I'm not done!" I yell at the blank phone. My hands curl into fists. "I'm not done," I repeat as tears start streaking down my face.

Sweeping my arm across the table's surface, I send the scattered pile of bills soaring off the table. I get up and stomp all over the mess and then take my checkbook, wind up my pitching arm and then send it flying down the hall toward the living room.

Fucking mother fucker!

I press my hands over my face and realize that despite my streaks of tears, my skin is so flushed with heat it feels like it's burning. Stepping up to the kitchen sink, I turn on the faucet and douse my face over and over with cold water. After about a minute I'm starting to feel human again, and I shut off the water, lift my wet face up and look out the window.

Through my blurry view I'm fairly certain that Joe is watching me from his kitchen window.

Yikes! I wonder how much he saw of my storming around my kitchen. I reach out for a dishtowel and blot my skin. When I look back up my vision is clear and Joe is smiling and waving at me. Just seeing him makes me feel better.

I squeak out a tiny smile as I wave back.

This time he motions for me to come over, so I set down the dishtowel and step out my back door. He's on his tiny landing as I approach.

"What's up?" I ask.

"You wanted to see the inside of my place. Do you still want to?"

I figure he either didn't see me throwing a fit or he's kindly pretending he didn't see it.

I shrug. "Sure."

He steps aside so I can pass through the door.

"Wow," I exclaim as I turn back and look at him.

"Please don't say it's tiny," he says.

I shake my head. "No. I think it's really cool." I take a couple more steps in to marvel at the craftsmanship of his place. It's like an intricate puzzle that someone put together. Every inch seems thought out as my gaze trails over the bookcase, fold-down table and chair, and miniature kitchen.

"Who built this?" I ask.

"My cousin's best friend designs and builds them. I helped some with the build. I brought it all the way down here from Portland after he finished it."

"That must have been some drive."

He grins. "Yeah, I got a lot of attention for sure."

"Where's the bathroom?"

He points behind us and I slide into the space that's smaller than my linen closet. "Whoa. No soaking in the tub for you!"

"No, but wherever I land next I want to build a deck, do an outdoor shower, and get a hot tub."

I nod, imagining it. "That'd be cool." I wiggle back out of the bathroom. "So you said you don't sleep in a loft."

He points to the other end of the structure and I see a surprisingly large day bed set in an alcove with bookshelves on either side. It's cozy and I have to resist the urge to crawl inside.

I let out a low whistle. "This is a much better plan than having to climb a ladder to go to bed."

"I had to give up having a couch or seating, but I'd rather spend my reading and thinking time sitting on top of my rig anyway. I like the open air."

I take note of the drawers and nooks which are built in everywhere, and everything seems to have a place. It's pretty amazing, and a complete contrast to my big empty house. I feel cozy in here, and I like it.

"Do you get claustrophobic?" I ask.

"Not really. I think the fact that I'm at the firehouse three to four days a week helps. It's good coming back here to simplicity and privacy."

"I can understand that. Maybe when the house is gone I should get one of these."

He doesn't say anything just opens the little fridge and

pulls out two bottles of water and hands me one. "Want to hang for a bit?"

"Sure."

We step outside and scale the ladder to the roof. We sit silently in the lawn chairs as I take in the daytime view of my neighborhood. When I turn back I realize Joe is staring at me. He smiles.

"Is this going okay?" I ask.

He gives me a confused look.

I wave my hand across his roof. "I mean with your being here. Is everything all right?"

"Yeah, it's great, and I think Betty likes it here, too," he says patting the deck railing affectionately.

"Betty? Your tiny house is named Betty?"

He scowls. "My *rig* is named Betty."

"Sorry . . . right, your rig."

He settles back into his folding chair. "Yes, and as I was saying, she's very happy here."

I take a sip of my water. "How can you tell?"

"It's just a feeling. Besides, she hasn't been creaking or groaning."

I grin. "Is that so? Well, I'm glad she's happy. So did you really help build her?"

He nods. "I would've liked to have done the whole thing, but I didn't have the time or all the skills necessary."

"I bet it's super complicated. It's so clever how they designed it with all those nooks, drawers, and fold-down thingies. It's like everything has a purpose and thought behind it."

He sits back and smiles with a satisfied look on his face.

"What?" I ask.

"I did the design."

My eyes grow wide. "Really? I'm so impressed. How'd you have the idea to do all that?"

"When I was a kid my parents had a camper, and I was obsessed with it, the way you could take such a small space and give it so much purpose. So when my cousin told me about carpenters building trailer-like houses—structures on wheels that had woodwork and architectural detail—I was all over the idea. It was during the beginning of my divorce and it gave me something positive to focus on. I was constantly doing research and sketching out designs."

"I'm so impressed," I say with a grin.

"I joke that it's my life's work, my masterpiece, but it truly is the thing I'm most proud of."

I reach over and push him in the arm. "See that. Now I really want my own tiny house, or rig as you call them. Maybe you'll design mine for me."

Tipping his head sideways, he smiles. "Maybe."

We look back out at the view, and he clears his throat.

"Hey, I hope you know how much I appreciate you letting me park here."

I study his expression. It's a simple statement but it feels like there's a lot behind the words. He hasn't mentioned when he plans to leave and I don't bring it up because I dread the day he does.

I smile at him. "Honestly, it's been good to have you here."

"How are you doing with all the changes?" he asks.

I shrug. "I'm taking things one day at a time."

Of course I don't mention that only a bit ago I was cursing out Mike's lawyer in a fit of rage.

"Have you talked to your ex?"

"Yes, but only once. He's apparently still in the denial stage. He says he wants to work it out so we can give our marriage another chance."

Joe's eyes widen. "Do you think that's possible?"

"No. I'm not even sure what our marriage meant anymore, and believe me, my ego's taken a real beating. It doesn't feel good at all to know you weren't enough."

"But—" Joe starts to argue before I cut him off.

"I know what you're going to say. What happened was about him wanting men, and not about me. But if deep down he's always wanted men then he should live that life and make peace with himself. I need a man who wants *me* one hundred percent."

Joe looks down as if unscrewing his water bottle is the most interesting thing on earth.

"Besides, fucking around when you're married is a deal breaker for me, no matter who he's with."

Joe suddenly looks up with a haunted look in his eyes, and it feels like I've struck a chord. I remember back when he talked to me in the office and suggested that he had been through something that made Chief think he could be a support to me.

"Is that what happened to you?" I ask softly.

His fingers work the bottle cap back and forth and his lips press down into a straight line. He nods.

"I'm sorry." I wait for him to say more but he doesn't. "How long ago did it happen?"

"Two years," he states in a tight voice.

"Wow," I whisper. It's unsettling that two years later he's still clearly really messed up over it. *Damn. Is that what I'm going to be like?*

He turns away like he wants to be lost in the view, and I lean forward in my chair. I have an overwhelming desire to comfort him and I'm not sure how but I want to try.

"Joe," I say softly.

His gaze darts back to me.

"I'm so sorry." I say each word slowly and with as much weight as a word can have.

We have that moment as our gazes lock, where I feel like we are coding a language between us . . . the sad murmurings of two broken hearts determined to keep beating against all odds.

He nods. "Me too. We deserve better, Trisha."

I have a surge of compassion for this wounded man. I want to go sit in his lap and hold onto him with my hand pressed right over his heart.

We are comrades now in our own private battles of the heart. I'm willing to fight alongside him because for the first time since I walked into my husband's flower shop to witness the end of my marriage, I think there's a chance I can win.

"Woman! Where've you been?" I grab my bestie Jeanine and give her a big hug. I've only talked to her a few times in the last few weeks, and it was always about my impending divorce. Bitch is traveling on business so much we barely get to hang anymore. That's what I get for having a high-powered lawyer for a best friend.

"What have I been doing? Oh, you know, shopping, eating bonbons by the pool. Oh and don't let me forget those pesky facials and massages. It's all so taxing." She lets out an exaggerated huff.

I lower my sunglasses, and narrow my eyes at her. "Who are you and what did you do with Jeanine?" I ask in a threatening voice.

She arches her brow and gives me a scowl. "I was in New York on business. I'm pretty sure at this point that the lawsuit with Aston Noveo is never going to end. I'll be an old lady still working on that damn case. They'll have to wheel me in to the courthouse and their lame-ass legal team will still be asking for extensions and pushing back the court days."

"That's messed up," I say with a groan.

She shakes her head. "You have no idea."

I take a long sip of my iced tea as Jeanine checks her cell phone. Everything about her is razor sharp and uncompromised. She's the most determined woman I've ever known, and I'm proud to call her my friend.

She sets down her phone and leans toward me. "Is the jackass still leaving you messages?"

She was never a fan of Mike's, nor he of her. It's a relief to not have to mediate them anymore.

"Um, actually I talked to him once, and talked to his lawyer once. Both ended really badly."

"I warned you not to do that!"

"I know, I know. I lost control. But believe me, I learned my lesson. I'm not doing that again. I probably made things worse, but I couldn't help it. I'm so full of rage, Jeanine."

"I know you are. If I weren't your lawyer I'd go off on him too. What an ass. You know how I feel, Trisha . . . you deserve so much more."

"I know," I say, and for the first time I think I've actually embraced that idea.

"And do not talk to his lawyer. You will only screw things up. I've already heard from him and had to straighten him out."

"Okay," I say quietly, with my proverbial tail between my legs.

"So William needs to know if you want him to fight for you to keep the house."

William is her firm's divorce specialist, so she's working with him to make sure I get the best outcome possible.

"How much money will I have to come up with to be able to stay in the house?" I ask.

She shakes her head. "Not sure yet. Naturally his

lawyer is undervaluing his floral business, so it's going to be a fight."

I look over at her with wide eyes as I bite my lip.

"Don't worry about your fees, babe. I'm taking care of you."

"Thank you, Jeanine. You're the best. "

She smiles at me.

"Can I ask you something?"

She nods. "Of course, anything."

"Is it going to be a problem that I let a friend park their tiny house on the property?"

She purses her lips. "What?"

"I'm helping out a friend from the station and letting him park his rig there until he finds a permanent spot."

"A *friend*?" she asks. "I thought you had issues with those guys."

"I do . . . well, except for him. He's really cool."

She leans back in her chair and observes me.

"What?" I ask, squirming in my seat.

"*Cool*? Have you slept with him?'

"N-nooo," I stutter.

"Do you want to?"

"Most certainly."

She grins. "This pleases me excessively."

I grin back.

She waves her hand dramatically. "Carry on, my dear."

Chapter 8: A Man with a Tool Box

I want to do it because I want to do it.

~Amelia Earhart

When my doorbell rings, I look through the peephole and smile to see it's Joe and not a creeper. I pull the door open wide.

"Hey," I say. "What's up?"

He holds up a mug of coffee. "Just wondering if you have any milk for my coffee. I ran out."

"Why are you drinking coffee at night?" I ask.

"Because I like to," he responds like my question is lame.

I pull the door open wider.

"Sure, come on in. Is low-fat okay?"

He nods, but I notice his gaze skims the living room before settling on the pile of sealed boxes. He silently follows me as I walk toward the kitchen. We're halfway through the dining room when he stops in his tracks.

I turn toward him. "What?"

"You didn't tell me that you're moving. When will you be out? Do I need to get out too?"

He looks a little frantic, his eyes wide and searching.

"I'm not moving. Well, not until the divorce is final and that takes a while. Why do you think I am?"

He waves his arm across the room. "Why? This place is almost empty, other than the moving boxes in the living room."

"Those aren't moving boxes. That's furniture my

brother's girlfriend made me buy from Ikea."

He rubs his forehead like he can't compute what I'm saying. I guess it does look pretty crazy to someone wandering in here the first time with no warning.

"But if you're not moving, where's the rest of your furniture?" he asks.

"Mike took it. Most of it was his."

His lips tighten and his face gets red. "What do you mean, he took it? What kind of an asshole leaves you in this situation?"

I'm taken back at how angry he is, but I've got to admit that I like it. It's hot.

"A Mike asshole," I reply. "But in fairness, I told him to take it."

"And what about the stuff in the living room?"

"What about it?"

"When are you putting it together?"

I shrug. "I have no idea. Frankly I'm not very inspired lately. This must be what depression feels like."

He gives me a concerned look, and then turns and starts walking to the door.

"Hey, where you going?" I ask.

"To get my tools. Ikea furniture won't do you a damn bit of good if it stays in the box."

I smile. "I guess you're right." I could tell him that I have my own tools and can take care of assembling the furniture, but he seems so pleased with himself that I keep my mouth shut.

He leaves the front door cracked open and returns a few minutes later with a toolbox. The sight is about the sexiest thing I've ever seen. Joe is a real man and he's going to tighten all my screws.

My chest feels hot and I unbutton the top two buttons on my Henley T-shirt.

After he sets down his toolbox, I hand him his coffee. He takes several long sips before handing it back. Next thing I know he's carefully laying out various tools from hex wrenches, to screwdrivers and a mat knife. He grabs the knife and slowly cuts open the first box.

"Shall I grab my tools and join in? I'm an Ikea master, you know, and you've inspired me."

"Sure, the more the merrier." He looks up at me and winks.

I grin back. "Okay."

When all the parts of the table are out, I get a kick out of how meticulous his approach is. While I dive in and start screwing in the legs, he carefully reads the instructions first and follows it to the letter. I've finished three legs by the time he gets one attached.

I step back with my hands on my hips. "Look at that, we made a table!" I tease as we stand it upright and move it to the dining room.

"Looking good, and in record time," he remarks.

I want to point out that if the assembly had been a race, I would've beat him by a mile, but decide I'm better keeping my mouth shut. Instead I show my appreciation.

"I'm going to have to make you dinner now," I say.

"Do you cook?" he asks with a hopeful look.

"Sort of. If you have low expectations, then my cooking should be tolerable."

He chuckles and shakes his head. "You're one-a-kind, Trisha."

"Hopefully in a good way."

"Definitely."

When we've finished screwing the squatty legs into the couch base and putting it into position, I turn to him. "Wanna take a break? How about a beer?"

He nods.

When I come back from the kitchen, he's sitting on the couch with his legs stretched out wide and his head leaning against the sofa's back. I have an image of myself straddling him, and I run my cold beer bottle along my lust-fevered forehead as I hand him his.

"Did I wear you out?" he asks with a grin.

"Hardly," I huff. "All that work and this damn room still looks empty."

"Maybe that's good. Frank Lloyd Wright said that 'space is the breath of art.'"

"That's the architect, right?"

"Yes. He was amazing. You know I wanted my rig to be in his organic architectural style, but we didn't quite achieve that. There really wasn't a practical way to achieve his low-pitched roof and casement windows."

"So I take it you read his biography, too?" I'm impressed to be learning all these things about Joe.

"I did. Did you know that two of his major homes were destroyed by fire and he rebuilt them both?"

"Wow."

"I had a dream once that somehow I got my rig perched over a stream. It was like the poor man's Fallingwater."

"I've seen pictures of that house. Actually, that would be cool."

He nods with a smile.

As we sit and drink our beer, I like that we've found a comfortable silence with each other. I notice him looking over at me.

"What are you thinking about?" he asks.

"I was thinking about how when I ask you that very question you always say 'nothing,' and now I see that couldn't be further from the truth."

He raises his eyebrows but doesn't comment.

"Thanks for helping me with this. I imagine those boxes

would've remained unopened for who knows how long."

He nods. "No problem."

"When you and your ex broke up, what did you do with your part of the furniture and stuff? Obviously it's not in your rig."

He turns the bottle in his hand a few times and I can see the tension in his jaw. I regret asking but I can't take it back. "Hey, we don't have to talk about—"

"I packed a bag, walked out of that house, and never looked back."

"Wow."

"Yeah. And I haven't spoken to her since. The lawyers can fight over shit. None of it matters to me anymore."

"Is she still in your house?"

"I don't know and I don't care."

My breath hitches. I didn't think the gentle giant had it in him to be so frigid. It makes me feel cold inside. Something really bad must have happened. My curiosity overtakes me.

"What happened?"

There's a long pause that's only broken by him finishing off his beer and setting it on the coffee table we just put together. Dragging his fingers through his hair, he clears his throat.

"My younger brother Jason and I were always close. So when his construction company started to do big projects in L.A., he was always welcome to stay with us. He was fun to have around, and Sharon liked having him at the house when I was at the station."

My stomach is churning as I begin to see where this is going. "Oh no," I whisper.

He nods. "I stopped at the house in the middle of one of my shifts to grab something, and they were fucking in our bed. Apparently it had been going on for a while. I swear, if he wasn't my brother I probably would've strangled him."

"I'm surprised you didn't anyway," I growl, not hiding the fury in my voice.

"I couldn't have done that to my mother. Her kids are her everything."

I can't help myself—I reach over, grab his hand and squeeze it, then lace my fingers through his. He doesn't pull back but instead his grip tightens over mine.

"I'm so sorry," I whisper. "And your family?"

"I'm sure my parents are completely ashamed of him, but we don't talk about it, and I don't go home anymore."

It all hits me hard. "You lost so much more than just a wife." I scoot closer to him and rest my head on his shoulder. I don't know if my comfort is helping him or making him uncomfortable, but I can't not offer it. I'm so heartbroken for him.

I get my answer when he tips his head so it's leaning on mine. He lets out a deep breath and it's ragged.

"The only person I've told is Chief. Not even the guys at the station know the whole story."

"I won't tell a soul, I promise."

He squeezes my hand. "I know you won't. You're a good woman, Trisha."

I blink back tears and try to keep my voice steady. "And you're a good man."

After sharing more of our stories, and drinking a second beer, we finally accept that we have no motivation to continue with Ikea parts. How can I care about a bedside table when we've laid out the broken pieces of our hearts? No hex wrench is going to put those parts back together. Things feel heavy and dark but at least we can share the pain.

When he gets up to leave, we give each other a long

hug, me on my tiptoes, him leaning down into me. I wonder when he was last hugged like this. I'm a good hugger
and I can tell he needs it.

His fingers brush my cheek when we part. "Thanks, I
needed that."

"I'm here whenever you need a shoulder or a hug," I
reply. I inwardly cringe at saying something so corny, but
judging from his warm gaze, it was okay with him.

When I close the door and walk through the house
turning off the lights and double-checking the locks, I feel
my pulse flutter.

What's happening to me? Is this feeling the desperate need to connect with someone who's merely willing to
listen, or is it the beginning of something more? The only
thing I know for sure is that when I get into bed, I'll be
thinking about Joe and there'll be a lot more than hugging
going on in my head.

Late afternoon the next work day, Joe and I give each other
knowing glances as the truck charges down Magnolia
Boulevard, the wail of the alarm amping our adrenaline.
Scott, sitting just to the left of Joe, seems particularly tense.
This kind of call, a child found at the bottom of the pool, is
particularly tough to control our emotions over. I grip my
fingers along the edge of my seat.

This is my third child drowning call since I joined the
force, and all three times I've felt sick inside because of the
senselessness of it. Mother fucking swimming pools.

We're the first to arrive, hauling up to a small ranch-
style home where an old man is yelling and frantically
waving his arms. Neighbors with frightened expressions
are gathering on the lawn of the house next door.

Joe and I are first off the truck, running down the

driveway toward the unmistakable sound of a mother screaming. My heart is thundering in my chest as my gaze scans the yard for our victim. Once I see her my brain computes: little girl, lifeless. There's a panicked man attempting to give her CPR. We are twelve minutes from the call . . . it may be too late, or we may only have moments left to save her. Focus, shut down surge of emotion, focus, *damnit,* focus.

Sinking to my knees before the little girl, I scan her head to toe. She's in a colorful swimsuit with a ruffle around her waist and appears to be about four or five, with soggy pigtails and blue lips. The man attending to her looks up at me frantically.

I wrap my hand around her wrist with one hand and press my fingertips against her neck with the other. I'm not sure if I'm actually feeling a faint pulse, or just want to so much that I imagine it, which makes my heart sinks.

I look up at Joe, who's flagging Alberto to get details from the hysterical mother, he glances down and I shake my head with a quick jerk. His jaw sharpens as he pulls the man aside and sinks down across from me to confirm her vitals. Scott is unwinding the cords for the defibrillator as I clear her airways for mouth to mouth. Meanwhile Joe starts the cycle of compressions to her chest.

Alberto rushes toward us, and leans down next to Joe. "The EMT team is just pulling up now." Everything is a mad blur around me and all I can see clearly is the little girl's unresponsive face.

Joe nods as he continues his counts with a steely focus. Alberto takes over keeping the mother back, while explaining what's happening. He has a gift for getting focus from the most hysterical victims and their families.

"Come on, come on," I whisper before I push air into her small, cold lips.

The next round of compressions start. "One, two, three," Joe chants as he firmly applies pressure to her chest. "Four, five, six."

I hear more screaming and the sound of the gurney rattling toward us.

"Seven, eight, nine."

I glance up at Joe and he seems determined, but I don't see the confident look when we know progress is happening.

"Come on, baby girl. Come on!"

I hear a gurgle, and we both arc up and turn her on her side while water starts cascading out of her mouth.

Joe checks for pulse and gives me a quick nod.

We settle her back down and continue, with a renewed resolve that she has a chance to pull through. She's still unconscious but there's a pulse, *there's a pulse.*

I glance up and recognize there's five of us around her now, working in a carefully crafted synchronicity.

The EMT, Brian, lowers his monitor. "Sherman Oaks, stat."

The ground crew backs off while she's lifted and secured on the gurney. As I watch them roll her down the driveway toward the ambulance with Joe by her side—continuing the compression—I feel the ache of knowing that we may not hear if she pulls through completely, or holds onto life in some compromised state.

Back in the truck, Scott and I are silent. It feels wrong not having Joe with us, but he'll return to the station after the hospital staff takes over. I'm exhausted, more emotionally than physically, and it leaves me haggard and down.

"Think she'll make it?" Scott asks.

"I hope so," I answer.

He nods. "Poor kid."

I kick my heel against the truck's floor "Fucking

swimming pools."

Chief checks on us when we return, his expression somber as he hands Scott a blank form. "Henderson, this report is yours."

Scott nods and takes the form.

"Joe is on his way back," Chief says to me.

I nod. "Any word on the girl?"

He shakes his head. "Too soon to know. Why don't you get some rest? It's a full moon tonight, it's going to be busy."

"Okay, sir. I'll go lie down."

"Good."

Twenty minutes later my door cracks open.

"Are you asleep?" Joe whispers.

"No, come on in." I get off the bed just as Joe slips inside and closes the door.

I blink at him with wide eyes. Him being in my room is risky business but I can't care about that when I want to know what happened.

"You okay?" I ask softly.

"Not really."

"How is she?" I ask.

"Too soon to say." He grimaces. "She's so little, Trisha."

He pulls me into his arms and holds me.

I press my face against his chest. "Chief says she has a fighting chance."

"They'll know after the tests and MRIs if her brain is damaged from the oxygen deprivation. I just always wish we'd hear afterwards if the people we've tried to rescue are okay."

I let out a long sigh. "Me too, but maybe we're better off not knowing."

Chapter 9: She's a Man-eater

The most common way people give up their power is by thinking they don't have any.

~Alice Walker

A few days later Joe and I both step outside of our homes at the same time, with our bags slung over our shoulders, ready for our next two-day stint at the station. The sun hasn't been up for long and everything still has a quiet blue cast leftover from the night. I give him a wave and he smiles as he climbs on his bike.

I follow him all the way to the station, appreciating the ease with which he handles his bike. I pull in the lot and park next to him. "You ready?"

"I'm always ready." He grins.

"Is that so?" I laugh and shove him playfully to the side.

"So what am I supposed to be ready for?"

"Our sensitivity training today." I roll my eyes. "Not like I'd ever need that. I'm just a big, mushy marshmallow on calls."

"Sure you are. Is that why they call you T. Rex?"

"Hey, don't *you* start!" I pout.

He pushes me back. "Just kidding."

We're about to go inside the station when I notice two of our guys standing on the edge of the lot—Bobo and Scott, and both of them should shut their gaping big mouths or they may start catching flies.

It's the look in Bobo's eyes in particular that make me

feel like I've done something wrong and just got caught. I guess they aren't used to me being so carefree. I glance back to see if Joe is wondering the same thing but he's holding open the door for me, and seems focused on something happening inside. I sweep past him, and he follows right behind me.

It's not until late in the afternoon that I'm reminded of that brief moment in the parking lot, with Joe and I laughing while the guys looked on. I'm in the hallway posting the notice of the firehouse visitor schedule when I hear my name in the day room. I step up just outside the door, debating whether I should go inside and face the music or not.

"So what's with you and T. Rex?" Bobo asks Joe in a taunting voice.

I have a partial view of the room from my position in the hall and I can see Joe's expression tighten.

"What do you mean?" Joe answers.

"Is something going on? You looked kind of cozy this morning."

What an asshole. I'm tempted to step in and tell him off.

Joe gives him a pissed off look.

"You know she's letting me park my rig on her land, right? Don't make anything more out of it than that."

"So you're just being nice to her because of that?" Scott asks. "Cause it seems like you're spending more time with her than you need to."

Joe folds his arms over his chest. "Is that so? Why are you so interested? Do you think it's any of your business?"

Scott shrugs. "We guys have to look out for each other and she's a bitch, a carnivore of the male kind. Look what she did to her husband . . . she made him gay. I don't want to see that happen to you."

"I appreciate your concern," Joe replies with a conde-scending tone.

"Uh huh," Bobo says tauntingly.

I hold my breath waiting for Joe to defend me for ass-hole's comment. *I made my husband gay?* I'm going to make Scott a ball-less eunuch if he doesn't shut the fuck up. *Why isn't Joe standing up for me?* A horrible feeling is creeping up my spine.

Joe's irritation is written all over his face. "Oh for fucks sake, has it occurred to you geniuses that Chief may have asked me to look out for her? She's been through a rough time. Or did you forget that? It's the same thing I'd do for any of you."

. . . the same thing I'd do for any of you . . .

"Well that makes sense," Bobo says. "You feel sorry for her. I mean why else would you spend time with T. Rex?"

I see Joe flinch, but it's so slight that I can't be sure. What I do know for sure is that he doesn't disagree with him and my cheeks sting like I've just been slapped. I was just about to charge in and go off on the assholes, but his pity suddenly deflated me.

"So there you go, you don't need to worry about how I'm spending my time."

"Okay. Good to know you'd never get involved with her. Gotta say dude, I'd be afraid she'd eat you alive."

"We've got your back, Joe. We'll make sure you don't get T. Rexed."

"No need guys. It's not going to happen."

The conversation moves to another topic, but for some damn reason my legs won't move. I've got my left shoulder pressed against the wall to hold me up, and my shaky right hand pressed over my mouth. If this is just another small death, then why does it feel so damn huge? What I just lost must not have been much according to Joe's account, but for me at this point in my downfall, it feels like everything.

It's at that very moment that Joe happens to look out the door where I've stepped out of the hall shadow. The moment our gazes meet, he knows I heard their revealing discussion, and his eyes shadow over with shame.

The betrayal feels huge to me, not just from my team, but most of all from a man I'd come to trust and thought was my friend. Feeling bile creep up my throat, I swallow it back as I turn and rush down the hall.

I hear heavy footsteps behind me as I fish my room key out of my pocket. Once it's in my grasp, I sprint down the last hallway, get the door open, and slip inside just in time to close and lock the door.

A second later I hear the knob being worked. I've never been so grateful for a lock. He twists it a few more attempts before it stills, and then there's a soft knock on the door and a muffled voice.

"Trisha, are you okay?"

I blink away tears as I take several steps back, until my legs make contact with my bunk mattress. I sink down, grab my pillow, and pull it to my chest.

He knocks again and the tears flow faster. "Go away," I whisper so softly I can barely hear my words.

As if he heard me, everything goes silent other than my occasional sniffle. I know I need to stop. I've got that Irish skin that gets pink and blotchy when I cry. I can hide in my room during dinner, but how am I going to look if we get a call?

I'm focused on willing myself to stop crying, when I hear a key slip in the lock and the door edges open. Joe slips inside and pushes the door closed behind him. Chief has copies of all our keys in his office. He must have gotten it there.

He studies my blotchy face, tears and all. "Trisha," he whispers, looking defeated. Why would he feel defeated? He certainly fared better than I did in that stunning character assassination I overheard.

I avert my gaze and curl over my pillow. I don't want him here.

"Please leave."

"I can't," he says in an uneven voice.

"I don't want you in here. Can you imagine what they'd say about me if they knew you were here?"

"I don't care," he says.

"Well I do. I'm the one that got slaughtered out there. Thanks for standing up for me. I thought you were my friend. I trusted you."

"Please," he begs.

"I thought you were my friend," I repeat as I press my face into my hands.

"They threw me off guard, and I didn't know what to do. Our friendship is private, between you and me. It's none of their business and I don't want either of us to be teased about it."

"What friendship?"

"Trisha . . . please don't."

"You mean T. Rex, the man-eating bitch?"

"Oh fuck," he groans.

"Don't worry. You can keep your rig on my land. I'm not that horrible, I swear."

He steps back and puts his hand on the doorknob. "I'm going to go talk to them. I need to fix this."

"It's too late for that. Besides, it's my turn to talk, but I'll be talking to Chief about changing stations. I can't stay here now. Everyone hates me."

"No!" he exclaims before pacing the room. "You're being dramatic. Can't you see that? The guys talk shit about each other all day long. You know that. Why did you think you'd be spared?"

"This felt like a lot more than that, Joe. Especially when you didn't come to my defense."

"I really fucked this up, didn't I?"

I just stare at him. What does he expect me to say? *It's okay, Joe. Don't worry about It . . .* Well, that's not going to happen.

I pull my pillow closer into my chest. "Can I ask you one thing?"

"Anything," he replies, seeming hopeful.

"Do *you* also think I turned my husband gay?" I know the look on my face is pathetic, but I have no way to hide my pain. This one is a sharp knife dangling over my heart.

"No! Jesus, Trish. That's crazy talk."

"Believe me, I've laid awake at night worrying about that very thing."

"Just take my word on this . . . you're wrong. A woman like you inspires a man, not turns him."

As much as I like hearing those words they're a little too late for me to not question his sincerity. "Thanks Joe, but I really think it would be best for you to leave."

"I'm not leaving. Not until I can make this right."

Putting his fingers under my chin, he raises it so we're eye to eye.

I shake my head. "There's no making this right. What's done is done. I need to step away before my spirit takes another hit." I lift my arm up and wipe my tears across my sleeve.

"No . . . no . . . no," he chants as he pulls me up off the bed into a tight hug against his chest. I squirm and try to extricate myself but he's not yielding.

"I thought you were my friend," I say again, but this time in a painful whisper.

"Please stop saying that. I *am* your friend. There's so much I haven't even said to you yet. This can't be it for us." He slowly cups his large hand over my head and then combs his fingers through my hair and down my back. He does this over and over until I start to calm and melt into his chest.

I should stop him. I have no idea why he's doing this. *Is he trying to torture me?* Despite my trepidation, I've lost the will to resist. It just feels so damn good to be touched and held.

My eyes are pressed shut as I remind myself that this may be the last time we'll be this close again. Suddenly I realize that his lips are pressed against my forehead.

My eyes pop open. "What—"

"Shhh," he whispers as he kisses me just above the eyebrows and then my temple. His lips are so warm, and I'm intoxicated just to have him holding me like he'll never let me go.

My brain and reason are battling with my heart. "But . . ." I murmur as I try to push him away so he can explain what's going on in his head.

"Shhh," he says again as he kisses my cheek and then the tip of my nose.

My legs wobble underneath me and his grip around my waist tightens.

"Oh God," I groan the moment I realize that he isn't just trying to soothe me . . . he's trying to tell me something without words.

He pulls back just slightly and my gaze settles on his lips, which I didn't notice were so perfect until now. I brush my fingertips down his chin.

"*This* is right," he whispers. He drags his nose along my jaw until his lips press against my other temple.

"It's not right . . . not when I feel like our friendship is broken," I say despite the fact that he's stroking the back of my neck and it's making me want more. This guy doesn't play fair.

"Broken?" he whispers. "Remember, I've got a tool box. I can fix anything. Please, Trisha."

When I comprehend the desperation in his voice, and look in his eyes I lose all reason. I have no idea why but the room appears to be brighter. I fall into his gaze, and it suddenly seems like anything is possible.

And that's when he kisses me.

His lips to my lips . . . honey sliding off a spoon as his sweetness fills me. I have a vague sense of my fingers gripping his shoulders and then getting tangled up in his hair as his lips consume me. I've never been kissed like this—a delicate twisting up of tenderness and a rough bass beat claiming me, as my heart pounds under his touch.

He steps back against the wall and pulls me to him, yet giving me berth to escape if I need to. Escape is the furthest thing from my mind. Each kiss and caress teaches me something about him, and I fold each detail up and tuck it in my heart for safekeeping. What I love best is how he cradles my face and whispers my name like it's sacred before he kisses me again and again.

Is this what it feels like to be reborn? This man had broken me completely, and in our resurrection, brought me back someplace new.

My knees are starting to buckle when suddenly the sound of the station alarm tone alerts us to the here and now. We listen carefully to the sequence, as he tightens his arms around me.

"Damn," he groans. "I'm on this one."

I nod, relieved that it's him and not me. I'm not sure I could be focused enough. "Go," I urge.

"I'll be back."

"I hope so," I whisper as irrational images of him trapped in a burning building plague me.

He takes my face in his hands. "Trisha . . . I'll be back."

I nod, crack open the door to make sure the hall is clear, and push him out the door.

"Be safe," I whisper.

He nods with a stoic expression and charges down the hall.

Chapter 10: The Dali Lama of Fire Fighting

It takes a great deal of courage to stand up to your enemies,
but even more to stand up to your friends.

~J.K. Rowling

It's a long night as I lie awake and wait for their return. This night could be any night at the station, but for me it's unlike any other. I feel desperately alive and it makes me want to do crazy things.

I want to climb onto the roof of our station and stand on the buildings edge, my jacket over my p.j.'s, rustling like a cape in the wind. From that vantage point I could see the truck as it ambled back home, the men weary from whatever crisis they faced. Joe would look up and see me cast in silver from the moonlight, and I would have all the answers I needed in his soulful gaze.

But with each hour passing the magic of his kisses fade and instead the reality of our situation takes over my spirit. Nothing has changed about the words that were said about me in the day room. Am I being overly dramatic? I don't think so. Am I being influenced by the blog of female firefighters I follow when women share stories about how they are treated as lower class citizens in their stations? I can put up with the guys taunting about stupid shit, but they crossed a line this time. I'm going to have to talk to Chief and make some hard decisions about my standing with our team.

As for Joe, there's no question that I'm infatuated with him. I still have a drunken hangover from his glorious kisses. But what can we be to each other? We're both dealing with a lot of relationship baggage. I'm not divorced yet and it doesn't sound like he is either, but much more than that there are rules about fraternization in the firehouse. What a mess. We can't be kissing in hallways or sneaking off to my private room.

Instead I finally fall asleep some time past three and wake up at 6:15 to my alarm. *Screw the gym,* I groan. I reach over and pick up my phone. There are three texts, all from Joe.

The first was sent just past four.

We're heading back. Can I come see you?

The next is at 4:20.

There's stuff I need to say. Please be awake.

The last is at 4:44.

I'll wait to hear from you . . . please Trisha.

I set the phone back on the side table and curl up under my covers. My mind is a whirling dervish, so I focus to calm myself and make a plan. I can't face Joe again until I've figured some stuff out. After considering different scenarios I finally decide that I have to speak to Chief first. I can't go back out and be part of the team after what I overheard yesterday without facing what was said about me head-on. I have to take care of this situation before I do anything else.

And however that conversation goes will undoubtedly have a big impact on my situation with Joe.

As I think I run my fingers over my lips, which still feel swollen with his kisses and it stirs me up. What would've happened if the station alarm hadn't gone off? How far would we have gone?

Something occurs to me and I scoot out of bed and open the bottom drawer of the dresser. I pull out the spiral bound book and run my hand over the front: Van

Nuys Department, Administrative Rules and Regulations. Climbing back onto the bed, I open the cover and lean back against the wall.

It only takes a few seconds of skimming through the table of contents to find the section I was looking for.

Section 1—Rule Violations

29. Sexual fraternization between members is expressly prohibited.

It's not that I'm surprised to read the warning. I've read it before. But last time it was of no consequence to me. I was a married woman with absolutely no interest in anyone on my team. Seemingly overnight, everything has changed.

I'm too nervous to eat, so I get dressed and pick up my phone to text Joe.

I need to decide what to do about the situation with the guys yesterday. I'm going to go talk to the chief.

After I hit send, I purposely set the phone down on my dresser, and step out of my room without it. I can't talk to him right now. My space is on the opposite side of the building from the guys' quarters, and sometimes I resent the isolation, but right now I'm grateful for it.

I know Chief is usually in his office at this time in the morning so it's time to deal with this head on.

His door is half open and I knock on the door jamb.

"Hey McNeill, what's up?"

"Got a minute, Chief?"

"Sure." He pushes away from his computer.

"Mind if I close the door?"

His eyebrows raise but he gestures his approval, so I gently shut it.

"What's up?"

My hands are already twisting together and I look

down to gather my courage. "There was an incident in the day room yesterday I need to tell you about."

"Okay. Have a seat," he says.

I lower myself into the chair and grasp my knees to keep my nervous hands still.

"I was in the hallway posting the visitor schedule on the board and I overheard a conversation about me, and it was really ugly, sir."

"I see. Can you tell me what was said?"

I nod and swallow hard. "I was referred to as a bitch, and a man–eater."

"That's wrong and I'm not minimizing your feelings about this, but I have to ask . . . you know how the guys are, right? They give each other shit all the time."

"But they do that to each other, face-to-face, not shit on someone who isn't there. On top of that there was something else said that really hurt me personally . . ."

"You mean something worse than bitch and man-eater?" he asks, seeming very uneasy.

I nod. "They said that I made my husband gay." I avert my gaze again.

"Damn," he mutters.

"I had no idea how they really felt about me, but it makes me wonder if they'd have my back if we were on a call and things went south. Did you see that article the *L.A. Times* did earlier this year about hostility toward women in the firefighting profession? It sure explains why we're still only three percent of the force."

"I did," he sighs, shaking his head.

He swivels his chair sideways as he studies the wall. I've seen him do this before when considering a difficult issue, so I know to just be patient as he chews on the end of his glasses and rubs his hands over his eyes.

"Who was it?"

"Bradley, Scott, and Joe."

Chief's gaze jerks over to mine, and his eyes narrow. "Joe?" He appears particularly displeased to hear his lieutenant mentioned.

"Well they were taunting Joe about being nice to me, but he didn't stop or correct them when they talked serious shit about me."

"I'm very sorry to hear that, McNeill. Are they aware you overheard all of this?"

I feel my cheeks heat up. "Joe is aware. He saw that I was there just as they finished talking about me. I don't think Scott and Bradley had any idea."

"Well, I'm glad you brought this to my attention. That isn't anything we tolerate here. I'm going to call them in. Are you okay with that?"

I nod. I know in my gut that their reaction to being called out on what they said will have a huge influence in my decision whether to stay or go.

After he puts the call out for the three men, it only takes a couple of minutes for Bobo to show up, with Scott right behind him. I don't make eye contact with them as they take their seats. When Joe walks through the door it takes everything I have not to look at him and there's a scramble since the room is short a chair, but he insists on standing.

Chief motions for him to close the door, then clears his throat.

"I called you here for a serious matter. McNeill overheard an extremely offensive conversation about her between you knuckleheads yesterday and is questioning if she still belongs in our department."

"What?" Scott sounds shocked. *What an actor that one is.*

"You heard me, Gallagher."

"But—" Bobo starts, but Chief holds up his hand to still him.

Joe remains eerily silent and my gaze runs along the floor to see his polished boots and the bottom edge of the dark slacks of his uniform. Just knowing he's so close is making my palms sweat and my heart skip.

"This is exactly why my dad says women have no business being firefighters. They're too damn sensitive," Scott says.

The bonehead's dad was a career Battalion Chief and he's always quoting him like he's the Dali Lama of firefighting. My fingers curl into fists.

"You're not helping your case here, Gallagher. It's not about someone being over-sensitive. This is beyond the shit you give each other hanging out between calls. Saying offensive things about one of your team behind their back is not just against regulations, it's damn wrong. Is she supposed to believe you have her back after you've talked smack about her?"

"Chief, it wasn't that bad," Bobo argues.

"Yes, it was," Joe says, "and I regret that I didn't defend her."

My breath hitches, and I look up at him. His arms are folded over his chest and his jaw has sharp angles as he watches Chief.

Chief gives him a long stare. "I'm disappointed you didn't, too."

"We were joking," Scott remarks.

"Do you think it was funny calling me a man-eating bitch who turned her husband gay?" I say with gritted teeth.

He fights back a smile and I want to knee him in the balls and say I was joking about that, too.

"How would either of you feel if you heard me talking serious shit about you and your wives behind your backs?"

The tips of Scott's ears turn bright red. "I wouldn't like

it," he admits.

"No, I'm sure you wouldn't," Chief replies

Bobo drops his head. Maybe he realizes that keeping his mouth shut is the best plan at this point.

"Are we going to be suspended or something?" Scott asks.

"I'm thinking about it," Chief warns. "I want to keep McNeill on our squad, but that's going to be her decision."

"Why don't you guys start by apologizing to her?" Joe suggests before he turns to me, and our gazes lock. "I, for one, am very sorry, Trisha. I wish I'd defended you. It wasn't right."

With a cautious, neutral expression I nod at him. His gaze never wavers as if he's looking into my head to try to figure me out. He also has the look of someone who never thought he'd be in this position.

Bobo turns toward me. "I'm sorry, McNeill. I didn't really mean what I said. You're not the easiest person, but you're not a bitch."

"Okay. I don't deny that."

"And I wouldn't want you to leave."

He seems sincere and it gives me comfort.

Scott lets out a long breath. "I'm sorry too, and I won't call you T. Rex anymore."

"I don't mind T. Rex, Gallagher, just not bitch."

"Understood."

"And do you really think I made my husband gay?"

His head drops down and his cheeks color as he shakes his head. "That was a stupid thing to say . . . a cheap shot. No, I know it doesn't work like that."

I feel relieved, which is ridiculous, but that was the comment which stung the most. "Okay," I say.

"All right, you guys are dismissed. McNeill still can decide to take this to a higher level. She also has to decide if she wants to stay here with us, or ask for a transfer. I'll follow up with you when decisions are made. Meanwhile, I don't want any more of this kind of crap from you."

"Got it, Chief," Bobo responds.

"Okay, get back to work. And Joe, I want to talk to you in a minute."

Joe's expression is completely neutral as he nods, leaving the office and closing the door without looking at me.

Chief studies me. "Well, I'm sorry that happened, McNeill. I think we still have a long way to go with the women in our force."

"I don't want special treatment, Chief. I just want to be treated fairly. If they have an issue with me, just talk to me face-to-face."

"Yes, of course." He straightens the pad he's just made notes on. "So what do you think? Do you want some time to decide if you're going to make a formal complaint?"

"No. This is finished, and I want to stay."

He nods. "Good, good. Let me know if anything else comes up."

"Will do. Thanks, Chief."

Reaching over, he pats me on the shoulder, and it makes me smile. "Send Murphy in on your way out," he says.

"Sure thing."

When I open the door, Joe is leaning against the hallway wall, all long and commanding in his black uniform and gleaming badge. Our eyes meet and his expression is somber, I have no idea what to say to him, so I say what I know I can. "Chief is ready for you."

He nods, walks past me, and steps inside—the door closing firmly behind him.

Chapter 11: Burning Man

I like people too much, or not at all.

~ Sylvia Plath

Although I can't help but be on the lookout for Joe, our paths never directly cross the rest of the day. We go out on separate calls, and I have a station tour to give while he has a presentation on smoke detectors. He's missing at dinner and by the time I get in my bunk I'm thinking that the kiss with him last night was just a dream.

That feeling continues the following day as I head home. I don't see his bike in the driveway, and as the hours continue with no sign of him I start to wonder if he's gone to visit the muffin lady, Nicole. Just the idea of it makes me queasy which pisses me off.

Is he mad at me for talking to Chief? Why, oh why, did I have to get the hots for this man? I sense I have nothing but a long tortured road of frustration ahead of me when all I want is to be kissed like that again.

That evening I head over to my parents' place. At least things are starting to feel more normal at our weekly dinner. As it was Mike almost never came with me, but now that I'm getting used to my new Mike-less life, everyone's not being so careful and polite with me anymore.

It's much easier being my usual Trish McNeill bitchy self when they aren't all being so sickly sweet to me.

Besides, tonight Patrick has brought his wacko girlfriend, Skye, to dinner, and that chick is all the entertainment we need. She's such a fruit loop. I used to worry that she was going to get Paddie to drink her Kool-Aid and then he'd run off and join a cult with her. But as the months have passed, the worry has faded. She seems harmless. The good thing is that she's loosened him up without making him a fruit loop too.

They join us right when we're about to sit down to eat, and all of our mouths drop open when we get a good look at them. Paddie may not have drunk the cherry Kool-Aid but it looks like he took a bath in it.

I lean back in my chair. "Dude! What the hell happened to you? You're beet red."

"I'm sunburnt," he answers, wincing as he sits down.

"No shit," I say and Dad scowls at me. "You've got those white circle raccoon eyes from your glasses."

He makes a face at me. I guess he didn't need to be reminded of that. I love taunting Patrick . . . it's kind of our special brother-sister bonding thing.

"Did you forget your sunscreen? You know how sensitive our Irish skin is," Ma asks.

He lets out a long sigh. "It wasn't waterproof."

" . . . and they kept hosing us down to cool us off," Skye says.

Dad presses his hand over his forehead and groans.

Elle leans forward with a curious expression. "If you don't mind my asking, why is your skin so shiny?"

I nod at Elle. "Right? I swear I can see my reflection in his face."

Paddie gives Skye an exasperated look. "I told you we shouldn't have come tonight."

She ignores him and turns to Elle. "I applied coconut oil to his skin. It's very soothing, actually great for a myriad of afflictions."

I lean forward and sniff. "You do smell like a coconut!"

Paul leans over and sniffs too. "He does."

Patrick ignores us, and starts eating his salad.

"So how was Burning Man?" Elle asks.

Skye sighs and gets a dreamy expression on her face. She looks positively beatific. "It was amazing. Life changing."

"Did it change *your* life, Paddie?" I ask.

He shakes his head. "No, but I was only there a day, Skye was there all week."

"What exactly happens there?" asks Paul.

"It's a gathering of people focused on every form of creative expression. All week long we express ourselves, create amazing art and music, and then we destroy it all by setting it on fire."

I hold up my hand. The firefighter in me has every hair standing on end. "Wait a minute . . . what do you mean *you set it on fire?*"

"That's why they call it *Burning Man*, Trish," Patrick explains.

I try to keep my voice modulated so I don't start yelling. "You burn a man?"

When Skye shakes her head, I hear the tinkle of her earrings. "No, of course not. It's a huge figure of a man. It's symbolic."

"Why do you burn it down? What about the safety of the other structures around it?" I'm getting really irritated, and I'm ready to call the department and make a report.

"There are no other structures around it, we're in the middle of the dessert. And the next night we burn the memorial temple down."

Are these people insane? "A second night of burning? Are there firefighters present when this happens?" I ask, making notes in my mind.

"Not that I could see," replies Patrick.

"What if a windstorm picks up and there's a sudden

shift and participants get caught in a firestorm?" I point out.

Skye nibbles on a carrot shred she's picked out of her salad. "You know Trisha, I think you probably wouldn't enjoy Burning Man."

I laugh just a little maniacally. Skye has a gift for observing the obvious. "And while we're at it, can I ask why you have dirt in your hair?"

Patrick reaches over and starts picking it out of her hairline near her temple.

"We had a celebration in a mud pit after the sweat lodge. I thought I washed it all out."

Mud pit . . . what the hell? I roll my eyes at that one. And was she high when she showered? How could she miss all that dirt?

"Oh, I've read about those sweat lodges," Elle says excitedly. "It's that American Indian tradition where you build a dome-shaped structure and sit inside in the dark, around a pit of hot stones, right?"

Smiling, Skye nods. "Yes! The heat makes you sweat profusely. It's a physical and spiritual cleansing."

"But how did you tolerate the heat if you were already in the hot desert?" Elle asks. She seems so calm—my family never seems to faze her. That Elle is really something. Paul is lucky he found her.

Patrick shakes his head. "She almost passed out when she came out."

"So you didn't do it?" Paul asks.

"No way, I'm claustrophobic," he answers.

Dad gestures to Ma. "Pass the potatoes, Millie."

Ma nods, lifts the heavy bowl and passes it to Paddie who passes it on. The table falls silent. *'Pass the potatoes'* is my dad's way of saying *enough*. I take a sip of my wine and dig in.

After dinner Skye tries to show my mom some reflexology for her sciatica. Meanwhile, Paul and Paddie load the dishwasher, so I drag Elle to the backyard under the premise of some girl time. Judging from her wide-eyed stare I guess I dragged her outside a little too forcefully.

After we stop in front of the garden she rubs her shoulder. "You may have pulled my arm out of the socket, Trish. What's up?"

"He kissed me," I whisper.

Her eyes grow bigger. "The firefighter guy?"

I nod.

"A casual kiss?"

"Oh no, this was a very serious, toe-curling kiss . . ."

She grins. "That good, huh?"

"Oh yeah," I hum.

"Excellent!"

"But we were at the firehouse and then he got called for a run."

"Bummer. But wait a minute, you were kissing in the firehouse? Aren't there rules about that?"

"Yes. It's against department policy."

"Damn! But wait . . . if you had a hiding place, how would they even know?"

"Maybe the goo-goo eyes I'd be giving him at the station. I'm having a hard enough time just acting normal around him as it is."

She bites her lip. "You really like this guy."

"Yes," I say breathlessly.

"Awesome!" she exclaims, and claps her hands together with glee. She's as happy for me as I imagine she'd be for herself. It's no wonder I love her like a sister.

"This is exactly what I told Paul! I knew he was the one."

I purse my lips together. "Don't go overboard. We've

only kissed."

She waves her hand at me. "Oh, I know that! What I meant is I think he's going to be the one to finally fuck you properly. It's a game changer, Trish. You'll see."

I bite my thumbnail. "Well first we need to get to second base."

She nods. "Let me know if you need a plan. I'm good at strategizing."

I fist bump her. "You're the best."

The next day continues to be Joe-less and I'm frustrated. I'll never get to second base with him at this point. Is he mad at me, or something? Because now I'm getting pissed at him. I mean, what the hell?

I channel my anger and do weeding in the garden and chores around the house. I'm climbing the walls by sundown so I go for a long run and come home to a hot shower. I've just pulled on my clean sweats and a T-shirt warm from the dryer when my doorbell rings.

His hands are jammed down in his pockets. "Didn't you hear me knocking?"

I shake my head.

He looks pissed all right. Well that makes two of us.

"What were you doing?" he asks.

"Taking a shower. What? Did you think I was avoiding you?"

He shrugs and averts his eyes.

"Well I could say the same about you. Where've you been?"

"Around."

I nod and look down. *Could this be more awkward?*

He rubs his hands over his face and then reaches his hand out toward me. "I came over to say something."

This doesn't sound good.

I open the door wider and gesture toward the living room. "Okay. Come on in."

He nods, and walks over to the couch and sits down.

"Want anything to drink? Water? Bourbon? Gatorade?" I ask.

His eyes widen. "No thanks."

I settle down on the opposite end of the couch from him. "So what's up?"

"Why didn't you talk to me—warn me, before that interrogation with Chief the other day?"

"Interrogation? Really?"

"Yes, that was shitty. And why didn't you respond to my texts on the way back from our call? I needed to see you, or at least talk to you."

"I was asleep."

"How about when you woke up?"

I shrug. I can feel his irritation.

"I see. So this is how it is? Can I ask you one thing?"

I shrug again. "Sure, what?"

"Why the hell did you let me kiss you that night?"

I purse my lips. "I don't know."

"You. Don't. Know." He says it again without the dramatic pauses, "You don't know."

"Nope." *Why the hell am I lying? What the hell is wrong with me?*

He turns to me with an infuriated expression and dark, angry eyes. I know it's messed up but I think he looks hot. I didn't realize how much I'd miss him and now that he's sitting in front of me every one of my nerve endings are on fire. He just looks so damn good.

What the hell is happening to me? I just took a shower, dried off, and now I'm wet between my legs. I want to climb his tree, butter his biscuit, and ride him like a stallion . . . all at the same time. *Good Lord.*

Leaning forward, he rests his elbows on his sexy knees. A second later he rips off his leather jacket, and as he pulls it off his sleeve pushes up and I see the edge of a tat. My nipples get hard. I swear they do.

"Okay, McNeill. Here's the thing. Have you read the Station Book of Rules and Regulations? There's a rule about fraternization on page twenty-eight."

"I know," I say with a sigh. "I reread it this morning."

He purses his lips and nods. "Okay. Then you know that as long as you stay at the station we can't fraternize. Are you staying?

"Yes, I am," I reply.

He's staring straight ahead, but he shakes his head and slaps his knees. "Okay then, so whatever happened between us the night before last, let's just pretend that it never happened okay?"

"Sure," I say.

"You stay away from me, and I'll stay away from you."

"Right," I agree while pressing my thighs together and wondering if I have a pair of clean panties. I hope so because the ones I'm wearing are getting wetter and will definitely need to be changed.

"So you're fine staying away from me?" he asks, his voice a little choked.

"Yeah. I guess so," I reply in a low voice as I rest my hand on his thigh. *Damn* his thigh is hard as a rock. I'm surprised but pleased that he doesn't push my hand away.

His gaze drops down to where my hand is placed and he lets out a long breath. "And I'm not going to kiss you, even though I knew you really liked it when I did, but I'm sorry . . . no can do." He shakes his head vehemently.

I want to laugh at that one, and how insincere he sounds, but I can't because I'm too busy trying to keep my panties from combusting. I'm pretty sure they're my only clean pair.

"You know, I'm pretty sure you liked it too." As I spread and tighten my fingers over his leg, I swear the heat rising up from him is burning my hand.

His jaw tightens and he rolls his shoulders forward.

My thighs are actually quivering. I look down to observe the phenomenon. I'm pretty sure they've never done that before. So to test them I rise up, swing my leg over and shift until I'm straddling Lieutenant Joe Murphy. When I fully sink down onto his lap I receive the information that maybe he likes me being there.

"Oh God," he moans with a dizzy look like he's going to pass out. "What are you doing?"

Leaning in, I whisper in his ear. "Sitting on you. I like how this feels." I wiggle and sink farther into his lap. He gets the idea.

He nods, closes his eyes for a moment and takes a deep breath. When he opens them again, I swear I see fire.

"What do you want?" he asks, his hands resting on my hips.

"How about just a kiss? Kind of to test things out again," I whisper as I place a hand on either side of his face and pull him toward me.

He's not resisting but he's not exactly helping get the party started either. I forge ahead because I've been holding in all these big infatuated feels and I need to let them out before they just burst out of me and scare him.

When our lips meet this time I'm the one kissing him and I kiss him like I mean business. I put my heart and soul into this kiss, my lips consuming his breath, his heartbeat, his heat. I feel his grip on me tighten as he presses his fingers into my flesh. I moan long and deep when he pulls me down over where he's hard for me. Damn, like everything about him, he's big. So big.

I kiss him again and again as I press against him. I'm stunned. Fooling around has never been even close to this desperate and hot, and even better . . . we're just getting started.

"Wait a minute," he says with a gasp as he pulls away from me.

"What?" I ask, feeling perplexed.

"You're so damn confusing. What's going on here?"

"I just really wanted to kiss you. You aren't enjoying this?"

"You need to ask me that? I thought it was pretty self-evident." His head falls back and he takes a deep breath.

"Why don't I keep going then? We can get each other so worked up that it won't matter if we're confused."

"Good God," he groans, rubbing his face. "You're wearing me out, Trish."

I'm pretty sure he doesn't mean the good kind of wearing someone out.

"Sorry about that," I murmur, although I'm not exactly sure what I'm apologizing for. I slide off his lap so that I'm sitting next to him on the couch.

He nods, his expression suddenly looking very far away.

"So where were you today?" I ask.

"With Nicole."

My porcupine spines prickle and stand up.

"And what were you and Nicole the muffin maker doing?"

"Talking about you."

"Really. What did she think?"

"Well at first she was surprised about us."

"Us?" I ask. I bite back a smile. I like the sound of that.

"She thought you're gay, but I assured her otherwise."

I scoff. It's not the first time nor is it the last I'll be called that. Any woman who is perceived as outwardly strong, and not overtly feminine is in question. It's bullshit but I refuse to be stereotyped. "Well she was wrong."

"Yeah, I'm pretty clear on that."

"Why did you talk to her about me?"

"I wanted to get a woman's perspective."

I suspect her perspective wasn't going to be helpful. "So what did she say?"

"That I shouldn't be with you—that there's too many reasons why I shouldn't."

"I not surprised at all. She doesn't want to share."

He huffs. "I told you I haven't been with her in a long time."

"Yeah, but that doesn't mean she doesn't want you to be. So what do you want to do?"

He rubs his hands roughly over his face. "Maybe we need to slow down."

I pull back. "Yeah. It wasn't smart, us kissing like that."

"No, it shouldn't have happened. I promise you that I'll control myself next time."

"Good. You do that," I say even though I know I'm the one who provoked him, not the other way around.

"But hey, you were the one who climbed onto my lap, straddled me, and wiggled all over me."

"Yeah, I probably shouldn't have done that either."

He shakes his head. "Nope."

I bite my thumbnail. "Okay, sounds like we have this figured out."

He nods. "Okay good."

I sort of thought we were kidding each other about not kissing me but now he seems pretty serious.

As he pulls his shirt down, I gesture to his crotch. "You're really well endowed."

He arches his right brow and side eyes me. "So I've been told."

"Maybe one day you could show me," I sigh.

"Trisha," he says with a growl. "Seriously, what's going on in that crazy head of yours?"

"I can't help it. You bring out this side of me."

He groans.

"You don't like that idea?"

"Oh believe me, I really liked kissing you and all. But I don't think either of us are ready for this. Besides, it's not smart for me to fool around with my co-worker and quasi landlord."

"Landlord? I hadn't thought of it like that. So that means I'm lord of your land," I chuckle.

"Are you high?" he asks.

I shrug. "Maybe on endorphins. Between the run and that awesome kissing I'm overflowing with them."

He stands up and straightens himself out.

"You leaving?" I ask.

He nods.

"So just friends from now on?" I ask, secretly hoping he'll change his mind.

"Yeah, just friends. No benefits."

My heart sinks but I put on a good face and give him a smile. "Okay then, guess I'll see you around."

Chapter 12: Crack in his Armor

Vulnerability is our most accurate measure of courage.
~Brene Brown

I have no idea how I'm supposed to act around him at the station anymore. Even though we agreed to be friends, I feel like I'm holding in the biggest secret of my life. To prevent losing control I don't watch him eat with that sexy mouth at lunch, or consider grabbing his ass when no one's looking. That stuff is kid's play, and my thoughts for him are a serious, class-A obsession.

Maybe this is just that worked-up time when you first start falling for a guy. Today you have him on your mind twenty-four, seven, and tomorrow you're bitching at him about leaving his crap all over your place.

But deep down I think this is something more.

I've never been amped like a billboard in Times Square. The most lust I ever had with a man was a buzz. Every night I'm alone in my station bunk is spent imagining him in bed with me.

So Friday morning I'm in the day room refilling my mug with coffee when Joe strolls in wearing his dress uniform.

"Going to a funeral?" Bobo asks.

He gives him a long look. "No. It's Bailey's retirement luncheon, remember?"

"From the Sherman Oaks station? Oh yeah, sorry, dude."

I try not to stare at Joe, but damn, that man with his perfectly fitting uniform, clean shave, and polished shoes makes me want to stare at him until the image is permanently etched in my brain. What is it about a good-looking man in a uniform?

It's sweet torture knowing how it feels to have him kissing me senseless with his arms around me, in contrast to how cool and controlled he seems right now. His gaze shifts over to me and I glance down, sensing that my cheeks are on fire.

"What are you working on, McNeill?" he asks.

I blink. "Finishing up a report from last night's call in Reseda."

He nods, looking official.

I'd like to put my fingerprints all over his shiny badge just to see a crack in today's armor. I bite my lip. He'd probably make me shine it up again.

Good Lord. Why does the idea of that make me hot? I avert my gaze again.

"We need you to go on the business inspection run today with Scott. Jim got called away."

"Okay."

"You mean, 'yes sir!'" Bobo teases.

I arch my brow at him. "Really, *Bozo*? You want to go there with me?"

I can tell Joe is fighting back a smile.

He throws up his hands, perhaps remembering our meeting with Chief. "Sorry, sorry!" he says.

As Joe walks out, I stand up and gather my things, then silently follow him out of the room. He's already several steps ahead of me, giving me a perfect view of his broad shoulders and perfect ass. He walks in a steady gait as if he isn't even aware I'm behind him, but when he gets to the office door, instead of stepping inside he turns and leans against the wall so he can watch me pass. When I'm by his side I pause, my gaze meeting his, but giving nothing away.

"You okay?" he asks.

I don't answer right away, just take in his presence and the faint smell of his cologne. I'm sure I'm projecting phero-mones like a cat in heat. It makes me feel reckless so I check the hall to make sure we're alone.

I give him a long look, letting my gaze slowly travel down his body and back up.

"Okay?"

He nods, his gaze intense.

"Well I still have my private thoughts about us. I won't ever forget how it felt sitting on your lap . . . kissing you . . . you kissing me back," I say quietly.

His sharp cheekbones color.

"But it's good we're friends. It's the smart thing. I know I can be reckless, but *you're* a smart man."

I give him one more look, hoping that he's feeling drawn to me, at least a little bit, since I'm so powerfully drawn to him. This time as I turn and continue down the hall he suddenly speaks up.

"You know, Trish, somewhere, something incredible is waiting to be known," he says.

I stop and turn around. "Is that from another one of your books?

He nods. "Carl Sagan."

I smile. "I like that."

The corners of his mouth turn up and there's a spark in his eyes.

His expression gives me a glimmer of hope, and I re-spond before continuing on, "Maybe one day you'll let me borrow that one too."

Later, Ma calls me, and it's clear she's cast her reel to go fishing . . . into my private life.

"So how are things at the station?"

"Fine."

"I hear your lieutenant has been very kind to you."

I'm going to kill Paul.

"Yeah, he's nice to everyone," I lie.

"Well, why don't you bring him to dinner this week?"

"No, why would I subject him to that? He's a nice guy, not a masochist."

"See, I told your father you wouldn't bring him. So I'm going ahead with my original plan that he tried to talk me out of."

"Which would be?" I break out into a cold sweat. Ma is unrelenting once she gets an idea in her head.

"I'm going to bake him a cake and write thank you on it with fancy lettering that I saw in a magazine. Is he on duty tomorrow? I'll bring it by then."

Thank you?

"Thank you for what?"

"Well, he's been nice to you in this difficult time. He must be a very patient man."

I'm about to drill her to find out what exactly she meant by the *patient* man quip, but I've got bigger fish to fry.

In my mind I picture Ma in the station's day room, cutting up pieces of cake for the guys while grilling them about their personal lives. Every tiny hair on my body is standing up from the sheer horror of the idea. I'd never hear the end of it.

Over my dead body is this going to happen.

"Ah, I don't think so, Ma. There are rules against that," I say.

"No there aren't. I already called your chief and asked if I could. Of course I'd include all the men, not just your lieutenant."

"He's not *my* lieutenant! Wait . . . you called my chief?" I can feel my eyes bugging out of my head.

"He was quite lovely about it. He said that if he was away at an inspection, to make sure and save him a piece."

Every muscle in my body is so tense that I may explode. I slip on my bullshit vest cause it's about to fly.

"You know, Dad's right. On second thought, it'd be nicer if I just brought him over. That way the whole family could meet him. He's a nice guy and a friend."

"Lovely," she says. "I'm so glad you agree."

Agree my ass. I just got my arm twisted out of its socket with her maternal subterfuge.

"And he *is* just a friend Ma, got it?"

"Whatever you say, dear. It's so nice that you have a new friend and now we get to meet him."

We're on the way to my parents' house and Joe's eye is twitching under his sunglasses.

"I honestly have no idea why I agreed to this," he murmurs, gazing out the window.

"So I wouldn't make you move Betty off my land."

He glances over at me with an irritated expression. "You were joking about that, weren't you?"

"Yeah. But I wasn't joking about Ma showing up at the station with a cake for you. I really don't need to give those guys another reason to make fun of me."

"I suppose not. They wouldn't be kind . . . to either of us, if she did that."

"So you're saving my ass and now I owe you big time. And look at it this way, it's a home-cooked meal with cake for dessert."

"And remind me what I'm being thanked for?"

"For being nice to me. My jerk brother must have told her that."

"Is it rare for people to be nice to you, Trisha?"

I chuckle. "Yeah. It's rare. I don't think I have to explain why. You know me pretty well at this point."

His eyebrows knit together. "You're not so bad."

"Thanks."

He taps his knee with his fingers.

"So tonight we will celebrate you," I tease.

"This is so weird. Seriously."

"Well it's true that you're a good man, and now you know that I need reinforcement from my family." I nod and grin.

He looks over at me with wide eyes. "Are they really that bad?"

"No, my family is great actually. I'm the problem . . . the black sheep, and they're always having to deal with my snarky attitude. I'm pretty sure I've exhausted them beyond measure."

He nods his head in agreement. "Oh, I get it. You exhaust me all the time."

"Shut. Up. You," I say, shaking a fist at him.

He points at me. "See, this is exactly what I'm talking about."

We're still bantering back and forth when we approach the front door of my parents' place and it swings open wide.

"Hey!" Paul leans back toward the entry hall. "They're here," he calls out down the hall before extending his hand out to Joe. "I'm the older brother," he says with a grin and they shake hands.

I roll my eyes. "Joe, this is my brother Paul."

"Good to meet you," Joe responds while I push them both in the house and toward the living room.

Paul looks over his shoulder with that stupid grin still on his face and his eyes wide as he waggles his brows. His expression of approval doesn't surprise me. Joe is very presentable. I just hope they don't all make asses of themselves making assumptions about us and saying things to embarrass me.

As we step into the living room I take a deep breath. "Hey Dad, I want you to meet my friend, Joe, from the station."

When Dad gets one look at Joe he sets down the remote and stands to greet him. I lose my chain of thought for a moment because Dad has usually been standoffish with any guy I brought home.

As they shake hands Dad asks, "Joe . . . ?"

"Murphy, sir. Joseph Murphy."

Dad's chest puffs out and he stands taller, but he's still not a match for Joe's height. "Yer family's Irish?"

"Yes, sir. Galway and farther North."

"Millie!" Dad calls out toward the kitchen. "Come meet Joseph."

"It's Joe, Dad," I correct him.

I've got to say, I'm getting a real kick out of the excited look in Dad's eyes. I've never introduced my parents to a guy they were impressed with right off the bat. This is new territory for me.

Mom knows something's up and skitters into the living room. She stops in her track when she sees Joe and her fingers flutter up to cover her mouth. "Oh my," she gasps.

I'm tempted to push her back into the kitchen. If she starts acting like that crazy Mrs. Bennett from *Pride and Prejudice* we're going to have to leave.

"Mrs. McNeill," Joe says with a smile. "Nice to meet you."

Mom smiles like she's meeting the non-asshole version

of Mr. Darcy. "So nice to meet you, too."

"I need a drink," I announce loudly. "How about you, Joe?"

He shakes his head. "No, I'm fine."

I shouldn't leave him alone with my parents but if I don't step away I'm going to say something bitchy. When I get to the kitchen Elle is slowly stirring the gravy on the burner. I fold my arms over my chest.

"You didn't tell them that I'm crushing on him, did you?"

Her mouth drops open but then she smiles. "Hey, Trish. No, of course I didn't tell them that. Paul hasn't either. We aren't idiots."

I shuffle my feet. "I suppose you're not."

She turns the burner down and sidles over next to me. "But holy hell, woman! That man is hot!"

I smack my lips and grin. "Right?"

"It's no wonder you want to climb his tree."

I sigh. "He'd be such a fine tree to climb."

Elle walks over to the door and peeks out for another look. "I think Millie's flirting with him."

"Ewww," I say, leaning into her to check out what's going on as well.

"She even took off her apron."

"And he brought her favorite wine. She'll never let him leave now."

"Whispering Angel?" Elle asks. "That's pricey."

I shrug. "He insisted."

Elle shakes her manicured finger at me. "Gurlllllll!" Apparently that's girl code that he's really impressed her.

"Don't get too excited," I say. "We keep agreeing to just be friends with no benefits."

"Are you nuts? Why would you agree to that?"

"The reality is I'm still in shock over Mike and not even

close to being divorced yet, he's damaged from his marriage, and to top it off, we're forbidden to be together because of our oath. We're kind of a hot mess."

"Oath?"

"We're firefighters, Elle. They forbid fraternization and for good reason. Complicated emotional relationships with people you could likely end up in a life-or-death situation with, is neither smart nor tolerated."

"Right," she agrees but I can almost see the wheels turning in her head.

"What if you were in different stations?"

"I don't want to be in a different station than Joe." I can feel my expression sag just at the thought of it.

Elle glances at me and then nudges my shoulder. "Well, let's not worry about that right now. You never know what will happen. Let's get out there and join them. Okay?"

"Sure."

"Can you pass the creamed corn?" Patrick asks. He keeps side-eyeing Joe but hasn't tried to converse with him much. He's never been so good with change, and this year between my marriage failing and Elle joining our clan, there's been a lot of it and that's not even counting his crazy girlfriend.

"So Trisha tells me you're an accountant," Joe says.

Patrick nods. "I work for one of the companies that insures the studios. I also have a side tax business with a number of clients."

"Cool," Joe says. "My dad was an accountant when I was growing up."

Patrick lights up and sits up straight. "What does he do now?"

"He's CFO at a hospital in Eugene, Oregon, where I'm from."

Patrick shakes his head eagerly and nods to Mom and

Dad. "See."

Confused, Joe looks over at me.

"We tease Patrick about his line of work . . ."

Patrick sighs. "All the time."

"Why do you tease him? Every family needs someone who has a good head for numbers. You're lucky."

Patrick looks over at Joe with so much appreciation that he almost has goo-goo eyes. If he weren't straight as a ruler I'd think he was crushing on our dinner guest.

"How did you end up in firefighting?" Dad asks Joe, changing the focus away from Patrick.

His eyes darken and his jaw tightens as he takes a deep breath. "I have a very strong sense of right and wrong, sir. I was a teenager when 9/11 happened and afterwards I wanted to enlist as soon as I was old enough, but my mother couldn't bear the idea of it."

Ma shakes her head vigorously. "Oh no, you could end up deployed to the Middle East. I don't think I'd be able to live with the fear if one of my boys did that. The stories I've read about it are horrible."

Joe gives her a knowing look and nods. "So she convinced me that there were other ways to make a difference. Firefighting felt like the next most noble thing."

Next most noble? My heart thuds at his confession. He's such a good man, far too good for me. Which is only confirmed when my next series of thoughts stray into my powerful attraction to him.

There's something about a real man, one who's strong and protective, and looking out not just for others, but for the greater good . . . it's so appealing. Like this man wasn't sexy enough.

I let out a quiet sigh of longing.

Dad appraises him with a serious gaze. "Our Trish says you're a lieutenant."

He nods. "I am."

"Your folks must be very proud of you, son," Dad says.

It's obvious how impressed my parents are with Joe. I'm glad they like him but this conversation has stirred me up, and I can't help but wonder about the different ways I've disappointed my parents. Yet what if my career choice has provided some measure of redemption?

I know this isn't the time or place to ask, but I'm compelled to seize the moment and ask the question I've often wondered.

"Are you proud of *me*, Dad?"

His eyes grow wide. "Of course I am. Why do you ask?"

I shrug. "I don't know. Maybe it's during those times on a rough call and the fear starts to wear you down . . . it's just good to know that what you do means something to the people closest to you."

There's a weighted moment of silence and then Ma looks at me with glazed eyes. "We're very proud of you, Trish."

The corners of my mouth turn up. "Good to know."

The conversation shifts when Elle asks Patrick to pass the salad bowl and Paul teases her about being a rabbit. As I listen I feel Joe's gaze on me before I turn to look and see his quiet smile. A second later I feel his hand reach under the table and wrap around mine, before squeezing it gently.

A warmth wraps around me, and I want to curl up inside of the feeling until my cold heart has thawed. The sensation is vaguely familiar yet completely new.

Joe rubs his thumb over the top of my hand and squeezes it one more time, before letting go. I have an overwhelming desire to kiss him and I look down at my plate and take a deep breath so I can get a grip.

The warm feeling hits me again and my brain starts to compute and immediately I feel concern and a bit of panic.

Could it be?

No.

That wouldn't be smart, and I need to be badass and strong-willed as I try to rebuild my life.

But then the warmth hits me again and takes my breath away. I'm left with an even stronger desire to kiss him. That's it . . . holy hell. There's no doubt. This is serious.

I'm friggin' falling in love.

We're halfway back to my place and Joe has barely said a word.

"A quarter for your thoughts," I say to break up the silence.

He glances over at me. "Quarter?"

I shrug. "Inflation."

"I liked your family," he replies.

"And boy oh boy did they like you!" I shake my head. "My mother was downright embarrassing."

He smiles. "Nah, she was sweet."

"In the kitchen after dinner my dad told me that you were welcome at our house any time. That's about equivalent to winning the Nobel Peace Prize in my family."

"I think he likes firefighters. You know that's nothing new. We get a lot of that from the public . . . like they think of us like we're superheroes or something," Joe says.

"Well, we kind of are, don't you think?"

"No. We're just well trained and disciplined about our job."

I roll my eyes. "Right. Just like the cashier at the drive-thru Starbucks is well trained. I like that you're so modest. It's very appealing."

He doesn't respond, which worries me, and when we pull up to the house everything suddenly feels very formal as he walks me to my door.

"Okay, I think I'm going to crash. Thanks for tonight."

My heart goes cold. *That's it?* Thanks for tonight? What the hell? Have I been reduced to being an annoying acquaintance? I'm suddenly wrestling with all these girly love feels and he's acting like he can't wait to get away from me.

I'm not willing to give up potential intimacy so easily so I gesture toward the house. "You want a beer or something?"

Slipping his hands in his pockets, he drops his gaze to the ground. "Not tonight. Can I have a raincheck?"

Damn, now he's being polite. I hate that shit. It riles me. "Look, Joe, don't worry about a raincheck, okay? I'll see you around."

I jam my key in the door, crank it open, and bust it closed in record time. I'm tempted to look through the peephole to see his expression but I resist the urge recognizing that it could potentially piss me off more.

God, now I'm becoming one of those desperate, dramatic women I detest. *Awesome.*

Once inside, I pace back and forth through the house cursing Joe and then my life, until I cycle back to Joe again. I take small moments to chastise myself . . . after all he's made it clear he wants to be friends. So just because I got love-struck goofy doesn't mean he wants to get goofy too. I know he's damaged goods from his divorce. He's probably more messed up from what his ex did to him than I realized.

Plus it seems unlikely that he's been "working on his issues" and seeing one of those pussy L.A. therapists that repeats everything you tell them back as a question and then charges you three-hundred dollars for their precious time.

I storm into the kitchen for a bottle of wine, before realizing that tomorrow is my Trader Joe's run and so I'm wineless and screwed. Then in a moment of brilliance I remember my secret stash of miniature airplane wine bottles. I dig through the cupboards until I find my hoard. They've been sitting there a while, but isn't that cool with wine? That shit likes to age, even if it's in a tiny plastic bottle with a screw-on cap.

I down the first one pretty quickly and storm through the house a few more times before stopping at the kitchen window to take in the view. Well, well, well . . . what is the big man doing in his tiny house? Apparently he hasn't *crashed* yet since I can see the flicker of a TV screen.

You can bet that pisses me off. I stuff a few of my tiny bottles in my pockets and storm out of the house.

I knock hard on his door, and a second later, knock harder still.

Come on, Joe. It's not like you've got to climb down a ladder from your loft.

I'm gearing up to give the door a swift kick when he shows up and opens the door halfway.

He looks irritated. *Well, join the party, Joe.*

"What's wrong?" he asks.

"I want to talk. Can I come in or do you have company?"

He squints and studies me like I've lost my mind. "No, I told you I'm going to crash."

"But not right away, obviously." I wave at his jeans and sweatshirt.

"Soon," he says.

I push the door open, and step past him until I'm inside. Digging into my pocket, I pull out a tiny bottle and then hold it up for him. "This is for you . . . a tiny bottle of wine for the big man in his tiny house."

He arches his brow and doesn't take it. "You seem very pleased with yourself. Did you plan this out?"

"Hardly. If I had planned anything tonight, it would've been something far more exciting."

Folding his arms over his chest, he shakes his head. "Really?

I give him a long look. "Yup."

I walk to the back of the rig, kick off my shoes, and climb onto his bed until I'm leaning against the outside wall. "So what are we watching?"

He slowly walks back to where I'm sitting and just stands for a minute surveying me, his arms still folded. "I'm sorry, but were you invited back here?"

I shrug, and hold the bottle out to him again.

He keeps staring. He clearly has no idea of my tenacity when I've made my mind up about something.

"Go on now, take it. Hopefully it'll cheer you up."

"Alcohol is a depressant," he grumbles as he apparently surrenders and climbs onto the bed. After unscrewing the bottle, he takes several long swigs.

Glancing over to my right, I notice that the shelves built into the sides of his bed are full of books. I wonder if they're those biographies he likes to read and I pull one out, holding it up toward the light so I can read the cover.

"Amelia Earhart?" I ask. "Really?"

"What? I'm not a misogynist, if that's what you're implying. I read books about women too, you know."

"Well . . ."

He narrows his eyes at me. "What?"

"Where's my quote?"

"Okay, let me think . . . how about this . . . *Never interrupt someone doing what you said couldn't be done.*"

Grinning, I fist pump the air. "Oh I like that!"

"She was tough, I'll have you know," he says.

"My kinda gal."

"You kind of remind me of her."

"In what way?"

He shrugs. "You're true to who you are, and you've forged your own path . . . so you're both trailblazers. That takes a great inner strength. As you know, female firefighters still aren't very common."

"It's still a boy's club—*girls keep out*."

He arches his brow at me but doesn't comment.

I fluff the pillows behind me and settle back before pointing to the TV. "The cooking channel? Seriously?"

"What did you think I'd be watching?"

"Well, I was hoping for cartoons." I crack open my second bottle and realize that he's staring at me with dark eyes as I slowly lick the wine off my lips. The way his gaze lingers as he takes a deep breath is only the smallest bit of encouragement, but I'll take it.

"I still don't understand why you've got this on. You like cooking that much? I know you do a great job when it's your turn at the station, but you don't really have a workable kitchen in this thing."

"I used to love to cook. I considered myself a gourmet."

"Really?" I try to picture him with a white apron and chef's hat and it makes me giggle.

But then I notice that he seems upset, and maybe there's more to his proclamation than I realized.

"I cooked for Sharon, she was a serious foodie. And now I don't cook like that anymore."

I fall silent as I grit my teeth. So now we can add another thing to the list of losses since Joe walked in on his wife and brother. It pains me to see him hurting. Lifting the miniature wine bottle to his lips, he finishes it off.

"Will you cook something fancy for me sometime?"

He pauses with a look of pain on his face. "Maybe."

I reach into my pocket and hold up the last bottle of wine. "Want this? It's the last one."

He doesn't even reply, just takes it from me and unscrews the cap with a somber expression on his face.

I look at his muscular legs stretched out in front of him and reach out to rest my hand on his calf. He flinches a little and then averts his gaze as he takes a long drink from the bottle that looks ridiculous in his large hands.

I gently squeeze and stroke his leg, sometimes trailing up as high as his knee, other times focused on the tight bundle of muscles on the inside of his calf. He leans back into the pillows and watches me, the corners of his mouth turned downward.

"Is this okay?" I ask, hoping my touch is giving him at least a little bit of comfort.

He nods and sighs. I can feel his leg relax and settle into the bed.

"Why do you look so sad?" I ask.

He shrugs. "I'm okay."

Okay, sure. He's rocking that stoic man thing.

I lighten my touch on his leg. "I'd really like to know what's bothering you. Maybe I can help."

After a long pause he finally speaks up. "I miss my family," he says quietly.

I nod. "I bet you do. I can't imagine being cut off from mine."

"Being with your family tonight, the way you tease each other, yet it's obvious that you love each other . . . I can't lie. It was tough for me. It reminded me of what I've lost."

"You really won't go home again?"

He shakes his head. "I just can't. It's been like a death for me," he says quietly. "I'm not sure I could take it."

"But—" I start to argue.

"It's like my heart is a stone now, Trisha."

That one shuts me up. *Damn.* I don't want to believe that his heart is impenetrable. I scoot toward him on the bed. "Come here," I whisper, holding my arm out.

He surprises me by surrendering, leaning into me so that I can wrap my arm around him.

God, I love this man.

I brush my lips over his thick hair. "I'll go with you for

moral support if you ever change your mind."

He tilts his head back and looks up at me. "Why would you do that? It could get really ugly with my brother."

"You know how strong I am, right?"

"Yeah, that's kind of hard to miss," he replies.

"So I'd have your back. You've seen me in those self-defense classes. They don't call me badass T. Rex for nothing."

He smiles. "You *are* badass."

I nod. "So maybe that would be a time you could let me be strong for the both of us."

I feel his shoulders tighten under my arms and he slowly pulls away, then turns until he's upright and facing me.

I wait for him to address me but instead he just studies my expression and I'm trying to project kindness, even though I'm not sure I'm succeeding.

"I worry that you like me too much, Trisha."

I nod slowly. What he said hurts to even think about. "I worry about it too."

"You know I'm not the kind of man you deserve. I'm bitter and there's no romance left in me. I'm not a hearts and buy-you-flowers kind of guy, and you deserve that."

"You aren't?" I half tease him, then immediately realize he's completely serious.

He grimaces. "Not any more. I did that with her and got burned."

I give him a long look.

"You know what, Joe? I've had that romance crap and flowers and it was all a lie. So I don't need that from you or anyone. I just want to be with a real man, a good man, and I want to feel the way I do every time you touch me."

His eyes are intense as his gaze moves over my features. He reaches out and cups my face with his large hands, his thumb skimming my cheeks.

"What?" I ask, wondering how I should interpret his tenderness.

He shakes his head silently, his gaze settling on my lips. Despite all of his warnings about having no romance left in him, he leans forward and gives me the most gentle kiss of my life. I melt like a pat of butter, letting a soft moan escape my parted lips.

"Joe," I whisper.

"Shhh," he says.

"Don't stop," I plead.

His thumbs are still circling my cheeks. "I won't," he whispers before kissing me again. His lips trail down the side of my neck. "My feelings for you are getting out of control, Trisha."

I swallow hard. "Really? I'm so drawn to you that I'm scared your rejection could break me, but I can't stay away."

He leans closer into me and skims his fingers along my temple and across my cheek. "I think about you all the time even though I'm not supposed to. I think about touching you like this. My want is big, Trisha. Really big."

"Mine, too," I whisper.

"Can I? Is this okay?" he asks, the intensity in his eyes making my heart skip as he runs his fingers along the edge of my sweater and lifts it up just enough for his fingertips to graze my skin.

"Yes," I whisper. He pulls my sweater up and over my head, as his gaze slowly moves down my neck, across my breasts and back up to my eyes.

He takes a sharp breath then brushes his lips along my shoulder.

With trembling fingers I undo my bra and slide it off as he pulls off his shirt. The cool air tightens my skin, my nipples hard as I ache for the caress of his warm lips. Pulling me onto his lap, he kisses me with a rush of emotion as desperate as I feel. I revel in the sensation of my breasts skimming his bare chest, and his big hand pressing into my back to pull me closer.

"Please," I murmur a blush burning across my cheeks.

He nods, helping undo my jeans as I rise to my knees. When he eases me back on the mattress to pull them off, he groans my name.

He gets off the mattress just long enough to discard what's left of his clothes. Back on the bed, he lifts himself over me and takes a moment to look deep into my eyes. I see all the hurt from earlier still lingering in his gaze. But desire is taking control now, fueled by his determination, and desire seems to have won the war in his heart.

He kisses me everywhere, tenderly and then hungrily until I'm lost in his touch. His hands ease my legs farther apart before his fingers lightly trail up my inner thighs, until they're gliding where I'm already wet for him.

"Are you sure?" he asks breathlessly. "I want you so much."

I nod, rocking my hips up to encourage him as he sinks into me in one fluid, powerful stroke. He pauses, his forehead resting on the edge of my shoulder, his hot breath warming my skin.

I wait patiently, every muscle in my body poised to hold onto him, including his cock now buried deep between my legs.

"God, you're so perfect for me," he says. The way his eyes appraise me makes my heart race.

I stroke my hands over him, imagining the strength under each ridge and muscle of his torso. I love everything about his powerful body, his weight securing me under him as he begins to fuck me slow and deep. My fingers dig into the muscles of his ass to pull him even closer. I feel every part of me opening up wider to draw him in. I wrap my legs around him possessively as I gasp his name.

A wave of ecstasy flows through me at the raw, pure

pleasure of this man making love to me, showing me a passion I'd only read about, but had never understood.

He lets out a low groan, and fucks me deeper as if he knows I'm near the edge of a cliff, each thrust pushing me closer. Moving in synchronicity, our strong bodies surge forward while our emotions wind and tangle together until they're a single strand that feels unbreakable.

He's attentively focused as I take him deep, every sense so heightened that I soar up and up until each nerve cries out. I'm suspended between light and dark, pleasure so profound it's teetering on the edge of pain.

When I tumble to my climax, every part of me lets go with complete abandon. As pleasure washes over me, I'm aware of his powerful thrusts and being held under the bright light of love.

"Trisha," he moans, and a moment later he joins me with equal intensity. As I float in his arms I realize that nothing has ever felt so perfect . . . something beyond the world I'd known . . . someplace I never want to leave.

I love this man. *I love him,* and to the depth of my soul I hope he one day can love me too.

Chapter 13: Topsy Turvy

She stood in the storm, and when the wind did not blow her away, she adjusted her sails.

~ Elizabeth Edwards

The next few days we fall into an effortless rhythm. While at the station we're professional, with only weighted side-glances stolen, which make us feel like we're in our own secret club.

The best part of the tension and unfilled want between us at work, is that our time back home is that much more amped up, both in bed and out.

On this warm spring evening we decide to barbeque, which for some reason brings out the alpha male in Joe.

Joe elbows me. "Move over. You're an amateur."

"Is that so?" I say, waving my tongs at him. "What is it about men and barbeques? I may be a female Bobby Flay, but now you'll never know." I wink at him as I pass him the tongs.

He rolls his eyes. "I'm not willing to risk these great steaks to find out if you're right about that."

"Your loss," I tease. "You ready for some wine?"

"Sure."

"I'll go get the corkscrew and glasses. Be right back."

He nods as he checks the steaks before seasoning them.

When I step back outside, I've got two wine stems in one hand, a corkscrew in the other, but I almost drop all of it when I see Joe talking to a man who's holding a big floral arrangement.

My gaze fixes on the flowers, all bright yellows, hot oranges, and soft peaches. I take a sharp breath.

Mike.

What the hell is he doing here?

As I approach I can see Joe gesturing to his rig. Is Mike giving him a bad time?

Damn.

I walk over to the patio table and carefully set down the glasses and corkscrew. To say I wasn't expecting my ex to drop by with flowers is the understatement of the century.

"What are you doing here, Mike?" I call out and he and Joe turn toward me.

He's thinner than the last time I saw him. And he's wearing a sports jacket. *What's that about?*

He takes a step toward me and holds out the arrangement. When I don't step forward he moves to the patio table and sets it down.

Joe is watching us with wide eyes.

"What are you doing here?" I repeat.

"I wanted to wish you a happy birthday, Trish. And I wanted to make sure you're okay."

"It's your birthday?" Joe asks, an incredulous look on his face.

I nod. "Yeah."

"Why didn't you say anything?"

I shrug. "It's not a big deal."

Mike points to Joe and then to his rig. "Who's this guy, and what's that thing doing in our yard?"

I fold my arms over my chest. "He's my friend, Joe. He's lieutenant at my station, and what difference does it make to you that he's parked here?"

"It's just temporary," Joe says.

"This is my house too, Trisha. I still have a say in what happens here."

I shake my head vehemently. "No. You gave up that right when you cheated on me, and shit all over our marriage."

He presses his lips together. "I know you'd like to think that Trish, but it's still half mine, and I don't want him here."

"Wait a minute—" Joe starts, but I hold my hands up, and shake my head at him and he falls silent.

"Look Mike, he's not going anywhere. Jeanine has it covered, so go crying to your lawyer if you want to spend a fortune to fight me about this."

Mike takes a deep breath with his eyes closed. I recognize it as his attempt to regroup. He was king of that shit, he even meditated to find his center. What a joke.

"Can I talk to you privately, Trish?"

"No. Say what you want to say. Joe can hear it."

He gives me a wary look but then pulls his shoulders back. "I'm not giving up. I'm going to give you some time to work through your anger, but I still think we can work through our issues . . . we're meant to be together."

I give him the most wide-eyed baffled look I can muster.

"You, me, and your gay hook-ups?" I remark. "I don't think so."

"I'm done with all that."

"Are you fucking serious with this shit? What? You just turned off your gay switch?"

"Trish, please don't talk to me like that," he says with a hurt voice.

My stomach is churning and I realize I've lost my appetite. "So did you really come over to upset me on my birthday?"

Joe turns off the gas, sets the tongs down and steps toward us.

"I think it'd be better if you take off," Joe says in a tight voice.

"She's my wife and this is my house. Don't tell me what to do," Mike snaps.

"Go, Mike." I lift my hand to my cheek. I feel flushed.

Mike stands his ground, but doesn't say anything and it's awkward as all hell.

Joe steps forward and folds his arms over his chest. The contrast between the two men is startling. Joe's at least 5 inches taller than Mike. "She asked you to leave. You've made your point, man. Now leave her in peace."

Mike stares at Joe for a moment, then over at me. "I'll be back, Trish. And when I am I want this circus shack off our land."

My legs are wobbly so I go sit down in a patio chair and lean forward, with my hands over my eyes. "Happy Birthday to me," I mutter. I know I sound pathetic, but what the hell.

With that I hear Mike let himself back out the gate. I drop my hands so I can watch his figure fade into the night.

I turn toward Joe. "You want some fucking flowers?"

He walks over, takes the flowers, and carries them around the side of the house. When he returns his hands are empty. He seems really pissed off.

"Thanks," I whisper.

He approaches my side and rests his hand on my shoulder. "I'm sorry, Trisha. That was rough. And I feel bad because me being here only made it worse."

"Yes, a real man grilling steaks for me must have been a little jarring for him. I can't imagine what he thought would happen with him just showing up like that."

Joe nods. "As for my rig—" he starts, but I cut him off.

A flurry of worry swirls in side of me. "Oh no. Don't worry about it. Jeanine has it covered."

"But maybe it'd just make things cleaner for your

divorce if I'm not here."

I try to imagine the empty space in my yard, and the empty space in my heart if he were gone. I blink back tears. "Please don't leave, Joe. Please."

I can't tell if his expression of concern is because I'm acting clingy, or if he's just worried about the situation. He squeezes my shoulder and leans over, kissing the top of my head. "Hey, birthday girl, I think it's time for some wine."

He takes the bottle and masterfully uncorks it, fills both glasses, and hands me mine.

"I'm sorry our dinner is ruined," I say.

"It'll be all right. I turned off the grill and with the lid closed the stuff is still warm."

I help him pull it all together and despite my lack of appetite, I shove extra sour cream in my damn baked potato.

He arches his brow as he watches me.

"It's my birthday," I explain, waving my sour cream coated spoon in the air.

He nods and fights back a smile.

"Indeed it is." He lifts his glass. "Happy Birthday, Trisha."

"Thank you. And you know what's cool, Joseph Murphy? Despite all this upset, and without even knowing it was my birthday, you made me feel like I really matter to you and that's the best gift of all."

I'm on my second glass of wine and feeling crazier than normal. Joe appears to be observing me with a watchful eye.

"You okay?" he asks.

I shrug. "Funny how you can think you have your whole life figured out and then just like that, it all goes topsy turvy." I snap my fingers for emphasis.

"Don't I know it," he agrees.

"Were you and your ex going to have kids?" I ask.

"Eventually. We wanted to be in the situation where she could stay home with the baby, and we weren't there yet."

His admission, which makes me picture him holding a baby in his arms, makes my stomach hurt. Mike didn't want kids and I went along with it. If I'd really pushed him, I wonder if he would've bended.

"You know how it is . . . L.A.'s an expensive place to live."

"True, but I bet you'd make a good dad."

He looks down and turns his wineglass in his hands.

I immediately regret talking about kids that he may or may not have now. It's only going to make him feel worse about his situation. As I look over and watch him take a sip of his wine I realize that there's so much I don't know about him.

"So tomorrow we're back at the station," I say with a sigh.

He nods. "And it's getting more and more difficult for me to keep my hands off you when we're there."

"Really?" I ask, secretly pleased, but worried too.

"Yeah. I even get jealous when the guys go on a run with you that I'm not scheduled for."

"Oh believe me, you have nothing to worry about."

"But what if it gets worse? I'll have to change to another station."

"No," I whisper, feeling unhinged at just the idea of it. "So what are you saying? You don't want to have sex with me anymore?"

He gives me a quizzical look. "That's not what I said."

The wine must be getting to me because suddenly I'm on a slippery slope in emo-land where logic is nothing but a five-letter word.

I swallow hard. What have I ever done that's so horrible that this is my karma? The sexiest man I've ever known, the man who says I make him wild, may avoid sleeping with me. This means that soon I could be sexless again, I'm on emotional overload.

The tears start streaming down my face as I surrender to the feeling of hopelessness and despair. Welcome to my pity party and it's a doozy. It's my birthday and there's no actual party . . . just the bleak stretch of an empty landscape . . . my forever emotional wasteland. I let out a quiet sob.

"It's my birthday," I whisper, when he reaches over to brush my tears away.

"Shhh," he says.

"But the idea of not being with you makes me feel so alone and I just want . . . I *need* to be loved."

"Oh baby," he whispers as he pulls me in his arms. Next thing I know I'm being lifted out of my chair and cradled against his chest. I love how this man holds me so completely. Sighing, I settle against him.

"It's my birthday," I whisper. I'm pretty sure the wine has set off my emotional babble.

"I know," he whispers back and kisses me on the top of my head. "I think I'm finally seeing the soft side of you, sweetheart."

My eyes grow wide. I guess he's right. I shiver at the idea of it and then reach up and kiss the patch of skin where his T-shirt ends and his neck begins. This man makes me feel so much, which only makes me want to kiss him more.

He looks down at me but instead of concern in his eyes I see something else. "Let's get out of the cold. I'm going to warm you up."

I nod, happy that I'm still tight in his arms.

The way he carries me across the yard makes me feel

protected. He pushes my back door open with his foot.

"Where are you taking me?" I ask.

"To bed."

"To sleep?"

He shakes his head. "No, birthday girl. I'm going to wake you up. Sleep is the last thing on my mind."

I groan and press my thighs together.

When we get to the bedroom he gently lays me down on the bed, then pulls his T-shirt over his head.

"Is this going to be a pity fuck?" I ask.

His eyes narrow. "Now, Trisha . . . do I look like the kind of man who would do that?"

"No," I admit.

"This is *me* taking care of *you*."

"But–"

"Shhh. This is also me *wanting* you." From the intense look in his eyes I'm inclined to believe him.

He reaches over and undoes my jeans, and I lift my hips so he can pull them, along with my panties, off with ease.

He unzips his fly, but right before he pushes his jeans down he pauses. "What are you doing?"

I blink at him as I continue to pull the sheet over my legs. "Covering up."

"Why?"

I feel my cheeks heat up. "I guess I'm feeling especially vulnerable tonight and I'm embarrassed about my thighs."

"Why?"

"They're thick."

He smiles. "All the better to be wrapped around me. Besides, they're not thick, they're shapely and strong."

"You're just saying that."

"Do you really think a man is going to prefer skinny thighs? I want something good to grab onto."

My fingers loosen on the sheet as I take in how he's

looking at me. It's like he's got ideas for all the sexy things he'd like to do to me, and the fun is about to begin.

"For the record, your strong thighs are sexy."

"Oh really?"

"I've been admiring them for a while."

"When?"

"When I've spied on you at the gym working out."

He takes the edge of the sheet in his grasp and slowly pulls it away from my body. "Oh yeah," he whispers as he trails his fingertips over the curve just above my knee and then slides them between my legs.

"These are exactly my kind of thighs. As a matter of fact, I'm in love with your thighs. Why don't you spread them for me and I'll show you how much?"

I reach a new level of hotness. For a man who's typically pretty reserved with his words, this man is the Shakespeare of dirty talk. With a few choice phrases he can transform me into a burning fireball of need.

I spread my legs slowly as he pushes off his jeans and joins me on the bed. He starts with my lips, kissing me senseless. His intensity, and the way he grabs my thighs with his strong hands, makes me feel wild. I moan and kiss him back, as my legs ease open wider. I'm pretty sure I won't feel complete again until he's inside of me.

"That's right, baby," he says in a low voice while he works his way back down my body until his lips skim my inner thighs.

"Oh God," I moan as he explores and teases with his mouth and fingertips. I arch into his touch, hungry for more.

"Aren't you going to fuck me?" I ask breathlessly.

"Maybe," he teases, his tongue circling my clit. "You know, you need to be more patient."

"It's my birthday," I whisper.

"You were very bad not to warn me about that." He shakes his head in reproach as he lifts up on his knees.

My gaze roams over the ridges and plains of his body, each muscle defined. He's hard everywhere Mikey was soft. I'm feeling primal urges, raw lust that I could smother myself in, just to take in every inch of this magnificent man.

"So sexy," he whispers as he runs his hands up and down my inner thighs. I'm panting by the time he rubs his cock against me in a slow tease. Seconds later he fills me and in that moment nothing–not Mikey showing up, not the rules at work, not his wife's betrayal that haunts him— matters. This time when my tears fall it's because sex has never felt even close to this, like the best gift in the world.

He builds slowly, then sensing my need, he begins to thrust hard, pressing me down into the mattress. He touches me all the places that make me crazy, kissing and embracing me like I'm everything.

I groan and I grind against him and hold on tight. "Don't ever stop doing this with me."

"I can't stop," he says with a groan, his gaze fixed on me because he knows I'm about to come and this man is all about following through and getting the job done. He knows how to really take care of his woman.

Oh good God. My head falls back as my body tenses, and then my climax roars through me.

Oh yeah, oh yeah . . . Happy Birthday to me.

Chapter 14: A Badass Queen

A queen will always turn pain into power.
~ R.H. Sin

A few days later, Jeanine is on her way over so we can finally celebrate my birthday. Every year she insists on me dressing up and then she takes me out somewhere fancy for dinner. But the annoying thing is she always insists I not just dress up, but wear a dress. I think it's a control thing with her, and she knows I don't like to be controlled and I feel ridiculous in a dress. It used to really piss me off but she wasn't backing off, so I finally decided to treat it like I was going to a costume party dressed like a girl that actually likes to dress-up, and it became fun.

The dress I'm wearing tonight Elle helped me find at one of those girly boutiques and she paired it with black heels from Nordstroms at the Grove. I zip up my new frock and turn to look at myself in the full-length mirror. I've got to say, this dress looks pretty damn good on me. It accentuates my curves while showing off my strong back and it even makes the few inches of my thighs that show look good.

I smooth my hair out and put on colored lipgloss before stepping out on the front porch to wait for Jeanine. When I turn around from locking the door I see Joe in the driveway with wide eyes and his mouth slack.

"Hey!" I call out with a wave.

He doesn't respond, just takes several steps closer with a dark look in his eyes.

"I bet you barely recognized me," I say before turning around carefully so I don't face-plant in the heels.

He swallows, and shakes his head. "Where are you going?"

"I'm being taken out for my birthday to Mozzo. Have you ever been there?"

He shakes his head. For some reason he's starting to look a little pissed.

"It's on Melrose and Highland. I thought you might know it since it's owned by those famous chefs, Mario Batali and Nancy Silverton."

"Is it?" he says with raised brows before he scowls.

Okay, I'm pretty sure he's pissed.

"Do you want me to see if you can come too? I'm not sure since you know how uptight those fancy pants places are, but I could ask."

Narrowing his eyes at me, he purses his lips. Geez, I'm trying extra hard to be nice and frankly he's being a moody ass.

I wave my hand at him over his T-shirt and jeans. "You may need to grab a jacket. I'm not sure if there's a dress code."

"I don't want to go with you on your date, Trisha."

"Ha!" I laugh right as Jeanine pulls up in her Jaguar. "You thought I was going on a date?"

"Well, look at you."

Descending the stairs, I grab his shirtsleeve and pull. "Come-on, I want you to meet my bestie, Jeanine."

A look of relief settles over his features. "Jeanine? You wore a dress for your bestie?"

"Yeah. So?"

"You haven't worn a dress for me."

"You haven't taken me out on a date."

"Well, maybe we need to rectify that," he says.

I grin. "Well she *makes* me wear a dress, but I'll gladly wear one for you if it means that much to you."

He leans closer. "I'd like that. You look good."

"Good?"

"Really good." His gaze trails across me with a slow simmer. "Gorgeous," he whispers.

I blink several times and press my thighs together. This man can look at me sideways and get me worked up. For a brief moment I wonder how pissed off Jeanine would be if I canceled. I can just imagine Joe's long fingers unzipping my dress slowly before pushing the fabric away from my shoulders so my dress falls to the floor. *Hot damn.*

Just then Jeanine blasts the horn of her car as she rolls down the passenger window. "Trisha, get your ass in the car!"

I look over at Joe and wink. "She's a charmer."

"I can see that."

I drag him toward her car. "You've got to meet her. She's so fierce; she makes me look like a wimp."

She narrows her eyes at Joe as he approaches. "Is this the man you were telling me about, Trisha?"

I nod. "Yes, this is Joe. Joe, meet my best friend Jeanine."

Joe approaches the car and reaches in through the window to shake her hand. "Nice to meet you, Jeanine."

She gives him a knowing smile. "Likewise."

Joe opens the passenger door and holds his arm out to guide me inside.

I slide in and pull down my seatbelt.

"Have a great time, ladies, and keep the men away from her, Jeanine. And by the way, thanks for getting Trisha in a dress."

"She's hot, right?" Jeanine says with a grin.

"Yes, she is. I'm looking forward to her dressing up like this for me. You promised, right, Trisha?"

I feel my cheeks color. "Yes."

"Excellent," Jeanine says. "And sometime soon let's all get together."

"Sounds good," Joe replies as he closes my door and steps back. He waves as Jeanine pulls away from the curb.

When she stops at the light at Laurel Canyon she turns toward me. "Are you kidding me?"

"What?" I ask, as I raise my hands in surrender. There's no point taking on Jeanine because she'll always win.

"That's the tiny house guy?"

"Yup."

"Holy hell! He. Is. A. Man. A big, healthy, real man, with a visible dose of testosterone, accented by looks and manners. Do you understand what a rare breed he is in this god-forsaken city? He's like an endangered animal and he must be treated like the treasure he is."

I laugh. I can't help it. Jeanine has never been this impressed with *anyone*. "You *are* treating him right, aren't you?"

My eyebrows knit together. "Can you explain how that works?"

She sighs with exasperation. "You're treating him right . . . keeping him happy."

"What about me? Shouldn't you be focused on making sure he's treating me right, and making me happy?"

"Well, judging from the way you were looking at him and the way he doted on you, it seemed obvious."

I smile widely and she glances over at me.

"It's a jungle out there in L.A., the dating pool is overrun with savages, and Joe could be your king. Treat him like one and I'm sure it'll be worth it."

I roll my eyes. "My king? So much for the advancement of women as equal partners."

"Just giving you a reality check, woman. The rest is up to you."

Leaning back into her Jaguar's lush leather upholstery, I gaze out the window with a smile on my face despite her crazy ramblings. Jeanine enthusiastically approves of Joe. *Hot damn.*

According to her I've got myself a king, and it makes me wonder while in the fantasyland of happy-ever-afters, if I could be his badass queen.

Joe is waiting for me when I get home later that night. I know because he's left a scrawled note taped to my front door.

Get you and that sexy dress you're wearing over to my place. I'll be on the roof waiting. I've got a bottle of wine and all the stars lit up just for you.

With my heart pounding, I unlock my front door and kick off my heels. One shoe lands on the coffee table and the other on the couch as I rush to the bedroom for my Keds and a sweater.

Less than a minute later I'm scaling the ladder along the side of Betty. I pause when I'm near the top. I'm excited—I've never wanted to see him more.

"Hey," I say as I finally step up onto the roof.

I know it's night, but his dark eyes are bright as his shimmering gaze moves from my face, slowly down my body. The corners of his mouth turn up when he sees the Keds. "Where are your heels?"

"I changed shoes since they aren't exactly ladder crawling friendly. Why?"

"I want the heels."

"Well, too bad. At least I kept the dress on."

"Hmmm," he says as he surveys me. "You have to know . . . you make me crazy, woman."

My breath hitches. "I do?"

"Hell yes. I've been up here imagining taking this dress off of you." His fingers tug on the bottom of the dress' hem.

"Are you going to take it off me up here?" I ask as I bite my lip.

"Perhaps."

He's such a tease.

I sink down into my lawn chair and watch him pour me a glass of wine. It's a warm night and moonless, the inky black sky dusted with stars. He hands me my plastic cup and I take a long sip.

"So did Jeanine keep the men away from you like I asked her to?"

"Well, Malcolm the waiter was a little overly attentive, but other than that, yes, we were in the clear."

"Good," he says quietly as he takes a drink of his wine.

I sit with my head tipped back to watch the sky. I love the quiet beauty of a night sky—some may find the darkness foreboding, but I find it hopeful. Sometimes your heart can feel things more clearly in the dark, when not muddled by the light.

"Can I confess something?" I ask after finishing off my cup of cabernet. My dress has inched up high on my thighs and his gaze continues to linger there.

He nods, his expression suddenly wary like he's gearing up for another one of my frank revelations. "Sure. What?"

"I've never felt like this."

"Like what?"

"Like I'd do anything to please you."

"Really?"

I notice his hands tighten over the armrests on his lawn chair.

"Yes, really. I'm starting to worry that I'm obsessed with you. Jeanine was impressed with you and warned me that I should do whatever I can to make you happy. And what's weird is that despite my self-protective nature, I want to do that for you."

"Trisha," he whispers.

I hold out my hand. "Let me finish. The thing is I have all these feelings for you and they're big and complicated. Remember a few weeks ago, when we went out on the child drowning call? After we arrived, I was side-by-side with you trying to save that little girl. I remember my overwhelming fear that we were too late, and our sheer determination to save her. I looked over as you did the compressions and I thought if this little girl has any chance at life, it's because of Joe."

He shakes his head but remains silent because he seems to sense that I'm not done.

I clear my throat. "And a moment later it hit me, that if I have any chance of finding love again, it's with Joe."

"Stop," he whispers.

I shake my head. "I know. You don't want me to fall in love with you. But sorry, it's already happened. And I know It's crazy and fast and illogical, and my divorce hasn't even started to hit its stride. But I can't help it. I love you. I do. I think about you every messed-up minute we're apart. I think of the way you held my hand under the table at my parents, I fantasize only of you naked across my bed, and I panic thinking of you riding a rig to the fire that could be the one to take you from me. It kills me . . . the idea of losing you. My head is spinning from all my feelings for you so you don't have to say a thing, just know that it's all very real."

He appears positively stunned, his eyes wide and fingers pressed against his thighs.

I look him straight in the eyes. "I'm a woman in love with you, and you need to know that I'm one hundred percent honest, real and honorable, and most of all . . . despite my longing, I'm willing to wait as long as it takes, for you to love me back."

He shakes his head, his eyes pressed shut. "You don't have to wait, Trisha."

"Really?" I ask, trying not to sound hopeful.

"I'm in love with you too."

My heart swells. "You aren't just saying that to be nice?"

He reaches out his hand and when I take it he pulls me over onto his lap and wraps his arms around me. "Believe me, I'm not that nice. If I were I'd say I didn't love you so you'd move on and find someone better. But the truth is that I've wanted you far longer than you could imagine."

I nuzzle my cheek against his warm neck. "Really?"

"I'll tell you the story one day, but not now."

I'm tempted to pressure him to confess, but everything feels so perfect in this moment that I don't want to mess things up. "I do want to correct you on one thing, Mr. Murphy . . . there's no one better, not for me anyway."

"I bet it's just that you like a man in a uniform," he teases.

I elbow him. "So you must really think I'm deep. Although you do look panty melting hot in your dress uniform."

"Panty melting?" he asks with a grimace. "So I've melted your panties?"

I grin. "Countless pairs."

He rests his hand on my knee and then slowly glides his fingers up my thigh until they trace the edge of the silky pair currently in question. He clears his throat. "Apparently

I've lost my touch. Your panties are intact."

"How about we go to my place and investigate this further?" I ask.

"You know that will involve me removing your dress very slowly, right?"

I bite back my smile. "Oh, if you must."

He eases me off of his lap and then stands up to join me. I gesture toward the sky. "Thank you for making the stars shine for us."

He rests his fingers under my chin and gently tilts my face up so that I'm facing him. "My pleasure. I love you, Trisha. I'd give you the sun and the moon too if I could."

Chapter 15: Our Own Hero

You gain strength, courage and confidence by every experience in which you really stop to look fear in the face.

~ Eleanor Roosevelt

I'm in the ladies bathroom with Elle at El Coyote in West Hollywood waiting while she touches up her lipstick. "So what's happening with the divorce? I bet you're anxious to get it moving along now that you and Joe have gotten so close."

"I am," I agree. "But William, the lawyer I'm working with from Jeanine's firm said he spoke with Mike's lawyer and Mike has stopped responding to our attempts to move things along. It's not that we're fighting over money or stuff even, he's just avoiding everything."

"That's probably not that unusual. I mean it hasn't been that long, and didn't you say he dropped by your place with flowers wanting to work things out?"

"He did. It pissed me off. I wasn't very pleasant about it, but I can't help it. I'm still angry."

"I understand. I would be too."

"He even got his mother to call me and guilt me out by saying how depressed he's been. I mean what does she expect me to say to that?"

"So what are you going to do to get things back on track with the divorce?"

"I may just have to show up at his shop and bully him. It's not like I was the one who cheated on him. He screwed up. He needs to let it go."

She nods, and I throw away my wadded up paper towel to join Elle out the door and return to our table. We pass arches filled with exotic fake flowers, crafty oil paintings of Spanish dancers, and lanterns lit with stained glass panels casting prisms of color . . . a paradise of Mexican kitsch. I love this place.

We slide back into the booth where our men are debating the upcoming USC, UCLA game. It makes me smile to see how easily Joe and Paul get along. These last few weeks have been so damn good, and I'm glad to be able to share this man with my family and have them enjoy his company.

Paul's expression is playful as he lifts his margarita to his lips. "So is it true the guys at the station call Trish T. Rex?"

Joe glances over at me with a look of concern. I shrug to let him know it's okay to talk about.

"Yeah, most of the guys think she's pretty fierce. But she's a better firefighter than the whole lot of them combined."

I lean over and give him a WTF look.

"It's true, Trisha," he insists.

I roll my eyes. "Just a little exaggeration, guys. Besides the new guy, Charlie, who transferred from West L.A. seems really sharp."

"He does," agrees Joe. "Do you know that I was talking to him the other day and he told me that his wife is a narc agent?"

Elle looks fired up. "Seriously? That's so hot! Let's have a dinner party and we can invite them and hear all the stories."

"There she goes," Paul says with a chuckle.

Reaching over, I rest my hand on Joe's forearm. "Maybe you could cook? I'd help."

He seems lost in thought for a moment and I can tell

Paul is trying to read his expression.

"He's a gourmet chef," I announce proudly.

"I used to be," Joe responds quietly.

He looks like he's in pain. I shouldn't have pushed so soon.

"You don't have to cook," Elle says.

"Maybe I will. Let me think about it."

I take a tortilla chip and scoop up some guacamole before offering it to him.

He takes it with a smile and settles back in the red booth.

We're good. Really good.

Two days later we're in the station and just finishing up the after-dinner clean-up when we get a call about a freeway crash on the 101. I hate freeway accidents in general, it's dicey dealing with injuries and drama while cars are speeding past mere feet away. Add in the dark at night and it can be especially harrowing. A few years ago a guy from our station was hit at full speed trying to get back on the truck. He lived, but he'll never walk again.

We've already been informed it's a multi-vehicle pile-up, and we speed into action. When we arrive we aren't the first truck at the scene, and the Highway Patrol is busy shutting down lanes. Jim, Charlie, Joe, and I jump off the truck to check in with the crew already at work, as the first ambulance arrives.

Jim and Charlie are directed to the third car in the pile-up and Joe and I move to the fourth. The airbags have been deployed and Joe gets busy deactivating them while I check on the passenger in the front seat.

"Ma'am, we're here to help you. Are you okay?"

She whimpers and looks down.

"Can you tell me where the driver is?" Judging from the bent metal and shattered window it appears that the door was kicked open so the driver could get out.

Lifting her hand, she points forward. I lean sideways and spot a large man yelling near the front of the pile-up. "The one in the black jacket?" I ask.

When she nods and closes her eyes tightly, I notice her eye is swollen and turning black and blue, and her lip is split open. I run my hand over the deflating airbag, trying to understand how she was injured, but then it occurs to me that an eye wouldn't be turning black and blue this quickly.

I lean in closer to her and gesture toward her eye and lips. "Ma'am, you're injured. Was this from the accident?"

Her eyes fire up with fear and I have a sinking feeling in my gut.

"This isn't from the accident, is it?"

There's a long pause, her eyes brimmed with terror as her gaze shifts to the distance where the man in black is still yelling.

I back away from the window and turn back to Joe. "See that guy in the black jacket. He's this vehicle's driver. Can you go see what he's up to?"

He nods toward the woman. "Is she all right?"

"I don't think so."

I turn back toward the woman. "Can I ask your name?"

"Katrina," she whispers.

"I'm Firefighter McNeill, but you can call me Trisha," I say gently.

She nods at me, casting her gaze downward again.

I notice her legs are bare, and her skirt is ripped. Her thighs have several dark bruises scattered over her pale skin.

I know protocol but I can't help it, whatever is happening here is too close to home for me, and protocol can go to hell.

I nod forward. "Did he do this to you? Is he your boyfriend?"

She presses her hands over her face as she nods, and I hear a muffled sob.

My fingers curl into tight fists. In the distance it looks like Joe is trying to calm the bully down. I want to kick his ass to the moon and back, but I bite down my fury.

"You know there are places to get help, Katrina. I can assist you in getting to the best services," I say softly.

She shakes her head vehemently. "He has a really bad temper."

"That doesn't mean he can get away doing this to you. It has to stop."

"He promised me."

"And he broke his promise. Katrina, I've been through this. I was beaten and sexually assaulted by my boyfriend and what I can tell you is that it will only get worse. You need to get help."

"He'll kill me," she whispers.

A chill runs up my spine as my emotions swirl into rage.

Joe returns to the car. "We need to get her out of the vehicle so she can be checked."

"What did he say?"

"He said a lot of things," he says with a grimace.

"Is Jared coming back for me?" she asks, her eyes filled with panic.

I look up and see the asshole walking our direction alongside the freeway.

"Not if I can help it," I say. "Joe, can you watch her for a minute?"

He narrows his eyes like he isn't sure of my plan, yet nods.

I start walking toward the beast and it suddenly hits me that he's three times my girth. He could take me out if I'm not careful. I need to stand my guard.

"Jared?" I ask. "I need to ask you about your girlfriend."

"What?" he barks with an aggravated expression.

"She's been battered, and not by the car accident. Are you responsible for her injuries?"

"Is that what she said?" he asks, his eyes wild with anger.

I grit my teeth. "Answer the question. Did you beat her?"

Joe, who until now had been leaning into the car talking to Katrina, suddenly twists to watch me. He rises up and starts walking toward us.

"I don't have to tell you anything," Jared spews. "What I do with my girlfriend is none of your fucking business. And if she didn't have such a mouth on her, none of this would have happened. So if she told you I beat her she can shut the hell up."

I lean toward him and slap my hand on his chest and push. "So is that it, then? Beating a woman makes you feel like a big man?"

He steps back with his eyes narrow and dark. "Keep your fucking hands off me, bitch!"

"Your momma must feel really proud of you, asshole."

He looks around angrily, and when he sees Joe he calls out to him, "Did you hear what she said, man? I'm going to sue the hell out of this broad accusing me of all kinds of shit she knows nothing about. I want to make a report!"

Joe's gaze is steely as he approaches. He ignores me completely and addresses the asshole, "I'll take care of this. Excuse us one moment."

He calls out to one of the medics, while pointing to Katrina. "She needs medical attention."

As soon as the medic opens Katrina's car door, Joe grabs my arm firmly and drags me several paces down the emergency lane.

I shake my arm free of his grip and storm farther away. If he's going to reprimand me I may have to punch him in the face.

"Trisha, stand to," he calls out in a tone I've never heard before.

I glance back at him with an exasperated look. "Are you fucking serious?"

"What the hell is wrong with you? You've just broken every protocol and put yourself at risk for suspension."

I fold my arms over my chest. "So now I'm the bad guy here? Well fuck you. He beat her, Joe. She has a black eye and bruises everywhere and she's terrified he'll do worse."

I turn and march away, knowing I'm acting unprofessionally, but I can't bear his censure.

He grabs me again, and pushes me back. "You know this needs to be handled by the police and social services. You could've just put her in serious danger with how you handled that. What the hell are you thinking?"

"I'm thinking that I can't just write a report and pass this into the system with the hope that she gets help. She needs help now, before something worse happens."

"This isn't your battle to fight Trisha," he insists.

I fight a tear back as my lower lips trembles. I can't be a coward now. "It *is* my battle to fight, Joe."

"No, it isn't."

"It is because I was *that* girl. I was beaten and sexually assaulted by my asshole boyfriend. I know what it feels like to not ask for help. Like it was my fault, somehow."

He looks like I punched him in the gut. "Who beat you?"

"It doesn't matter anymore," I insist.

"It sure as hell matters to me," he says.

"His name was Sam. I haven't seen him for five years but I'll hate him the rest of my life. He broke me, and if it hadn't been for Mike and my family, I may never have gotten back on my feet."

Joe drags his fingers through his hair before glancing back at the rest of the action around the accident. It hits me that I was so absorbed in my vengeance, that I missed all the other chaos that needs our attention.

He gently rests his hand on my shoulder. "Please just do this for me, and don't argue. Okay, Trisha?"

"What do you want me to do?"

"Go sit in the truck, and wait for us to finish up what we need to here. Can you do that?" he asks.

I nod, feeling hollowed out and entirely defeated. Dropping my head, I walk to the truck.

The ride back to the station is silent. I'm sure the other guys are wondering why I was sent to wait in the truck, but no one asks. When I finally have the courage to glance at Joe it's hard to read his expression. Somewhere under his exhaustion I see what I imagine is a mix of anger and pain. I've never seen him look so dark.

After the rigs are in the bay Joe gets off the truck first, and then turns back toward the rest of us with a stern look.

"Meet me in the office in five minutes, McNeill."

"Yes, sir," I say quietly as I watch him walk away.

"You in trouble, T. Rex?" Jim asks.

"Yeah, and it's not looking good."

"What'd you do?"

"Went off on an asshole at the scene. He was a victim in the pile-up but he had beat up his girlfriend earlier, and let's just say that pissed me off."

"Yeah, that's one of those jacked up situations that pisses me off . . . what did you do?"

"I did what I had to, but I'm going to pay for it now."

"Well, good luck."

"Thanks."

It's a long, dread-filled walk to the office. I knock on the closed door.

"Come in." His muffled voice sounds stern.

I close the door behind me and sit in the chair in front, on the opposite side of the desk to him. We sit silently staring at each other for at least a minute.

"Are you all right?" he finally asks.

"Not exactly," I answer. "I'm worried about the woman. Leaving her with that asshole is every kind of wrong."

"I alerted the medical team, and they assured me that her injuries would be under scrutiny by the sexual assault team at the hospital."

"Good," I sigh. "That makes me feel a little bit better."

"Do you understand how serious your infractions were tonight? You endangered a victim, nearly endangered yourself, and then you were belligerent about it. What the hell, Trisha?"

I glare at him but keep my mouth shut tight.

"I had to give you a time-out in the truck, for God's sake. We sure as hell expect more from you than this kind of behavior."

Something about hearing that I've let Joe and my team down hits me and I feel my guard falling. I'm starting to see things from his point of view. I try to think of how I can explain my enraged response at the scene.

"I'm sorry, but that asshole acting like he had a right to do that to his girlfriend . . . it was a trigger for me."

Joe takes a deep breath and spreads his fingers slowly over the desktop. I'm just as distracted by his big manly hands as the first time we met alone in this office.

"I wish you'd told me about your past, Trisha. I would've understood what was happening with you tonight. And not just tonight, but what about when we've been intimate? I would've handled things differently with you."

"How so?" I ask, trying to stay calm. It sounds like he has regrets.

"I would've been more careful." His voice is quieter now, no longer harsh.

My eyes grow wide. "Careful? What does that mean?"

"I would've taken things much slower with you, and I would've been more gentle."

"Please don't feel that way, Joe. Besides, that would have made me crazy."

"But that first time I kissed you at the station. I was too aggressive. I was all over you . . ."

I sigh. "That was so hot."

"Did that make you feel bad after?"

"The way you were all over me? Good God, no. Why would I have felt bad?"

"You know, post traumatic stress or something like it. Is that why you were so distant with me after?"

"I was distant because I was still mad over the stuff I overheard with you and the guys. You know that. As for the kissing, I think it was very clear that was consensual. As I recall, I had my hands all over you and was kissing you back."

"You were," he agrees.

"I trust you, Joe, and you've never given me a reason not to. So please don't regret a thing in that regard."

"I don't know, Trisha. I don't think it's as simple as just telling me it's okay."

I let out a long breath and look up at the ceiling, like I'm asking God for guidance. I'm also wondering why there's a popcorn ceiling and horrible fluorescent lights in our nice station. I guess I'm tired and just want to think about nothing of consequence for a while. I look back at him.

"Joe, do you even begin to understand how strong and tough I am?"

"Do you always have to be so tough? It's okay to be soft once in a while, you know."

"I suppose, but that's not me. So are we done here?"

He studies me silently. I swear his hair is turning gray the longer we sit here. "No, we're not done. We need to talk about this so-called boyfriend who abused you."

"But I told you, I don't want to talk about him. It's over . . . old news. I've dealt with it and moved on."

"It's not old news to me."

"Okay. Honestly, I'm sorry I told you. I don't want you to see me as a victim. You don't need to feel bad for me."

"Feel bad for you?" he asks with wide eyes.

I shrug.

"I'm gutted because something horrible happened to you, and there's nothing I can do about it. Sharon used to accuse me of having a hero complex, and right now I have to wonder if she was right because I desperately wish I could've been the one to save you from being victimized."

"Sometimes we have to be our own hero, Joe."

He looks at me with a measured gaze. I swear I see admiration reflected in his eyes. I'll take it. I worked hard to get myself back on my feet.

I fold my arms over my chest. "Honestly, I'm glad you weren't around for that. It wasn't pretty."

"No, it's raw and ugly and there's no protocol for what I would want to do. 'Cause actually I'd like having a baseball bat and five minutes alone in a room with the bastard. I'd hit a home run with his fucking head and he'd no longer have the ability to hurt you or any other woman again."

My mouth gapes open as I picture his description in my mind.

"Sorry," he whispers.

"Don't be sorry. That was a very satisfying thing to hear."

He stands up, moves away from the desk, and holds his arms open. "Come here, sweetheart."

I fight back a swell of emotion. *My God, what did I do right to deserve this man?*

I walk straight into his embrace, and allow myself to be wrapped in his warmth. "I'm sorry I'm not easy," I say with a sigh.

"I don't want easy. I want real. You are real. I want you."

"Is that a haiku?"

"Shut up, woman."

Fighting back a smile, I press my lips together. "Did you forget how good my pitching arm is? Tell me to shut up again and I'll nail you with that stapler on the edge of your desk."

While still holding me, Joe opens up the desk drawer, sets the stapler inside, and closes it.

"Shut up and kiss me," he whispers with a teasing tone, and a twinkle his eye.

And I do.

Chapter 16: The Babysitter

We don't know who we are until we see what we can do.

~Margaret Grimes

The next afternoon at the station Jim and I are checking in some repaired equipment in the bay when a striking blonde holding a small boy steps into our view.

"Can we help you, ma'am?" Jim asks.

She drops a large canvas bag on the floor of the bay and moves the boy to her other hip. "Yes, thanks. Can you get Charlie for me? I'm his wife."

"You're Sue the narc agent?" I ask with wide eyes.

She nods impatiently.

I approach her. "Sorry, I'm Trisha, and Charlie isn't here."

Sue looks alarmed. "Oh no, is he on a call?"

"He and Joe left about ten minutes ago for a bad car wreck off Ventura Boulevard."

She steps over to the bench and sinks down, moving her son who's starting to squirm to her lap. He points to the fire engine excitedly. She checks her phone and groans. "Oh no. I can't believe this."

"Is there something I can do to help?"

"I got called in. A major bust we've been working on for six months is going down in a few hours. I have to get to the station. Our nanny has the stomach flu, and our back-up babysitter is in Florida visiting her mother. Babysitter number two said she could come, but just let me know it won't be for two more hours. I thought since this was major

I could leave him with Charlie until the babysitter could show up. He said afternoons are usually training sessions, but I should have still checked. Now I'm screwed."

Her son is really squirming and whining now.

"What's his name?" I ask as I step closer to them.

"Spencer. He loves fire trucks. No surprise there."

"Can I?" I ask, as I nod to the truck.

"Yes, thank you. I can make a few more calls. Charlie's sister might be able to step in."

I sink to my knees and look at the little boy. "Hey, Spencer, I'm Trisha, your dad's friend here at the station. Can I show you the fire truck?"

He nods, wiggles off mom's lap, and rushes over to me.

"Here, take my hand I'll show you."

He folds his little hand in mine as he bounces all the way to the truck.

"I don't know, T. Rex," Jim warns. "Chief may not like this if you didn't get approval ahead of time."

I give Jim the evil eye. "He doesn't need to know then, does he?"

Jim shrugs. "It's your suspension. You're such a rebel."

"And proud of it."

When I open the door and lift little Spencer up on the first stair to the cab, he scrambles right up with me right behind him. Once inside I put my hands on his shoulders. "Okay, I'm going to sit in the seat and you can sit on my lap and I'll teach you how the truck works, okay?"

Spencer nods, and his gaze has the same serious expression his dad has during meetings. He's like a mini version of Charlie.

I like that he's taken to me right away; I haven't scared him off like I scare the grown men around here. He sits on my lap with his little hands clutching the huge steering wheel and repeats the name of each dial and knob as I call it out to him.

"Do you want to be a firefighter when you grow up like your dad, Spencer?"

He nods.

"You'll be a really good one I bet."

"What's this?" he asks, pointing to the button I've avoided mentioning. It's the Q2 siren switch on the control panel.

"That's the siren. It's really, really loud."

He twists his head and looks up at me. "Can I push it, Twisha, please?"

I hold my breath for a second, wondering the worst that can come out of it. *Oh, what the hell.* "You've been such a good boy that we can push it, but only once. Okay?"

He nods anxiously. I take his hand and help him stretch far enough that with my help he's able to push it down and a second or two later I snap it back off.

Holy hell. I forgot how loud it could be when the truck's in the bay. I press my lips together waiting for whatever hell I'm going to get.

"Okay Spencer, you did a great job. Now we need to get down and check on Mom."

I think he's so stunned from the siren blast that he agrees without any hesitation and as we work down the stairs Jim is scowling at me.

"You really did it now, T. Rex."

Several other guys enter the bay. "What's going on?" asks Bobo.

"I was showing Charlie's kid, Spencer, the truck. Got a problem with that?"

Bobo rolls his eyes and turns around. "It's okay, guys, just T. Rex making trouble like usual."

I narrow my eyes at the bunch of them.

"Everything okay?" Sue asks.

"Oh sure. Don't worry about them. And Spencer was great. You're going to make a great firefighter one day, aren't you dude?"

"Yeah!" He jumps up and down, and his mom smiles.

"Hey hold on a sec, I just thought of something." I go to the cabinets on the far wall, open one, then pull out a little red plastic fire hat. "Look what I've got here, Spencer . . . your very own hat."

He scampers over to me and I place it on his head before giving it a pat down. "There you go."

"Thank you, Twisha."

"Sure thing, dude."

Sue looks at me with a warm expression. "Thank you for being so kind, Trisha. Charlie has told me how highly he thinks of you."

"Thanks, but don't thank me—he's a great kid. Hey, did you find anyone to watch him?"

Her expression falls. "No. I don't know what I'm going to do. We've never had all of our back-ups fall through like this."

"I can watch him if you want until Charlie gets back."

"What? Are you sure?"

"Yeah, it's not a problem. I bet they'll be back within the hour anyway."

Sue lifts up the canvas bag. "I brought snacks for Charlie to give him, and stuff like his coloring books and stickers."

"Cool. Hey, Spencer, can we hang together for a while until your dad gets back? That way mom can go to work, and I can have fun with you."

"Sure!"

I turn to his mom. "I worked for a pre-school during the summer before my first year of college so I'm good with kids this age."

Sue lets out a sigh of relief. "I can't tell you how grateful I am. Truly."

Kneeling down to her son's level, she takes his hand. "I'm going to work Spence, so have fun with Trisha and then Daddy will be back soon. Okay?"

He smiles and nods and walks over to me. "Okay, Twisha."

I grab the canvas bag and give mom a wave. "Good luck with the bust. I hope you take 'em all down."

Her expression gets hard as she nods. "We will."

I take Charlie up to the dayroom and ignore the looks the other guys give me. "Look, Spencer, these are your dad's friends, the other firefighters."

Bobo gives him a thumbs up and the others wave. "I'm watching him until his dad gets back."

No one says anything and they turn back and continue their conversation. I plop Spencer's bag down on the table and unzip it. "Hey Spencer, let's see what cool stuff you have in here. You want to show me?"

He climbs up on the chair and starts pulling things out of the bag, and dropping them onto the tabletop.

I let out a low whistle. "Wow! Look at all this fun stuff. What should we do first?"

He slaps his hand on the jungle animals coloring book. I dig the crayons out of the bag. "Do you want a snack while you color?"

He nods so I pull out the juice box and insert the little straw, then pour the crackers on top of a paper towel.

And that's how Joe and Charlie find us when they get back from their call. Spencer, having finished off the crackers and juice, moved to my lap so we're coloring together, me on the right side page, and he on the left. The two men just stand and stare at us for a minute, their mouths practically hanging open. I wait for Spencer to notice them but he's too absorbed in his work.

I nudge him gently. "Hey, Spencer, look who's here!"

He looks up briefly. "Hi, Daddy." And then goes right back to coloring.

I hear Joe chuckle.

"You've got a great kid, Charlie. Spencer and I are buds now, aren't we, dude?"

He nods, his hat crooked on his little head. He points to the lion I was coloring. "You didn't finish, Twisha."

"You're a detail man I see," I say to him with a wink. "You want to see if Daddy will finish the lion?"

He looks up. "Will you, Daddy?"

"Sure, little man." He takes a seat next to us and I scoot Spencer over.

"Did Sue get ahold of you?" I ask.

He nods. "Thanks so much, Trisha. Really."

"Any time, Charlie. He's a really cool kid."

"McNeill," Joe says, "a word with you in the office."

I shrug. "Sure."

Charlie looks up, concerned, but Joe nods at him. I have no idea what's going on but I guess I'm going to find out.

I say good-bye to Spencer and silently follow Joe to the office. He closes the door behind us, then leans back with his ass against the front of the desk and his arms folded over his chest.

"Is it true you let him play on the truck and blast the siren?"

I can feel my cheeks turning red and it pisses me off that my skin gives me away. "Yeah, I did. And I already got grief from the guys, just so you know."

He shakes his head with a stern expression. "What am I going to do with you, McNeill?"

I shrug. "Whatever you want I suppose. I'm yours after all." I give him a wide grin.

His smile finally cracks through. "I wish I could have been there to see it, Spencer pretend-driving the truck."

"Oh man, he loved it. He's going to be a firefighter one day, just like his dad."

Joe nods. "Probably a safer bet than narc agent."

"Speaking of which, have you ever seen Sue?"

"No, why?"

"She looks like a model who happens to tote a gun in her Coach handbag. How badass is that?"

He steps closer. "No one's as badass as you, T. Rex."

"I'm flattered you think so, Lieutenant Murphy."

He pulls me into his arms and kisses me, gently at first and then hard and urgent. I'm breathless when we finally pull apart.

"Whoa, what's that about?"

"It's crazy, but there was something about seeing you with that kid, how natural and great you were with him. It just stirred me up."

"Apparently," I murmur as he presses against me and I realize how stirred up he really is.

"I want more than anything right now to take you to your bunk, pull off your uniform, and make love to you."

My eyes grow wide as he leans down and kisses my neck. "You're acting like you want to put a baby in me."

"Yeah, I bet that sounds crazy, huh?"

"No. Not crazy at all."

"How do you feel about that?"

"I think it's great since you'd make an amazing father. You're serious daddy material for sure."

"Do you want to have kids?"

"I do. You know I'd tried to talk myself out of it since my ex was anti-kids. But in my heart I've always wanted a family."

He runs his finger under my chin and kisses me again.

"Good to know. Now you go back out there and pretend that I scolded you. And I'll stay behind until I calm down."

"Yes, sir," I say with a wink and salute as I slip out the door.

Chapter 17: Have a Little Faith

I'm not afraid of storms, for I'm learning how to sail my ship. ~Mary Louise Alcott

"You may want to slow down," Joe warns me as I take the curves of Laurel Canyon's winding road in my pick-up as fast as my truck will handle. "There's usually traffic cops hiding on the turn-offs."

"Let 'em catch me," I tease. I've got the truck's windows open and my hair is whipping around my face as I speed around another curve on the way to Jeanine's house off La Cienega.

I can't help it. It's fun driving this road when it's not weighed down by rush hour traffic. The sharp twists heading up-up-up the hill, and then down-down-down are thrilling, and then suddenly you cross Sunset Boulevard into the land of Oz.

It's fun chasing convertibles with the tan beautiful people in their expensive sunglasses, Hollywood producers showing off their Teslas, and the Valley people clinging onto their Honda and Ford Fiesta's steering wheels until they're safely back on flat land.

I also love the funky mish-mash of houses perched on the edge of the canyon road: everything from English-style cottages that look like they belong in fairyland, to ultra-modern concrete boxes with checkerboard windows of frosted glass, to Spanish haciendas with crumbling terra cotta tile roofs. Wild bougainvilleas trail delicate fuchsia blooms up Juliet balconies and along the stucco walls edging the road.

Joe scowls.

"You don't have to do this, you know that, right?" I ask as I make an extra sharp turn.

"I know," Joe says.

"Paul and Dad are going to help me."

He nods. "Paul, your dad, and *me*." He folds his arms over his chest.

I shake my head. "I shouldn't have told you all those nice things Jeanine said about you. Is that why you're helping us with her landscaping? She's not even going to be there today. She's on another business trip."

"Ha, surely not that. You told me that the landscaping work is part of how you're compensating Jeanine for her legal expertise. I'm helping because the sooner your damn divorce gets wrapped up, the happier I'll be."

"Oh. Does it bother you that I'm technically still married?"

He shrugs.

"'Cause it shouldn't. I don't think of myself as still married to him . . . at all."

I almost bring up his divorce which I don't believe is done, but that seems like old news, since he hasn't even talked to her in over two years.

"So what's taking so long?"

"I had no idea that you were so old-fashioned."

He folds his arms over his chest.

"What, do you think I'm somehow cheating on him with you? I sure hope not because that's just bat-shit crazy. He's the one who cheated on me, as you know."

"I know," he grumbles.

My mouth drops open. "You don't think it's me that's dragging my feet, do you?"

"No," he says quietly, sounding a little too half-hearted

to me.

"Oh for fuck's sake." I jerk my car to the right and turn onto a side-road before slamming on the brakes. I shut off the engine, leaving the car parked in a wonky way, and hand him my cell phone.

"Okay, find my ex in the contacts, and then hit dial."

His eyes narrow and darken. "Why?"

"You'll see. Don't worry you don't have to talk to him."

He presses various buttons and then looks up at me. "He's not in the 'M's. Where do you have him?"

I roll my eyes. "Oh yeah, sorry I forgot that I moved him. He's listed under Dickwad now."

"Dickwad," he repeats as he presses more buttons. He accepts the news like it's the most natural thing in the world. I bite my tongue to keep from laughing.

He hands the phone to me. I listen as it rings and rings. Finally, I get his voicemail and it pisses me off. I make a fist with my free hand while I wait for the message prompt beep.

"Michael, why the hell don't you answer your phone anymore? Are you trying to piss me off by not getting back to the lawyers? I mean what the hell? I want this divorce done, like yesterday, and you're holding everything up. If this is some kind of fucked up strategy to take my money or something, can you just give it to me straight so I know what's going on? Get back to me, man. I mean it."

I thrust my index finger over the hang-up button about five times as I grip the phone hard so I don't hurl it out the truck window. Instead I slam it into the tray on the center consol.

After I calm down enough to drive, I look over at Joe and his arms are still folded across his chest but his index finger is pressed over his lips as he stares straight ahead.

"Now what?" I challenge him.

"Oh, nothing. Shall we get a move on?"

"Do you believe now that I'm dead serious about getting this divorce finished?"

"I never doubted it," he says quietly. "But now he knows it, too."

As soon as we arrive, Joes goes over and shakes Dad's hand, and then Paul's. They look pleased that he's joined us. Secretly, I'm also pleased.

"Glad for the help," Dad says.

"Anything for Trisha, sir," Joe replies with a smile.

Geez, he's laying it on thick.

"Besides, I'd like to learn more about landscaping. I plan to own some of my own land one day, hopefully by the end of the year," Joe says.

My ears prick at the comment. It kind of bugs me that he has plans I had no idea about. I mean, I knew him staying at my place wasn't forever, but it sounds like he's had a plan for a while.

"Where are you thinking?" Paul asks as he hands him a shovel.

"I have my eye on some property in the hills above Burbank."

"Burbank is a solid investment," Dad states as he nods. "Can't go wrong there."

I like Burbank but it makes me think of Michael and his floral business. His business is far from the hills but still too close for comfort. Maybe Joe doesn't care what matters to me. Feeling a dark mood settle over me, I grab a shovel and get to work while the boys stand around gabbing.

The sun is hot and I'm glad I slathered sunscreen on every exposed inch of my pale skin. I've only turned the soil on one small bed, and I'm already sweating.

Every time I look over the men are working and talking

like old pals. I should be glad that my family likes Joe so much but the tick about his future plans is moving up my spine.

I remain quiet when we stop for a break, eating cookies that Ma made and drinking cold bottles of water. Paul gives me a curious look; he knows something's up but I'm not spilling.

After our break everyone focuses in with the last group of stuff to be planted and works hard to finish, while Dad double-checks the irrigation system he installed for the new design. With the first round of plantings placed, we wrap up the day, depositing empty bags of soil, mulch, and plastic tubs in the back of Dad's pick-up.

I give everyone a semi-embrace since we're all sweaty. "Looking good. Jeanine is going to love this. Thanks, guys. I owe you. "

Dad brushes me off like I'm being ridiculous. "You don't owe us, Trish. We're family."

I smile. "And you guys are the best."

I'm quiet in the truck on the way back and thankfully Joe doesn't push it. When I pull up to the house and park, I ease out the truck door. "Thanks a lot for helping, Joe. It was really cool of you."

"You're welcome. I'm glad it all worked out. Her yard looks great now."

"It does. I think I'm gonna jump in the shower."

"You okay? You were quiet today, especially on the ride home."

I shrug. "Just stuff on my mind. I'm okay. So see you later?"

He looks bewildered but nods as I turn and head for the front door.

I've got the water running and am about to step in when I hear a knock at the backdoor. *Really?* Shutting off the water, I wrap a towel around me so I'm covered before going to see what Joe wants.

I pull open the door to find him buck naked except for a towel cinched around his waist. He's holding a bar of soap and has a sheepish expression.

I arch my brow, giving him a curious look.

"Some days I really hate my tiny shower."

I'd laugh at him if I wasn't in such an emotional mood. "It's tiny all right."

"I thought maybe you'd share your shower with me."

"You did, huh?" I fold my arms over my chest, partially to keep the towel from falling down.

"I could just stand in your backyard and use your garden hose, but I'd really like a hot shower where I'm not in a sardine can right about now. I got really sweaty helping you out with all that yardwork."

"True. I guess sharing my shower is the least I can do."

He nods with a smile. "I brought my own soap."

"What about shampoo?"

"Well, if you won't share yours I'll just use soap."

I roll my eyes playfully and pull the door open wide. "I'll share. Get in here you hot, sweaty man."

He follows me into the bathroom and stands back while I get the water running again. "So what was up today, Trisha? I've never seen you that quiet."

"I dunno. I'm feeling emotional. I think I'm about to get my period."

His eyes grow wide. "Thanks for the warning."

I pull off my towel and set it on the counter before stepping into the shower. The spray feels so damn good on my skin but I'm waiting for Joe to get in and he's taking his own sweet time. I stick my head out. "Hey, what's up? Aren't you getting in?"

Chuckling, he shakes his head before joining me.

"What's so funny?" I ask, trying to focus when all I want to do is watch the water cascade over his broad shoulders and down his washboard abs. We take turns getting under the water spray until we're both thoroughly soaked.

"Nothing's funny, I just love how comfortable you are in your own skin. It's sexy."

"Well I'm still not crazy about my thighs, but you clearly like them so I've made peace with them."

"Yes, I love your thighs. Do you want me to soap them up?"

"Sure." I hand him the fancy mango vanilla bath gel Elle gave me for Christmas. "Have at it."

He squeezes a liberal amount in the palm of his hands and suds it up, then starts by rubbing it into my shoulders working the sore muscles from our landscaping work. When I let out a low moan he steps up behind me so my back leans against his front.

"Good?" he asks.

I nod and lean back farther into him.

His hand trails down along my midriff. Meanwhile, with his other hand he's stroking the outer part of my thigh, and then he leans over and slowly starts kissing my neck and along my shoulder.

I shiver under his touch. "You getting sexy with me, Lieutenant Murphy?"

"I am," he whispers before lightly biting my earlobe.

I close my eyes as his hands slowly stroke up and down my thighs and across my belly and up to my breasts.

"Does this feel good?"

I nod. "Yes," I whisper. I'm glad he's behind me so he can't see that I'm starting to tear up from all the pleasure of his hands, and the pain of his future plans coursing through me. I bite my lip when I realize that his fingers are trailing up my inner thighs. *Oh God*, now he's stroking me between my legs.

"Joe," I moan.

He slips his slick finger inside of me, while his thumb rubs me in the most distracting way. *Whoa . . .* this teasing just makes me want more. I feel his erection pressed against my ass.

"Relax, baby," he whispers in my ear as the water falls around us like warm rain. "I just want to make you feel good."

I take a sharp breath, which becomes a sob, and he freezes, then turns me around. I feel the foam slowly slide off my skin.

"Trisha, what's the matter?" he asks.

"You're leaving me and moving to the hills of Burbank."

His eyes bug out. "What are you talking about?"

"You told Dad you were looking at property in Burbank. When are you planning on leaving me?"

He pulls me tight into his arms. "Oh sweetheart, I'm not leaving you. Why would you assume that?"

"Because you said—"

"But I said by the end of the year. And you said this house would be sold as part of the divorce. When that happens do you really think I wouldn't take you with me?"

"Really?" I ask with a frown. *Why am I acting like a spazzy little girl?*

"Don't you understand how I feel about you?"

"Why don't you tell me so I can make sure I have it straight."

He reaches over, turns off the water, and opens the shower door. A moment later he's gently rubbing the towel across my skin before he wraps me up like a burrito. He then does the same to himself, just rougher and faster, but the towel can't cover his tall frame, so he wraps it around his waist.

Next thing I know I'm being led into my bedroom and being pulled into his arms and lifted onto my bed. He joins me there and pulls me tightly against him, kissing me on the forehead as I nuzzle into him.

"So you don't want me to move away?" he asks.

I shake my head. "No, I don't."

He rakes his fingers through my damp hair. "Will you come with me, then?"

I start to cry again. *What the hell is wrong with me?*

"Shhh baby," he says. "Don't cry. I want you to come with me."

I hiccup as I gasp for air. "But Betty isn't big enough for the both of us."

"How do you know?"

"We'd end up killing each other."

"Aww have a little faith, sweetheart."

"You don't know how I get. I can be scary."

He shrugs. "You don't scare me, but if it makes you feel better I'll lock the knives up at night."

"Quit teasing me," I grumble.

He pulls back and looks down at me with a worried expression. "I've never seen you like this. Do you always get this way before your period?"

I burrow my face into his shoulder. "Only when the man I love says he's moving away from me."

I silently gasp as I bite my tongue. *Oh. My. God.* I slipped and used the L word in a clingy context. I'm so screwed. Who needs knives when you can scare a man away with desperate clinging, cinched tight by misuse of the dreaded 'L' word?

I wedge my eyes closed tightly as we both lie still—the

silence between us so big it's loud. I remind myself that he told me he loved me during that romantic night under the stars. So maybe this faux pas won't be too damaging.

He pushes me away far enough so he can turn me toward him. "Trisha, I love you too, and that's why I want you to come with me. What can I say to make you believe me?"

I'm feeling like such a pussy that my cheeks heat up.

"I believe you," I whisper. "I'm sorry for being so emotional."

"Don't be sorry. Being vulnerable around the people closest to you is part of being strong."

"I much prefer being the badass version of strong."

"Believe me, you're still badass. And you shouldn't think twice about it. When it comes to strong women, you own your own category."

I sniffle. "Oh I like that. You're not just saying that?"

"Nope. I mean it."

I tilt my face up and kiss his jaw. "Thank you."

"Sure thing."

"And I'll go wherever you and Betty go, and you won't have to lock up the knives. Okay?"

He grins and pulls me close. "Deal."

Chapter 18: The Walking Dead

Don't be afraid your life will end. Be afraid it will never begin. ~Grace Hansen

Two weeks later it's a low-key evening in the firehouse. A bunch of us are in the lounge watching the latest episode of *The Walking Dead*. I'm not into zombies too much, but naturally Bobo is, and he won the coin flip.

We all groan when at a really suspenseful part of the show the dispatch tone goes off and starts getting louder. So much for zombies.

As we climb in the truck Jim asks, "What's the call?"

"Reported possible suicide in North Hollywood. We're the closest so we'll be the first responders. Step on it Henderson."

We're silent on the short ride to an apartment complex on Oxnard. We pull up to a tan stucco box of a building that looks like every other apartment building on this street. It's an usually warm night, the air thick with the scent of blooming orange blossoms.

As soon as we come to a full stop, Joe and Jim jump out of the truck and hurry to the upstairs apartment where the apartment manager is waiting for them with the door wide open. Meanwhile, Bobo and I grab the medical kit and equipment. We're halfway up the stairs with the gear when Jim steps out the door. "McNeill," he yells, "we can't get a gurney in here. Hurry and grab the long spine board."

My eyes widen, wondering what the scene is inside. But I nod and run back to the truck.

When I return and finally pass through the front door I stop in my tracks. *Holy hell.* Whoever lives here must be the neatest hoarder we've ever seen—and we've seen all kinds. Pristine moving boxes are stacked floor to ceiling. To add to the problem, furniture covered with moving blankets is bunched up in some weird puzzle around the boxes, leaving only a narrow path through the apartment.

"I've got the board!" I call out, but there's a flurry of activity in the back so I wait for more instructions.

A minute later Jim steps into the path from what I assume is the bedroom and takes the spine board. "Is the person alive?" I ask.

He nods. "Just barely. Pills. Damn good thing we got here when we did. We just intubated him."

When Bobo finishes using the radio to contact the hospital, I turn to him. "Who called this in?"

"Apparently the dude called his mom and was saying stuff that made her suspicious. She called the apartment manager to check on him, and then we got the call."

I nod, feeling sorry for the poor guy. "A cry for help."

"Sounds like it. What a sad loser. The guys almost have him ready to go but they'll have to get him through this narrow path first."

He lifts up a frame that's face down and perched on the edge of a stack of boxes like it could fall into their path. He turns it around and stands it upright on a shorter stack of boxes out of harm's way.

From where I'm standing, and the look of the black and white shapes, I assume it's a wedding picture. Jim leans into it to look closer and then pulls back, glances over at me, and leans down to look at it again. My stomach falls when his face pales, like the blood has drained from it. He carefully turns it back face down.

"What?" I ask, pointing to the frame.

His doesn't look at me but his eyes are bugging out. "Um, nothing, T. Rex. Just a picture."

My gut is telling me otherwise and I march over and grab the frame before he can stop me. When I turn it around it almost slips from my fingers and my breath catches in my throat.

This picture has haunted me before and it all computes instantly. How can I forget the damn cascade of starched curls that the perky wedding coordinator talked the hair lady into doing to me? I hated it . . . I looked like a fucking poodle standing next to Mikey looking all proud and debonair in his tux on our wedding day.

Mikey always insisted that I looked beautiful that day and kept the fancy framed portrait hanging in this office. What straight guy does that? Just another gay clue that I managed to be oblivious to and now apparently we're paying dearly for.

I feel an imaginary blow to the gut and I almost lose my footing. My stomach lurches and I choke back the bile as my wave of guilt roars over me.

Oh my God . . . What if Mikey's in the next room on the razor's edge between life and death because I abandoned him when he needed me? What if we can't save him? Or what if we got to him late enough that the liver and brain damage has set in?

Pressing the frame to my chest, I barrel toward the bedroom.

From inside the bedroom, Joe looks up with an alarmed expression and points my direction. "Stop her!" he yells at Jim who turns to block me before I can pass through the door. When I see Mikey pale and lingering in the shadow of death the picture slips out of my hands and crashes on the floor.

Joe barks at me as he rushes forward. "McNeill!"

I struggle to push past Jim who seems equally deter-mined to keep me back.

"Let me pass!" I cry out.

Joe grabs my shoulder. "Wait outside, Trisha. You don't want to see this."

I shake his hand off of me. "I've got to so get out of my way! He's my husband, for God's sake, and he needs me right now."

Joe's expression falls but I don't pay attention as I push past he and Jim until I'm at the head of the bed with Mikey. I reach out and place my hand on my husband's cold fore-head, feeling almost out of my body as if I'm observing the macabre scene from above. Scott is rechecking the breathing tube as the other guys strap him on the board. I'm hearing commands somewhere in the back of my consciousness.

Tears sting my eyes. *No. No. No.* He can't die.

"Mikey," I cry out as I lean in close to his ear, "I'm here. It's Trish. Listen to me . . . you need to hold on and fight. I'm here . . . I'm here." I brush my arm across my face, wip-ing my tears away.

I vaguely hear gasps around the room.

"Jesus," Bobo chants. "He's her husband?"

"Yes," I wail. "You gotta save him."

"We're doing our best, McNeill," Scott replies breath-lessly. "Heading down, ten-four," he says into the radio.

There's a rumbling voice which breaks through my daze. "Someone get her out of here!"

"Don't you fucking dare," I growl, warning all of them.

I'm running my hands through Mikey's hair over and over and chanting commands to him. I'm the only one he ever really listened to, so I'm making sure he's going to hear me loud and clear.

"Fight, Mikey! Fight!" I cry out as he's lifted to be evac-uated. Right before they carry him out I look up through glazed eyes and my gaze connects with Joe. He's staring at me like I'm a stranger, and a deranged one at that. It's all too much being in Mikey's bedroom with my lover trying to save him. I blink several times and reach out to the bedpost to steady myself. When I look up again Joe has turned away as they carry Mikey out of the room. I rush up behind them. "Hurry! Hurry!"

They ignore me, being well-trained to stay focused and not drawn into the drama of freaked out family members. I'm now one of them, on the outside looking in.

The tunnel of boxes and furniture we rush past have new meaning now that I realize that Mikey tried to fit our entire house into this small, bleak apartment. All the things he loved so much, tumbled together like a discount chain's sorry warehouse. Our life together once had meaning and now it's just a cardboard jungle of lost dreams.

When the ambulance with Mikey, the attendant, Scott, and Joe pulls away the sirens ring in my ears as I retch into the gutter, my dinner coming up violently mixed with my tears and snot. When I'm done Jim hands me a towel and bottle, so I can rinse out my mouth and wipe my face. I nod with gratitude.

"Damn shame," I hear Bobo say to Jim.

I silently follow them onto the truck with my head down.

We're almost to the station when I turn to Jim. "Can you drop me off at the hospital? I don't think I can drive right now."

He glances nervously over at Bobo. "Sure thing, Trisha."

"Thank you," I whisper as I close my eyes and focus, praying for Mikey the rest of the ride.

"When was the last time you talked to him?" Jim asks as we pull out of the station driveway in his SUV.

My brain is so numb I can't even remember. When?

When? I left him that message recently, but he never responded. Then I recall my birthday and Mikey showing up with my favorite flowers and the awkward and angry scene that followed. "It was weeks ago. I should've realized that something was up. He wasn't getting back to anyone and he's normally really on top of stuff."

"Weird," he says, probably just trying to be conciliatory.

"He told me that he didn't want a divorce."

"Damn, that's messed up. What did he expect, considering?"

I shake my head. "I don't know. Apparently he was conflicted."

"Shit like this ain't always black and white," Jim murmurs.

I nod silently.

We're almost to the hospital when I realize that I can't be alone. I call my brother, Paul, and he assures me he's on his way.

Jim hesitates when he drops me off at Providence Saint Joseph's entrance. "You okay, McNeill? I can wait with you 'til your brother gets here."

"Thanks. I appreciate it but you should get back to the station. I'll be okay."

Since I'm in my gear I play it professional as I approach the admissions desk so I'm directed right back into emergency. I'm about to pass through the doors when Joe approaches from the other side. He puts his hand on my shoulder and pulls me aside.

His expression is troubled, and his face haggard. "About back at the scene . . . I'm sorry about snapping at you."

"Don't be. You were doing your job, Joe. It was necessary."

His shoulders soften a little, sagging down.

"What's happening now?" I ask, nodding toward the ER.

"They just finished pumping his stomach, and he's still sedated. He was breathing faintly before we intubated him, so I imagine his brain is okay."

I shudder. "Thank God."

He nods and looks down at me with a concerned expression. "How are you doing?"

"Not so good. I'm feeling really shitty . . . like why did I have to be such a bitch to him? If I'd known he was so frail—"

"But you didn't know," Joe points out.

"Still . . ."

Joe seems pissed and folds his arms over his chest. "What about what he did to you, Trish?"

My head drops and I shrug. "I know. I haven't forgotten."

"I haven't either," he says.

I don't want to think about all that right now so I focus back on the situation. "Once he's stable, do you think he'll be going to a psych ward?"

"Probably, at least for a few days. They have to evaluate him first."

I jam my hands in my back pockets. "You should get back to the station."

"I don't want to leave you here. He's in good hands, Trish. Come back with me. You need to be around friends right now."

I shake my head. "I can't leave him here alone."

Joe studies at me, his eyes clouded with concern. "What about you? This has been a fucking nightmare."

Straightening up. I square my shoulders back. "Joe," I say in a tone that warns him to let it go. He can say whatever he wants, I'm not leaving Mikey here alone.

He glances over my shoulder and squints and I turn to see Paul walking toward us.

"You called your brother?" Joe asks with a frown.

"He said he'd stay with me."

"I see," Joe mutters, sounding hurt, like he should be the one.

"I knew you had to get back to work."

Paul steps up to us and slides his arm over my shoulder and pulls me against him, then reaches out to shake hands with Joe. He looks pale, his hair uncombed and wild. He must've gotten out of bed to come here.

"How's he doing?" he asks.

"He's stable," answers Joe. He rubs his chin roughly and studies me one last time before looking up at Paul. "Well, now that I know Trish is in good hands, I'm heading back to the station."

I step close enough to him to give him a hug. When his arms tighten around me, it's the first warmth I've physically felt since everything unraveled after seeing Mikey and my doomed wedding picture.

"Thank you, Joe," I whisper.

He silently nods, tips his head to Paul, and then walks out the door. He doesn't look back and I watch him as he descends until he fades into the darkness of the moonless night.

After I check in at the nurse's station I rejoin Paul. He glances around and then gestures toward the waiting area. I follow him and we take a seat on the side of the room as far from the droning television as possible. I couldn't give a damn about the evening news. My life is dramatic enough.

"I made Elle stay home. She wanted to come," Paul says as he squeezes my shoulder. "She's worried about you."

"I'm okay. It's Mikey I'm worried about."

"Oh, so are we, Trish. I mean, holy hell. I never would've expected this from him. He's full of jacked-up surprises lately."

I nod, and lean forward with my face in my hands and my elbows on my knees. "I can't help but feel like this is my fault. He could never handle it when I was angry with him, and I've had nothing but rage since our marriage blasted apart."

"But you've had every right to be furious. He lied and cheated on you."

I take a sharp breath at his brutally frank words. "Yet, he keeps saying he wants us to try again. What's going on in that head of his?"

"Being sexually attracted to men, and being okay with being gay, are two different things," Paul remarks, as he rubs the back of his neck, a heavy sadness in his eyes.

My brother is a compassionate person and I've never appreciated that quality in him more than tonight.

Maybe it's because I'm focused on Joe now, or maybe the passing of time has enabled me to look at things differently, but I can think about Mikey's confusion with perspective, like from a distance.

I look down at the faint mark of lighter skin from where my wedding band used to be. "I can imagine that coming out wouldn't have been easy for him. We never talked about it, but his dad was very conservative and probably wouldn't have accepted him if he was openly gay. Mikey always seemed scared of disappointing him."

"It was just about a year ago that he passed away, right?"

I nod. "Heart attack. Now that I think of it, there was a shifting in Mikey after his dad's death. He seemed a little lighter."

"Maybe all of that led to this."

I shrug. "Maybe." I feel a sharp sting at the idea that Mikey may have chosen to be with men much earlier if his dad weren't in the picture. Was I always just a beard?

"So how's Joe taking all of this?" Paul asks.

"What do you mean?"

"It's obvious he's in love with you, and now here you are, focused on your ex's well-being. That can't be easy for him."

My eyebrows knit together as I try to imagine how I'd feel in Joe's shoes. I'd feel like an outsider, that's what. I kind of regret not asking him to stay.

"I hope he can understand why I need to be here."

Paul gives me a hard look. "I'm going to be straight with you, Trish. You're dealing with a really complicated situation here considering that Mike is unstable. You and he weren't even talking before last night, and the divorce had the potential of getting really ugly . . . and now you're trying to take care of him."

He shakes his head. "You're in a new relationship. If this was Elle and her ex I wouldn't want her here, and I sure as hell wouldn't want her helping her unstable ex like some friggin' Florence Nightingale. Take heed, Sis. Pay attention to your future, because Joe's your future, and Mikey's your complicated past."

"I'll try, Paul. I promise, I'll try."

We've been sitting for about a couple of hours, nursing our Styrofoam cups of lukewarm coffee laced with Amaretto Coffee Mate and watching some late night show when one of the ER doctors approaches us.

"Mrs. Castallani?"

"Yes," I say, standing. No point correcting her about my surname at this point.

"Your husband's conscious. Are you ready to see him?"

I smooth down the wrinkles in my uniform slacks. "Yes, thank you."

I look over at Paul but he gestures for me to go ahead. "I'll wait here for you."

The attendant pulls back the suspended curtain, and I still for a moment adjusting to the image of Mikey, looking frail and defeated, hooked up to a plethora of beeping monitors. He blinks several times as if he can't believe I'm here.

"Patricia," he barely whispers, and my breath catches to hear him call me what he did when we first met.

I force a smile on my face, even though I don't have the energy to smile. "Hey you. What the hell were you doing, scaring us like that?"

His gaze drops down and he tries to lick his parched lips. "I'm sorry."

"I'm sorry too," I say with the most gentle tone I can muster.

He tries to clear his voice, but it still sounds like it's been rubbed with sandpaper. "I've just been so sad and I didn't want to be sad anymore."

"Well, dude, you know I'm not going to put up with that." I shake my head at him.

His eyes brighten the tiniest bit. "No, I suppose you won't."

"Did you know our station would be the one to respond?"

His eyes cloud with confusion. "Who reported it? I was wondering why I wasn't dead."

I feel a surge of everything from acute irritation to relief. "That's not funny, Mikey. You almost did die. What the hell?"

"Would you have been sorry if I'd died?"

"Would you stop with this shit! Of course I would've

been sorry . . . gutted. Do you really think I'm that heartless?"

He closes his eyes for a few seconds, and when he opens them he looks exhausted. "No, I just thought that I didn't matter anymore."

"You matter, you big lug."

He gives me a half-smile. He always used to laugh when I called him that. "And you care?"

I narrow my eyes and give him a stern look. "Of course I do."

He closes his eyes again, this time for about a minute, and just when I think he's asleep, he opens his eyes half-mast. "I'm so tired, and so damn sore. Everything hurts." He weakly runs his hand up his neck and tries to swallow.

I walk over by the side of his bed. "I'm tired too, Mikey. I'm going to go crash now that I know you're going to be all right. I'll be back in the morning, okay?" I reach over and smooth out his hair, then rest my hand on his cold forehead.

"Promise?" he whispers.

"Yes. I promise."

Chapter 19: The Return of Sasquatch

*A really strong woman accepts the war she went through
and is ennobled by her scars.*

~ Carly Simon

The next morning I feel like shit . . . like a truck ran over me, backed up, ran over me again, and repeated several times more. As I fire up the coffeemaker I wonder what in the hell I'm going to do.

I sit at the table nursing my first cup of java with my heavy head resting in my hands. After pouring myself the second cup I decide to call Jeanine. Like usual I have to go through the receptionist, her secretary, and her legal assistant before I get her.

"Still haven't heard from him, woman," she offers, assuming I'm calling for an update on my divorce.

"Yeah, well you won't hear from him today either. He's in the hospital on suicide watch."

She snaps her phone off speaker. "What the hell?"

"He overdosed last night, Jeanine. Pills." I blink back tears, surprised by my anguish. Why is it hitting me in full force now?

"Mother of Jesus, how did you find out? Why didn't you call me?"

"It was late. We got the call at the station. I had no idea it was him until the guys had already intubated him."

"Oh, Trisha, that's how you found out? On a call? I can't believe it. What was he thinking?"

"I don't know. But now we know why he wasn't responding to our calls."

"How is he physically?"

"I think we got to him early enough that he's going to be okay. They still have to test him for liver damage. As for his mindset, I just don't know."

"What about Joe? How is he handling this?"

I huff. "What about him? Why is everyone worried about Joe?"

"Oh, don't be pissed," she warns me. "I'm worried about the whole lot of you. Well, so much for wrapping this divorce up quickly. If nothing else, he's going to need your health insurance after this stunt. Emergency room visits and ambulance runs are bank breakers."

"Right," I say, resenting having to even think about shit like health insurance.

"You working today?" she asks.

"No, I was at the hospital really late and I'm going to call Chief next. I'm going back to check on him this morning."

Jeanine doesn't respond and the air is thick with all the things I'm sure she wants to say to me. I've got to give her credit, this is one of the only times I can remember that she's held her tongue.

"I just have to Jeanine. I'm a firefighter, and what do we do? We save people's lives."

"I get it, my friend. I understand your instincts to save him, to fix him. You're that good of a person. But just re-member that you aren't the one who's going to fix him."

"But if not me, who? His mom is afraid to leave her house."

Jeanine lets out a long-suffering sigh, laced with frus-tration. "You're getting a free pass today. But if this keeps going on I'll be all up in your business, woman. Do we have an understanding?"

I sigh back. "Yes," I agree, knowing that my under-standing something and my following through are two different things.

"Okay good. Then I'm heading to my meeting. I'll check on you later."

I don't set the phone down after we disconnect, but instead dial our captain.

"Captain Handley," he answers. I feel relieved to hear his gruff voice.

"Chief, it's McNeill. I'm sorry I didn't call earlier—"

"No worries Trisha. Joe filled me in. I'm damn sorry you're dealing with this."

"Thanks. I think I'm still in shock."

"Of course. I see you're off the next two days, I'm sure you'll need that time. Just give me a call if you need more time after that."

"Thank you, sir."

"And is there anything else we can do? I called my friend who oversees the ER at Saint Jo's to keep an eye out for him."

My heart swells. "I really appreciate that. I'm going to the hospital now. He needs help, and I want make sure the right decisions are being made. The thing is, I understand him better than anyone."

Or at least I thought I did.

"Of course. Please let us know if you need anything, Trisha."

"Thank you, I will."

After I set the phone down my head feels so heavy, crammed full of thoughts and feelings, and I lean over and rest my cheek on the cool wood of the tabletop. I let out a long sigh. Things had been going good for me—better than good, thanks to Joe. And now Mikey's cry for help has turned everything upside down again. I sigh once more knowing I have no idea what I'll face when I return to the hospital.

Maybe Mikey woke up with regret and a humble determination to get back on his feet. Maybe he's gone off the edge and they've already transferred him to the psych ward to be monitored. As well as I thought I knew him, it's weird realizing that I'm just not sure what to expect.

I place both of my palms firmly on the table, on either side of my resting head, and then push up with more strength than necessary. Just moments later I'm standing tall and stepping away from the table. It's time to be strong and face this head on. Somehow I need to get things moving back in the right direction.

As I approach the hospital room I was directed to for Mikey, I hear a woman giggling. I almost turn back, convinced they gave me the wrong room number, but I peek inside just in case.

Sure enough some bubbly redhead is blathering on about something as Mikey is boosted up with pillows in his bed, a weak smile on his face. *What the hell?* I may not have been sure what to expect, but I sure as hell didn't expect this.

When Mikey sees me standing in the doorway he gestures for me to come inside. "Trish, come meet my friend, Carmella. She works here."

I narrow my eyes, and it feels like heat is rising off my pupils. He should be resting not taking random visitors. I want to let the snarky out, unleash it in a big way, but I bite my tongue and count to three. Whomever this woman is doesn't change the fact that Mikey almost ended his life last night and he needs to be handled delicately.

Stepping into the room, I extend my hand. "Carmella?

Sorry to say I've never heard of you. How do you and Mikey know each other?"

She dabs the corner of her lips with her index finger and smiles before shaking my hand. Her fingernails are long and the tips are painted pale ivory with tiny rhinestones on them. She has showy rings on several fingers. I can only imagine what she thinks of jewelry free, make-up-less, me.

"I'm the Facilities Director here. Our office orders all the flowers for the hospital public areas, and I was the one who brought in charming Michael and his gorgeous work. Bloomsbury Gardens is my go-to floral shop now."

"Tell Trish about the last florist you used," Mikey says.

I study him. He may be weak but his coloring is definitely much better than it was last night.

"Oh my goodness, they were leftover from my predecessor, positively tacky . . . carnations and baby's breath for days. Their stuff looked like those arrangements you pick up in gas station parking lots on holidays.

Mikey smiles. He was always such a charmer. "Thank you for lifting my spirits, Carmella."

Her expression suddenly turns somber, and she glances over at me and then back at him. "Of course. We're friends, Michael. I'm glad I could help today, but I don't want to ever see you in here again as a patient—only as our floral designer, okay?"

He suddenly looks somber too, and he nods.

"And you promise to keep your appointments?"

"I will. Thank you again."

"You're welcome." She turns to me. "And nice to meet you, Trisha."

"Likewise. Thanks."

I wait until she's halfway down the hall before I turn to Mikey. "What was that all about?"

"They wanted to lock me up at the psych ward at

UCLA, Trish, and I can't bear the thought of that. I know it would only make my depression worse."

Just the idea of a psych ward sounds creepy, like Stephen King kind of creepy. Honestly, if it were me, I'd refuse, too. And knowing how sensitive Mikey is, I think it could do him more harm than good.

"So is this an optional thing? I thought they just went ahead and committed you if they thought you needed it."

"Well, after I met with the ER doctor I called Carmella since I was freaked out and I knew she had relationships with everyone in this place."

"Why have I never heard of this woman before?" I ask.

"I'm friends with a lot of my clients but I don't like to talk about work at home, so you don't hear about them."

I take a sharp breath. Just another thing to add to the list of things I didn't know about Mikey, the secret keeper.

"Anyway, she stopped in after I was evaluated and she convinced the doctor that I wouldn't handle hospitalization well, that regular sessions and family supervision would be the better plan."

"Family supervision?" I ask, my stomach tightening into a little ball. I hope he's not thinking . . .

"I told her I'd be with you, that you'd look out for me."

I want to yell at him, but considering how fragile he is I have to swallow my fury.

"Michael—"

"Please, Trisha, please. You're a firefighter so they know you're trained with this stuff. Being locked up in a psych ward would kill me, and I can't take that apartment anymore. The walls were closing in on me. I think that's what pushed me over the edge in the first place."

"Well it's no wonder with all your stuff stacked up like that. Why didn't you get a storage space?"

"It's crazy to spend money to store that fine furniture in

a metal shed. Besides, everyone I know gets robbed in those places."

"What about your mom's garage?"

His face turns red. "I haven't told her about us . . . you know . . ."

I can feel my eyes bug out. "You haven't told her we've split?"

"Well, I was still hopeful we'd work things out, so why upset her?"

I press my hand over my forehead. "Good Lord."

"Trisha, please. Please let me come home."

The pleading tone in his voice breaks me.

In my frustration I'm determined to give him a dose of reality about us, tell him that I'm in love with Joe and everything. But the longer he gazes at me the more I realize how frail he is. He put on a good face for Carmella to get out of the psych ward, but I can tell he's far from being in the clear and on stable ground.

"How long are we talking about?"

His gaze suddenly brightens looking hopeful. "A week or two?"

A week? Two? How will I ever explain this to Joe?

"I've got to warn you . . . if you think your place is depressing you must remember how the house looked after you cleared it out. It's still pretty much empty other than a few basic fillers from Ikea."

"I could bring our furniture back?" he asks, his eyes wide with hope.

This festering feeling bubbles up in my gut. You know the kind of unsettling feeling that later you realize was a sign you should've paid attention to.

Later, when he's finally too wiped out to keep his eyes open I leave with instructions how to get into his apartment, along with a list of what he'll need during his stay at my place. I also leave with a sharp feeling of dread.

Joe swings by the house to check on me right as I'm unloading Mikey's things. He doesn't take the news well.

"What do you mean he's staying with you?" Joe asks, his teeth gritted and his eyes dark as coal.

"If I didn't say yes he was being locked up in the psych ward."

"Which is exactly where he should be, Trisha. He intended to kill himself. This is not a stable, or well man. And now you're telling me he's moving back in with you?"

"Just for a week, or so."

"And sleep where? In bed with you?" He has a scarlet flush working his way up his neck. I'd think it was hot if this were another circumstance and if his rage wasn't so scary.

I give him a stern look. "Of course not in bed with me. I was thinking I'd sleep on the couch in the living room."

He rolls his eyes. "Yeah, that makes perfect sense. You're taking care of him and then sleeping on a little loveseat you can't even stretch out on. Why are you allowing yourself to be a doormat?"

"Hey!" I snap, folding my arms over my chest and scowling at him. "I'm not a doormat. I make my own decisions."

"I guess you do, whether they make sense or not," he mumbles.

"What if I'm just being a good person? Is that really so awful?"

"It's more complicated than that, Trisha, and you know it."

"I know," I mutter looking down.

He stands waiting for a minute. I'm not sure if he's

waiting for me to have an epiphany or if he's trying to figure out what to say next. But I've got nothing left to say
right now. I'm on overload.

He pulls out his keys. "I'm heading back to the station.
Will he be here tonight?"

I shake my head. "They're watching him one more
night, and then I pick him up in the morning after I meet
with his therapist."

Joe looks off in the distance and then back at his rig.
"Okay," he says so softly it's almost a sigh. Turning, he
walks over to his bike, climbs on and roars off.

I'd be upset that he didn't at least kiss me, or say good-
bye, but I don't have a single free space left in my heart to
hold the hurt.

The next day feels like it will be the longest day of my
life. I'm apprehensive the whole way to the hospital, and
Joe's words from the day before echo in my ears. I numbly
meet with the psychiatrist to go through all the issues and
patterns that could come up once Mikey leaves the hospital.
I'm also carefully instructed on his meds and I take notes,
before going to collect him to head home.

As soon as I have Mikey settled in the bedroom and he
falls asleep, a feeling of panic stirs me up. I know it was
the right thing to want to help him, but it was a knee-jerk
reaction I hadn't really thought through. My house is my
safe refuge, where I've had peace and quiet and where I've
learned how to live without Mikey. Now he's here in my
space and I'm already agitated, and it's only been a couple
of hours. What am I going to be like in a week?

I'm also missing Joe, and I'm worried he's still mad at
me. I haven't spoken to him since he rode off on his motorcycle yesterday, and he was supposed to be home today. I

keep looking out the window hoping to spot him.

I've been sorely tempted to call him, but I've stopped myself since maybe he just needs to process all of this on his own. It's not like Mikey being here will be a permanent thing.

After about an hour of wandering around the house trying to figure out what to do, I grab a bottle of water and go out to the front porch and sit. With any luck Joe will finally show up and we can have a talk.

I'm halfway done with my water when a Jeep pulls up across the street. Through the tinted window I can make out that it's a very tall guy behind the wheel. My heart thumps. Maybe it's Joe, and he borrowed the Jeep for an errand. I set my bottle down and stand up so he can see me when he approaches.

But by the time he's halfway across the street my fingers have curled into fists. It sure as hell isn't Joe. What is that bastard, Stanley, doing showing up here? I'm tempted to go inside the house and bolt the door, but my twisted sense of curiosity gets the better of me. Whatever he has to say, it better be good to justify coming over and pissing me off. As he approaches I narrow my eyes and fold my arms over my chest.

"What do you want?" I yell out when he's close to my walkway.

"I was hoping I could talk to you, Trisha."

Sure he wants to talk to *me*. I roll my eyes. "He's asleep, and I'm not waking him up for the likes of you."

He glances down at his work boots, and then back up at me. "I swear. You're the one I'm here to see."

"Well, I sure as hell don't want to see you. So you can turn around and go back to where you came from. Besides, shouldn't you be minding the shop?"

His expression becomes muddled, like he can't

understand what I'm referring to. "Of course I'm not mind-ing the shop," he says.

"Why not?"

"I quit weeks ago. Didn't Mike tell you?"

I shake my head. "No he didn't. So who's there taking care of business? He won't be back for at least a few days still."

"Melissa. But she's totally in over her head. That's why she called me and asked for help, and then she told me about what happened."

I just stare at him, trying to compute everything.

He jams his hands in his pockets. "I understand why you hate me, but can you tell me if he's okay?"

"It's none of your business." I know it's cruel to say but right now I'm not subscribing to the decorum of friggin' civility.

"Trisha, please," he begs. "Melissa said he's been such a mess lately. I've been so worried."

I hear the anguish in his voice and realize that being cruel to him only makes this situation worse. Taking a deep breath, I try to calm down.

"Well, thank God we got to him in time. According to the tests he doesn't have any brain damage, and his liver weathered it. But I'm still not sure where his head is at."

Stanley nods. "He's always so hard to figure out. He puts on that upbeat, positive front, yet he can get very dark inside."

As I gaze at Stanley I realize that I haven't really looked at him eye-to-eye since the scene in the back office of the flower shop went down. That night after seeing his hairy ass I don't remember looking at him again since all my fo-cus was on Mikey as he fumbled to pull his pants back up.

Stanley and I had always been friendly. Hell, he worked for Mikey for years. He's a big, strong guy, but right now he looks defeated with dark circles and bags under his eyes, and his broad shoulders hunched over. It's as if he's a broken man instead of the upbeat jokester I'd always known.

Releasing a long sigh, I point to the porch chair to my right. "Have a seat."

He gives me a grateful look, and sits, twisting his hands together before turning toward me. "I've been wanting to tell you, Trisha, that I'm sorry for what happened. You didn't deserve to walk in on that. You've always been kind to me, and I know how Mike feels about you."

I give him a side-glance with a lifted brow. *He knows how Mikey feels about me?* "How's that?" I ask, not sure I want to hear the answer.

"He loves you more than anyone or anything, which is why he kept that side of himself so hidden. He was devastated that you walked in on us."

I lean forward in my chair and stare at the yard. So it sounds like Stanley knows a lot about my life with Mikey . . . more than just an employee would. A question starts to fester in the back of my mind.

"So why'd you quit your job?"

Stanley's head drops, and he rubs his face roughly with his hands. "I'm not here to tell you my story."

"Maybe you should."

He gazes off into the distance. "I quit because I love him."

"I see," I whisper, letting the hurt of his words sink in. It was one thing that my husband cheated on me for sex, but the idea that love was involved is something else. If Mikey knows Stanley loves him, and still had sex with him, Mikey must have those kind of feelings back. He's not the kind of asshole who would openly toy with someone's deepest emotions.

"Did you quit that night?"

"You really want to hear all of this, Trisha?"

I flex my fingers that have been gripping my knees. "Maybe I need to."

He crosses his arms over his chest and squeezes like he's holding himself together. "After you left the shop and Mike went after you, I fell apart. I was inconsolable and too upset to drive. I just couldn't believe that we'd finally been caught and would now face the consequences. What if he didn't acknowledge our relationship? When Mike returned in a state after you threw him out, he found me sobbing and we had an argument that escalated."

I can almost picture the scene in my head and it makes me feel incredibly sad.

"You see, this on-and-off stuff with Mike had been going on for a while. His needs, well *those* kinds of needs would build up and when they did he would come to me, and I helped him."

"Helped him?"

"Do you really want specifics?"

"I do."

"Sex, I gave him whatever he wanted or needed . . . whatever gave him relief. I told myself that it was like my Grinder hook-ups or bar bootie calls in West Hollywood and getting off was okay because it was what both Mike and I needed. I was lying to myself, but that's what we do when we're losing control."

I blink several times, trying to push the picture of Stanley and Mikey having sex out of my head.

"So last year after Mike's dad died, things changed. He let his guard down more and suddenly there was emotion, and at times what felt like love. He finally was getting comfortable about who he was."

"I know his dad had a big issue with gays, so are you saying that when he died Mikey felt free from his guilt about wanting men?"

"Yes," Stanley replies with dark eyes. "And as Mike changed so did I, and I allowed myself to want more from him . . . ask more from him. He started making me promises like we'd be together soon, but then he'd say that he loved you and didn't want to hurt you. It made my head and my heart fucking spin."

"Really?" I say, blinking back tears hearing he was trying to work up the courage to leave me all along. Could that really be true?

"So stupidly, that night after everything went down and he was unwillingly thrust out of the closet, I assumed that this was going to be the turning point for us to become a couple. Instead he assured me, with many cruel accusations and insults that he was going to get you back no matter what it took. It was like the whole thing had been a lie."

"Mikey knows what I'm about. Surely he knew I'd never take him back."

"You really won't?" Stanley asks, seeming surprised. "I'd take him back in a second if he'd have me."

"It's different for you Stanley. You both have the same needs. I know now he's not meant to be mine."

His mouth goes slack, as his eyes cloud with desperation. "He'll never forgive me for making him lose you, Trisha."

"Well, he has a lot of work to do, and that should be one of the things you guys have to work out. We all have the truth now and what matters is what we do with it."

We sit quietly for a few minutes, then Stanley stands up and thanks me for hearing him out. I assure him that once Mikey is stable I'll tell him that he came by. So much of what happens now is up to Mikey.

I sense that it's hard for Stanley to leave, perhaps because Mikey is just through that front door and down the hall. But at least when he walks slowly back to his Jeep he's standing a little taller than when he arrived.

That evening, after getting dinner for me and Mikey and then cleaning up, I realize I still haven't heard from Joe, so I call him on his cell.

"Hey," he says, with a neutral inflection in his voice.

"I was just wondering where you've been. I thought I'd see you today."

"No, I'm staying here. I took on some overtime. I'm working straight through the next four days."

"Were you going to tell me that?" I inquire, biting back my frustration.

"Does it matter? I imagine you're plenty busy there."

I let out a long frustrated sigh. "Of course it matters. Are you mad at me? Is it your intention to punish me? Because it feels that way."

"I'm not punishing you, Trisha. I just don't feel like being around your husband and his drama."

"Oh."

Geez, that makes me feel just great.

"How *is* the patient?" he asks.

"Sleeping a lot. I guess it's the medication they have him on. He has another appointment tomorrow. I'll know more then."

"Okay. Well, I better go."

It's lousy how distant and cold he's being, and I can't believe how much it hurts. I guess based on what the others were saying I should've expected something like this, but I didn't. I had just hoped that Joe would be a big person about all I'm dealing with. Now it seems it was too much to ask.

"Okay, goodnight then. And I hope you miss me a little,

because I sure miss you."

I don't wait for his reply and end the call immediately because I can't bear to know if he didn't respond. Right now my heart can't take any more bruising.

A few minutes later I set up my bedding for the night on the living room love seat. Once under the covers I lie for hours with my eyes wide open, wondering what I should do about Joe pulling away from me. I also think about my conversation with Stanley and what I should say to Mikey about it. His frankness about their sex life was startling and it made me wonder what it must be like to prefer having sex with someone similar to you, rather than your opposite. Do all men have desires to sleep with other men and just don't act on it? Does Joe? I can't imagine him with another man, but who knows. I don't have any interest in having sex with a woman. But maybe anything is possible if your path is crossed with that certain person. Who knows?

I continue to toss and turn, thinking again about Joe being distant, and how I'd give anything to have him holding me right now. It feels like my whole world is upside down again just when everything was starting to feel so right.

What if Mikey hadn't taken those pills? I probably would've been with Joe on top of his rig watching the stars tonight. And I'd be happy—so very happy, not blue and defeated like I feel right now.

As my mind whirls, sleep doesn't come to me until almost dawn.

I wake up to my shoulder being gently shaken.

"Trish, Trish . . . wake up."

I hear Mikey's voice as my mind clears. I blink and then try to stretch out my legs, but my feet are stopped short by the end of the love seat.

"What time is it?" I ask.

"Almost nine, and my appointment is at ten."

"Shit!" I cry out as I sit up and swing my legs down to the floor. I notice he's fully dressed and his hair is combed back. "Why didn't you get me up sooner?"

"You looked like you really need the sleep."

"Did you take your pills?"

"Yes."

"And did you eat first?"

"I did. But I appreciate how thoroughly you're taking care of me. Thank you for that."

"Sure, I guess," I mumble.

I throw some clothes on, brush my teeth and grab a granola bar while Mikey fills my travel tumbler with coffee. My head is still foggy as we load into the car so things almost feel normal until I remember that we're headed back to the hospital for a follow-up for my gay husband following his suicide attempt.

What is my life?

Mikey is more lively today, especially after his session with his shrink. He agrees to a stop at the market on the way home, and follows me around the grocery store making suggestions, and only stopping to rest once.

"When do you think you'll be going back to the shop?" I ask as we wander through the produce section.

"I'm thinking about going in a couple of hours tomorrow. You know, easing back in."

"Sounds like a good idea." I try to sound casual but I'm desperately hoping this means he can transition back to his place in a few days. I need to get my life back.

Later, we're both quiet at dinner, but after we've cleaned up I sit down at the kitchen table to pay bills and he joins me at the table.

"You okay?" he asks.

"Sure, yeah . . . I'm fine," I stutter.

"Trish . . ." he says in that knowing voice.

I look down at the table and shrug. "I've been better."

"I wish none of this had happened," he remarks, the corners of his mouth turned down.

"Wasn't it kind of inevitable? You can't stay in the closet forever. Well, I guess you can, but that shit always catches up with you. You know?"

"I know, but I liked our life."

"So did I, but our life was cloaked in secrets, and so we're someplace else now."

He looks down at his hands, his gaze shadowed by sorrow.

"If I ask you something do you promise to be honest with me?" I say.

He purses his lips like he just bit into something unsavory. "Do I have to answer if I don't like the question?"

"Yes, you do. I think you owe me an answer for this."

He looks off to the side and huffs. "Oh Lord help me . . . here we go. What is it?"

"Did I make you gay?"

His eyes grow wide. "I'm not sure I heard you right. Can you repeat the question?"

"Did being with me, and you know . . . how I am and stuff. Did I make you gay?"

"Is that what you think?"

"Well, I overheard a guy at the station say that and I've wondered ever since."

He looks pissed off. "Are you serious? Someone actually said that?"

"I always told you they're assholes."

"Is the tiny house guy also an asshole or is he an exception?"

"Except for him."

Mikey sits up tall, like he's exerting authority. "Well let me set you straight on this . . ."

"Straight?" I ask with an arched brow. "Nice double entendre."

He smiles and nods but then his expression gets serious again. "This is really hard for me to talk about. Especially with you, but Joanne, my psychiatrist, said I need to."

"I know. It's not easy for me either but I think we both need to be honest about all of it."

He nods. "Actually the truth is that you made me bi, Trish. I'd only ever really wanted men before you."

"But—" I start to say.

"Look, I made up those previous girlfriends that I told you about when we met."

"No shit?"

"I'm telling you the truth now."

"Wow. I thought maybe there was something wrong with me."

"There's nothing wrong with you. As a matter of fact, you're the only woman I ever wanted to have sex with, well except for Jennifer Lopez back in the day. So take that as a high compliment."

"JLo? Well, she's got a great ass. And apparently you like ass," I tease.

His eyes light up. He always liked it when I teased him.

"Guilty as charged. And may I point out that you have a great ass, too."

"Um, thanks?"

"Seriously, Trish. You're amazing . . . one of a kind in every way. And for the record, I'm still attracted to you. If you'd ever . . ."

I roll my eyes at him. "Well, don't hold your breath on that one."

He narrows his eyes. "So does Mr. Tiny House want to have sex with you too?"

I nod. No reason to hide that fact now.

"And have you?"

I give him a look, my brow arched.

Folding his arms over his chest, he gives me a pretend stern look. "We're still married you know."

"Don't even go there with your double standards," I warn him.

He rolls his eyes. "Okay, okay. So how tall is he anyway? I bet he's a handful."

I ignore his questions and pose one I really want an answer to. "You know what I don't get? Why do you act like you want to stay married to me, Mikey?"

"Because no one keeps me on my toes, makes me laugh, and loves me like you do. And you're strong enough for the two of us."

"I'm not sure those are the right reasons."

"They're as good as any others. And you should know, I'm up for negotiating. We could be very modern and do an open marriage if you still want to get it on with Mr. Tiny House."

With every minute passing he's sounding like the old, outrageous Mikey. Well, the gay version of the Mikey I used to know and love.

"Open marriage? That would certainly be convenient for you and your men interests. But it's not anything I could ever see me going along with, and I know for a fact Joe wouldn't either. Besides, you should know that Joe makes me happy."

He shrugs, and reaches over, gently tucking my hair

behind my ear so it's not hanging in my face. "Don't blame me for wanting everything. I still love you, Patricia McNeill."

"Hmmm." I cup my chin in my hand. "Last night as I laid awake I came to some conclusions about all of this. You want to hear what I came up with?"

He raises his eyebrows. "Of course, you normally aren't one prone to philosophizing."

I smile, knowing he's right. "Separate from whether someone is established as gay or not, I believe two people can discover a powerful connection and attraction with each other that leads to falling in love, which has nothing to do with gender. And I also believe we can love more than one person, perhaps in different ways."

He nods, animatedly. "Yes, and all those years ago, I fell in love with *you*. That will always be the truth regardless of the rest of it."

I look at him eye-to-eye. "And who else have you loved since? Stanley?"

He swallows hard but doesn't answer.

"He came to see me yesterday. Melissa told him what happened."

His expression falls. "He shouldn't have come here."

"Apparently Melissa called Stanley for help because she was so overwhelmed at the shop. By the way, I had no idea he'd quit. It sounds like you really need him there."

"He can't come back to the shop. He wouldn't want to anyway."

"I think he does. That was the impression I had, but you'd have to talk to him."

He shakes his head. "What else did he say to you? I'm so mad he showed up here . . . he has no right."

"Look, I was very unhappy when he drove up, but by the time he left I knew that talk needed to happen. He was very brave."

Mikey's eyes soften.

"He loves you. I can't imagine why, but he does," I tease with a smile.

Mikey averts his gaze, with a guilt shadowing his expression. "He does."

I lean back. "What a fine mess we're in. I think you should talk to him. And I also think I should talk to Joe."

He lets out a long sigh. "I suppose you're right."

"Yes, I am," I agree.

He makes a face. "I never liked change, you know."

I nod. "I know. And this is a lot of change, big change. But I think you'll be happier after things settle."

"And what about us?"

"We could try to be friends. I still have some rage to work through, but I think it's a possibility."

"And the house?"

"I think it's time to sell it. We both need a fresh start."

"Maybe you're right, but that's a hard one for me. I need to process all this."

"Well, talk to your shrink about it. That's why she's making the big bucks."

Scooting forward, he places his hand on my forearm. "You know, I'm so glad we're talking again. Thank you for that, Trish."

"Well, next time a little less drama to get my attention, okay? I care about you, Mikey. I always will. Don't forget that."

His gaze is intense, a mix of gratitude and tenderness. "I won't," he says.

Chapter 20: The Open Door

We must believe we are gifted for something and that this thing must be attained.

~Marie Curie

A while later, Mikey falls asleep in bed while watching a movie on his smartphone. I'm not ready for bed. Instead, I have a strong urge to sit outside with a glass of wine, and unwind from all that happened today.

When I step into the back patio I realize that the top of Betty is where I want to be most of all. After transferring my drink into something more portable, I grab my jacket and head back outside.

Once I've scaled the ladder and settled into the lawn chair, I take a deep breath. The sky is black velvet, scattered with pinpoints of starlight. I open up my wine and take a long sip. Damn, I wish Joe were here.

After enough stargazing and wine to inspire me to stir up trouble, I pick up my phone and turn it in my hand. I'm so tempted to call him but considering how things are going, maybe texting would be safer. I quickly tap out my message before I lose my courage.

Hi Joe . . . you'll never guess where I am

Several minutes pass before my phone pings.

Where?

On top of Betty.

You scaled my rig without me there?

I did. Are you mad at me?

Are you alone?

Of course.

Then I'm not mad.

I wish you were here with me. I have wine.

Don't fall off the roof.

Not that much wine.

Good.

I miss your kisses.

I bet.

Do you miss my kisses?

Maybe, from what I can remember of them.

You're so mean.

I warned you that I was.

If you were here I'd remind you about my kisses . . . over and over.

Hmmm. Maybe I do miss them.

When are you coming back to me?

When you can't take another moment without me.

Oh good. So you're on your way?

I'm in my bunk, just back from a call

Are you naked in your bunk?

No.

Can you just lie and say yes?

I'm naked. Buck-naked.

Sigh. See now you're getting me worked up.

Is that so?

It is, and I'm getting cold. I wish you were here to warm me up.

Don't you have a jacket? What are you wearing?

Just the moonlight falling over my shoulders, and my memory of you.

Slow down with the wine, Trisha.

Make me.

You aren't really up on my rig buck-naked putting on a show for the neighborhood, are you?

Maybe you should come by to see for yourself. It's worth the trip, I promise.

You're making me crazy, woman.

Good.

No, not good.

Hey, I want to break into your tiny house.

Oh, good God. Why?

Because tonight I want to sleep in your bed.

Is that so?

When did you wash the sheets last?

Seriously? I had no idea you were that prissy.

No. Not that.

Then what?

I want your scent on the sheets so I can wrap the sensation of you around me.

How much wine did you bring up there with you?

I lick the last bit of Pinot Noir off my lips. I'm a little buzzed. Gotta say though, this recklessness makes me feel like I'm letting my hair down in gale force winds, and damn, I like it.

I look back down at my phone.

I brought enough wine for the two of us, but you weren't here.

I'm worried about you getting back down on solid ground.

Don't worry. I'll land on my feet.

I'm sure you will, T. Rex.

So how do I break into your house?

You turn the doorknob and push.

The door isn't locked?

No, it never was. The door was always open.

Damn you. All the tears . . . I miss you.

Don't cry. You'll fall off the ladder.

I'm going down. Since your door is open guess where you'll find me?

In my bed?

Yes. Buck-naked.

Damn, Trisha.

Waiting . . .

Patiently?

Impatiently waiting for you

I take it slow heading back down the ladder, and get all the way down to the ground before I realize my jacket is still on the roof, next to my chair. I wobble a little as I approach the ladder to go back up, and then it occurs to me that I don't give a flying fuck where my jacket is.

Instead I do what Joe said—I turn Betty's knob and push, then step inside.

There's just enough moonlight for me to feel my way through his tiny house after I pass through the tiny door. It never occurs to me to turn on the lights Pulling off my clothes, I dramatically throw each piece aside as it parts from my body. Every step takes me closer to his bed.

I get a warm feeling just pulling his bedding open. Knowing Joe's been in this bed with his skin against the sheets, his scent lingering, makes me wild. I climb inside his man-nest of a bed and roll around like a joyful puppy, pressing my face into his pillow to take deep breaths. I'm the happiest I've been since that day he joked with me about breeding and kissed me silly in the station office.

As the minutes pass, the sheer rightness of being in his bed, combined with the emotional exhaustion of the day, makes me drowsy and I doze off.

Some time later I wake up to a tall figure at the end of his bed.

"Joe?" I whisper.

He's silent as he pulls off his clothes.

Is this a dream? I hope so because this has the potential to be a really good one.

"I'm dreaming, aren't I?" I ask.

"Maybe, maybe not," Joe says as he joins me under the covers. When he rolls me to my side so he can spoon me, I revel in the warmth of his body pressed against me.

I let out a happy sigh.

"Sorry I woke you."

"Never apologize for that. I'm just glad you're here."

His hand runs along my hip, and slides over to my midriff so he can pull me closer.

"Glad to see you got off the roof in one piece. What else has been going on? Anything I should know about?"

"Mikey and I had a serious talk tonight. I hope you don't mind, but I told him that I love you and I'm having sex with you. He knows we're involved now."

I can feel his smile break against the back of my head. "I don't mind."

"Good."

"I think he's ready to move things along with the divorce. We talked about selling the house and he didn't say no."

"Glad to hear it."

"So you're going to have to find a place to put me."

He chuckles. "I will, but I don't want to talk about the future now. I just want to be."

"Be? Like, with me?" I ask, wanting clarification even though the answer is pretty obvious.

"Yes, with you."

I feel him getting hard against my backside and I figure it's a good sign. I wiggle my butt against him so he knows that I'm extra glad he's here.

His hand moves up to cup my breast and I feel his lips on my neck.

"God I've missed this," I whisper, my body humming for him.

"Me too," he says, his breath hot on my skin.

His fingers slide up my inner thighs. He's really handsy tonight and I like it. I lean into his touch.

"So were you really up on my roof?"

I nod and swallow hard, as he slides his fingers between my legs.

"On your roof, inside your bed, in your arms. I'm all over you, Joe. It's the only place I want to be."

"Hmmm." He tugs on my earlobe with his teeth.

I suggestively part my thighs and tilt my hips back. "You know what I need."

"I do," he says as he takes his cock in his hand and rubs it against me.

I almost cry it feels so good. "More," I whisper.

"So demanding," he moans, and then excruciatingly slowly, he pushes inside of me.

Every feeling is intense, and there's something about my back pressed to his chest, and being held so close against him as he moves inside of me, that's perfection.

In this late hour, I push away my fear that my life is too complicated, my personality too much for this man who's looking to find peace in his life. Instead I bind myself to him with threads of hope as he makes love to me with not just his body, but his heart too.

In turn, I love him back with everything I have and keep faith that we will find our footing again in the light of day.

I'm sad that the next time I wake up he's out of bed and putting his clothes back on. It's still dark out but he's turned on a low light somewhere past the bed in his rig.

"Stay," I murmur.

He shakes his head. "I've gotta get back to the station. Go back to sleep."

I watch him with sleepy eyes as he pulls his jacket on. In the faint amber glow my heart skips as I look at his messy hair and shadow along his jaw where a beard is beckoning. Even half asleep and rumpled, this man has become the sole focus of my desire. I'm so powerfully drawn to him and grateful that apparently he feels the same about me.

"Today I'm going to work on getting things finished here so it's just you and I and Betty."

He nods, and leans over to kiss me good-bye.

"I love you," I say.

He pushes my hair out of my eyes and the intensity in his gaze startles me. "I love you too."

Even when he's out of my sight, I resemble a burrowing woodland creature as I listen with pricked up ears for the click of the door shutting, his engine firing up, and the fading roar of his motorcycle as he rides away.

What's that saying about 'if you love someone set them free, and if it's meant to be, they'll come back to you,' or some shit like that?

Yeah, I never liked that lame-ass saying, and especially not now.

The next morning at breakfast Mikey seems nervous. He keeps stirring his oatmeal over and over without taking a bite. I'm pretty sure it's going to turn into cement if he doesn't leave it alone.

"You all right?" I ask as I refill my mug with coffee.

He nods, and keeps stirring.

"Hey, what did that oatmeal do to deserve such a beating? Maybe you should just calm down and eat it."

He smiles and lets go of the spoon.

"So I was wondering . . ." He pauses, his eyebrows knitted together.

"About?" I wave my hand in small circles to encourage him on. Otherwise, knowing Mikey, this could take all day.

"Well, I was wondering if Stanley can come over this evening when you're at your parents, so he and I can talk? He thought it would be better somewhere neutral like a restaurant, but I'm not comfortable with that idea and his mom is staying with him through tomorrow."

Wow . . . It seems like our talk last night inspired Mikey.

I pause to think about it and realize at least this should move things along, one way or another. "Okay. I'll be heading over to their place at six-thirty."

"Are you sure this is okay?" he asks.

Like how much weirder can my life get?

"It's not a problem. You know I'll be at their place at least a couple of hours."

A thought occurs to me, and I crinkle up my nose. "But no sex in my bed."

His eyes grow wide with horror. "Oh no! Of course not."

I nod. "Speaking of Stanley, did he ever get another job after he quit the shop?"

"No."

"So he could come back to work for you if you wanted him to."

Now I'm encouraging a multi-faceted hook-up for my husband and his gay lover.

"Would it upset you if he did?"

I purse my lips as I consider the question. "Actually, I'd be relieved. You always talked about him like he kept the place running like a well-oiled machine. It only makes sense to bring him back. The last thing you need right now is added stress at work."

"True."

Could this mean we have figured things out so we can clearly head down our separate paths? The feeling makes me melancholy for a moment as I remember our good times but then I give myself a swift virtual kick in the ass. *This is now, Trisha.*

I clap my hand. "Okay, let's get this show on the road. Your appointment is in forty-five. And if she clears you for driving we can go pick up your car. Right?"

He nods with a hopeful smile.

I raise my fist in the air. "Onward!"

Ma brushes her hair off her forehead with a huff. Her face is still flushed from standing over a hot stove, but the spread tonight looks extra good. She's even used her favorite tablecloth on our old oak table that has been the stage for the drama of our family dinners over all these years. It makes me wonder if we're celebrating something?

Dad, on the other hand, seems grumpy as all hell. "What's the matter, Pa?" I ask. "You look like you've got your knickers in a twist."

"Meat pie, dear?" Ma asks him with a wide smile that looks overdone.

Why is she trying to butter him up?

He taps his fork on the table next to his plate and then sets it down. "I'm not going to stay quiet, Millie. It's just not right."

Her shoulders sag in defeat and Dad turns toward me. "Patricia, as your father I have to step in. I will not let you take that cheating scoundrel back."

Ma lets out a long sigh, and I hear Paul mutter under his breath, "Here we go."

I narrow my eyes. "Are you serious with this?"

"Yeah, when does she ever do what you want her to?" Patrick asks, pushing his glasses up his nose.

"He's got a point," adds Paul.

Meanwhile, Elle looks like she's fighting back a smile.

Skye pushes her long, wild clumps of hair off her shoulders. *Does she even own a brush?* It looks like small animals could be living in that mess and she wouldn't know it. She lets out a long sigh. "I think Trish taking her husband back is beautiful . . . so loving and beautiful."

Patrick looks down at his plate and pushes the carrots around.

It feels like the dining room walls, with their faded floral wallpaper, are closing in on us. I roll my eyes upward and notice that the frosted globes on the brass light fixture could use some dusting.

"What do you mean, beautiful?" Dad says, his face getting red. "It's desperate and pathetic maybe, but there's nothing beautiful about it."

Now my face is heating up too. "Gee, thanks a lot, Dad. Really, that's an awesome thing to say about your only daughter."

"Patricia . . ." Mom says in her warning voice. She knows how explosive my temper can get.

I fold my arms over my chest. "As long as we're throwing around insults, let me ask you, what in the world gave you the stupid idea that I'm taking him back?"

"Did you just call your father stupid?" Ma asks with a scowl. For sure that's a hard-limit for my parents.

I shrug. "Let's not get caught up in semantics. I'm not taking him back, Dad. I let him stay for a week or so because if I didn't he would've been taken to the psych ward."

"Where he should be! Lock him up and throw away the damn key! What kind of man marries a good woman, and then runs around having sex with other men? A man who's out of his gourd."

"I'm not sure what a gourd is, but I do know one thing. From what I've heard about Mikey, his soul was bruised, and Trish is helping heal him," Skye says pressing her hands together. "She's giving him the most soulful gift."

I look at her with wide eyes wondering what planet she came from. I glance over at Dad and sure enough, his face is now more of a scarlet hue.

"There's going to more than just his soul bruised by the time I'm done with him," Dad grumbles, and cracks his knuckles like a cartoon villain.

Paul nods over to Dad and winks at Elle. "Two peas in a pod. Now you know where Trish gets her badass edge from."

"Daddy's girl," Ma says, shaking her head, as if she's teasing us for being so much alike.

"Well, since my personal life is now fodder for tonight's family theater, I'm happy to share that right now Mikey is meeting with Stanley to talk about their relationship."

Ma's mouth falls open and she presses her hand over her heart. "I don't understand any of this," she says.

"Stanley, is that who you referred to as Sasquatch?" Patrick asks.

"The one and only."

"Wow. How modern of you, Trish," Elle says with a sympathetic gaze. "It sounds like you've come full circle to some kind of acceptance about the situation."

"I can't deny that his suicide attempt forced me to see everything differently. There's so much I loved about my life with Mikey, but now knowing his truth, I realize that I want more than he'd ever be able to give me."

"And has Joe played a part in figuring that out?" Elle asks.

My heart swells at the mention of Joe's name. "He has."

"Joe's a real man," Ma says with a sigh.

I nod. "But Mikey's a real man too . . . he's just a real man that's more into men, than women."

"We love who we love," Skye remarks. She reaches over and takes Paddie's hand.

Dad drops his head into his hands and rubs his face briskly.

Picking up the open bottle of wine to my right, I pass it to Paul. "Pour Dad another glass, will you? Looks like he could use it."

Patrick points to my phone. "Hey, Trish, your phone is flashing."

I look down and sure enough the red light on the back of the phone winks up at me. I normally keep the phone out and close to me in case there's a call from the station.

When I flip the phone over, the screen reveals that it's not the station, but Mikey calling me. I push my chair back and step away from the table toward the living room. There must be a good reason he's calling me now, and at this point I don't want to discuss anything in front of my parents.

"What's up?" I ask after I swipe the screen.

"Trish!" he howls. "Oh my God, what do I do? It's on fire!"

"What? What's on fire?" I yell.

"A candle fell over in the backyard and the grass caught fire. The grass is almost dead and dry as timber. Why hasn't it been watered?"

He has some fucking nerve to be asking me this.

"Have you heard about the drought? What the fuck do you mean the grass is on fire? And what the hell was a burning candle doing out there?"

"Stanley's out back with a hose but it's getting worse!"

"Have you called 911?" I can feel the rage surging

through me.

"No, I called you first."

"Damn! I'll call," I snap.

I hang up on him, and dial 911 dispatch with a tight grip on my phone to steady my hands from shaking.

When the operator answers I cut her off. "Reporting an out of control fire in the backyard at 2710 Addison, Valley Village between Laurel Canyon and Ben. This is Patricia O'Neill, firefighter from the Van Nuys station, thirty-nine and it's my house. Please dispatch the crew from there. My husband is on site and I'm headed there now."

I grit my teeth and pace the living room as she repeats the information to me one damn detail at a time. I know they have to do this, but it's making me want to hurl my phone against the wall. As soon as I hang up, I storm into the dining room.

"Paul, I need your help. There's a fire at my place and I need you to drive me. Now!"

Ma gasps. "Oh no!"

Paul leaps up, pushing his chair back so forcefully that it almost topples over. He turns to Patrick. "Take Elle home after dinner."

Elle leaps up. "No! I'm coming with you."

Patrick jumps up. "Me too!"

Skye seems to think that she's automatically included. I want to snap at her to back off so that her spiritual observations are not included in this frantic chase to my burning house, but there's no time to argue.

Thank God Dad and Ma stay seated with concerned expressions on their face, but no proclamations about joining us.

"Paul, call us!" Dad calls out as we grab our stuff.

I'm first out of the dining room.

"Get a move on, guys! This is a race for time, not a

traveling circus," I curse as we rush to the front door.

We pile into the car with Elle and Patrick in the backseat, and Skye squeezed between them. It's a somber clown car, with everyone giving each other worried looks as I rant under my breath about idiots and their candles.

Paul floors the gas pedal before we've even put our seatbelts on. I've never appreciated his inclination to speed more. As soon as I buckle up I start to call Joe, but then realize that I need to update Mikey on what's going to happen next, so I dial him first.

"Trish, what are we supposed to do? The hose is barely doing anything!" His voice is high-pitched and tight with panic.

I gasp and swallow my wrath. "The trucks are on their way. Are the side gates open? Go stand out front," I bark at him.

I look up just as Paul guns through a light that's past yellow, and turning red. Elle let's out a squeak.

"I think I hear the sirens," Mikey says in between pants.

I press my phone tighter to my ear and I can hear the faint wail in the background.

"Lead them to the backyard. How the hell did this fire start anyway? What were you doing with a fucking candle in the backyard?"

"We were sitting on the back patio talking and the mosquitoes started up, and Stanley is allergic to mosquito bites. So I lit a couple of those citronella candle torches and one must have fallen over when we went inside after it got cold."

I wonder how a big, hairy Sasquatch can be appealing to mosquitoes but there's no damn point in wasting my time on him.

"And you didn't blow out the fucking candles?"

"Obviously I forgot, Trish. It wasn't until I went to the kitchen to get some water that I saw the fire."

"Is the house on fire too?" I question calmly like I'm asking if he picked up the dry cleaning, but in reality I'm gritting my teeth like a wildcat.

I hear the sirens much louder now in the background.

"No, but I've gotta warn you, Trisha. That trailer thing of Joe's . . ."

My stomach lurches. "What? What Mike?"

"The trucks are pulling up. I've gotta go."

The line goes dead.

"I'm going to kill him!" I yell out, and Paul's grip tightens on the steering wheel.

I look out the window and realize we're being slowed down by heavy traffic on the 101 passing Universal City. The colorful lights of City Walk and Universal Studios with all the knuckleheads going there to party are annoying the hell out of me, with the hard reality of what I'm trying to rush home for.

"What, Trish?" Paul asks.

"Mike says Joe's rig may be on fire." I shake my head and slap my free hand on the dashboard.

"Damn," Paul says, and I sense murmurings in the backseat that I'm better off not hearing.

I pick up my phone again but this time I dial the station, knowing that if Joe is on the truck heading to my house, he won't be answering this call.

Scott picks up. "Van Nuys Fire, Station Thirty-Nine."

"Scott, it's McNeill. Is Joe out on the call in Valley Village?"

"No, he's here. You want to talk to him?"

"Yes, thanks."

He puts me on hold and I try to swallow back my dread about telling Joe what's going on.

"Everything all right, Trisha?" he asks, knowing I wouldn't call him at the station without a good reason.

"No, and Jesus, Joe, I don't know how to tell you this but I got a call that there's a fire at my house and Betty may be involved."

"What the hell? Where are you now?"

"I'm on my way home. I got the call while at my parents. We're close to the 101 at Laurel Canyon and I'll be at the house within ten minutes if this traffic doesn't get worse. Can you meet us over there? Mike said the trucks just arrived."

"Wait . . . does this mean your *husband* is at the house without you there?"

Husband? I'm sure he's thinking the worst—how can he not? "Yes," I murmur.

"I'm on my way, and you better warn him that I'm coming," he snaps and then hangs up.

I'm not sure what I expected, but the cold, steely tone in his voice is a hit in the gut.

Chapter 21: The Three-Ring Circus

He who believes is strong; he who doubts is weak. Strong convictions precede great actions.

~ Louisa May Alcott

When Paul turns onto Addison, it's a relief to see several rigs up ahead, their flashing lights reflecting off the shiny red metal of the trucks. It's hard for me to process that they're at my house . . . *my house* for God's sake. Paul has barely parked when I fling my car door open and jump out. I see Joe's motorcycle just beyond the second truck. I also see the blur of random groups of neighbors gathered to watch the drama unfold.

Something seems off as several of our guys scramble around the trucks. My adrenalin is pumping so hard that I can barely see straight, so instead of stopping for an update I run down the driveway. I need to see for myself exactly what's happening.

I'm halfway down the drive when I realize I'm heading into a fire zone and I'm not in my gear. The realization only heightens my rage, but I don't give a damn about my personal safety. There's so much at stake.

As I charge into the backyard my gaze darts across the chaos. The yard around the backend of Joe's rig is burning, as are patches across the yard. I'm distracted for a moment when I notice that Betty's front door is flung open, but then I focus back and realize that Scott is the only one working a hose and it's half-assed. Meanwhile sparks shooting high threaten the parched surrounding shrubs.

What the fuck is going on?

Despite the crackle and roar I hear the static filled radio callouts and turn to see Jim responding to the transmitter in his hand. I rush over to him waving my arm toward Betty. The crews have to have been on the scene at least fifteen minutes before our arrival, why the fuck is this fire still so hot?

"What the hell—" I yell but before I can finish Jim holds up his hand. His brows are knitted together and his scowl doesn't help calm my panic.

"Hydrant fail, McNeill. We've already emptied the tanks on the trucks. But that was Charlie on the radio. The closest tap was the street behind, and he said they've just busted through your neighbor's side gate to pull the line through."

I hear the sound of wood splitting and through the smoke I can see one of the guys taking an ax to our wood fence. My brain starts computing.

"Goddamn hydrant fail? This area was checked less than six months ago." I picture the hydrant and I feel my blood pressure soar. "It's in front of the construction site," I say, and Jim nods.

"What do you bet those assholes fucked with it?"

Jim's narrows his eyes. "I thought it was because the probie, Carter was on the line, but I checked it myself and almost lost it. A dead hydrant on *your* street? You're one of our own, McNeill! This just can't happen."

His words hit me hard, *you're one of our own.* Was the truth always there and it took my property catching fire for me to really see it.

I belong.

Jim gives me a sympathetic grimace. "And we didn't know at first it was yours. We'd called for back-up and suddenly Joe shows up on his bike, ahead of the trucks, and that's when we knew."

My eyes dart across the scene. "Where is Joe?"

Jim turns back and I follow his gaze, only to see Mike cowering on the back porch. Stanley is in the shadows behind him. My blood boils.

"Damn!" Jim curses. "Did he go back in that trailer? We told him to get out. He doesn't have his gear on either."

I turn back and see Alberto on one side of the yard dragging the line forward as its passed through the busted opening in the fence. On the other side tall flames roar up the backside of Betty, and I can see the orange flicks of hot light dance just about the roofline.

All the breath whooshes out of my lungs and my knees almost buckle as this surreal scene stops seeming like a made-for-TV-movie, and the sharp edge of reality cuts right through me.

Betty is on fire and Joe is inside.

I take off across the yard ignoring Jim commanding me not to. I have to get to Joe.

A wall of heat hits me as soon as I pass through his rig's door. "Joe!" I yell, but my voice seems lost in the roar of chaos. Then I hear a thud farther back. With only the faint yard lights and flames casting light into the dark interior everything looks creepy and smoke is already burning the back of my throat.

"Joe," I cry out again as I step farther inside, my hands reaching as if he's within my grasp.

A bright light flickers through the window and a few feet away I see the outline of Joe's long legs stepping down a ladder. He jumps the last few feet and leans over, grabs a box, and lunges toward me.

"Joe," I say, and then pause when I see the fury in his eyes. It feels like hate and it makes me feel raw, like my skin's been peeled back.

"Get out of here," he commands in a rough voice.

"What's that?" I ask pointing to the box, trying to imagine what's so precious that he risked getting it.

His eyes narrow. "My safe box. For fuck's sake move over or get out before we both go up in flames."

Suddenly everything feels hotter and I see sparks hitting the nearby window.

I can't bear his disdain but I have to say something, anything . . ."Joe, I'm so sorry."

He pulls the box closer to his chest. "Not half as sorry as I am for ever bringing Betty here. This was my home, the only thing I had left and now . . ."

A boom like a gunshot blasts and we both jerk toward the sound to see the window above the sink has exploded and the flames are curling inside.

"Out!" Joe roars and we charge toward the door as the burst from the new hose line hits Betty and water sprays through the broken window. We tumble down the stairs one after the other and out of our team's way.

Joe keeps on, marching down the driveway. He's halfway to the street before I stop following him and watch him put his box in the truck where it's safe. He then hurries back up the driveway.

"Joe," I say as I follow after him. He ignores me and keeps moving back to the fire. It's that moment that I realize my family is huddled together on the front lawn. They look like lost children, with no idea where to go or what to do. I'm sure they can read the defeat in my expression as I join them.

Paul speaks up first. "How bad is it, Trish?"

"Really bad. The hydrant was dead and getting backup cost dearly. At least Stanley and Mike were able to keep the fire from spreading to the house. So the backyard is gutted but worse, Joe's rig is on fire. They just got the live line so they'll get control and it should be out soon. By then I'll know how bad things are."

"He didn't look good," Elle says, before biting her thumbnail.

I shove my hands in my pockets. "No, and I think he blames me. I guess in a backwards kind of way he can, but I'd never do anything to hurt him and his rig."

"Of course you wouldn't," Elle agrees.

"In time he will hopefully find forgiveness in his heart," Skye says.

Patrick shakes his head. "I don't know. He looked pretty furious."

"This isn't your fault, Trish. He'll calm down and see that," Elle says.

I think about the conversation we had the night he saved the homeless man, and his comments about his home being all he has. "I don't know . . . this means something more to him. He may not bounce back."

Paul steps up and gives me a hug. "I'm sorry."

"What can we do?" Patrick asks, resting his hand on my shoulder.

"Maybe you guys can get Mike and Stanley to leave. I think them being here makes things even worse."

Paul nods. "I'll talk to them."

A few minutes pass as we discuss where I'll stay tonight, and what the next steps moving forward will be.

Scott approaches me as I step away from the family. "I know this looks bad, McNeill, but you guys are safe and the damage could be worse for sure. We have to see about Joe's rig, but I bet it can be repaired. And at least your house is safe. It just wouldn't be right to have it go up on our watch."

I take a ragged breath, all my swirls of emotion starting to weigh down heavily on me. I give Scott a weak smile and thank him. If he only knew that the worst damage here won't be covered with ashes that can be brushed off before rebuilding. If Joe never forgives me, the damage tonight could be irreparable.

I look over just as the front door opens, and Paul follows Mike and Stanley out. Stanley stays back while Mike approaches me.

"Paul said it would be better if we left," he says. He appears distraught. Now that I've calmed some I know how bad he must be feeling about the fire.

I nod. "Joe's really upset about his rig. I need to do whatever I can, considering everything. We can't stay here tonight anyway."

Mike nods. "Paul said he was going to have you stay with them. What about Joe?"

"He's actually on duty. He'll go back to the station."

He looks down. "I can't bear to stay at the apartment tonight. Stanley said I could stay at his place. Would that upset you?"

"No. It makes sense despite how crazy all of this is."

His eyes soften. "You have to know Trish, I'm just sick about what happened. I'm so sorry."

"I know. I know it was an accident, Mike. You've always loved this place. You'd never do anything to damage it."

"No I wouldn't. And although I've screwed everything up, I love you and would never intentionally hurt you or Joe."

I let out a sorry sigh and nod.

"I'll call the insurance company first thing in the morning. Can I be here for their inspection?"

"No, it's better if it's just me since Joe will have to be here, too. I'll get the station report. Just get them here as soon as possible."

"Okay. I'll let you know." He holds his arms out and I

accept his hug. Over his shoulder I see Stanley watching us, looking relieved. I nod at him.

After they've driven off in Stanley's Jeep I slowly walk to the backyard to see the state of things.

As I suspected the flames have been doused. Now it's just the bitter stench of random material burnt to a crisp. Smoke still slowly rises from all areas of the yard, most from Joe's rig. I look at where a good part of his wood siding is charred and the window is blow out, but at least the structure is intact.

Jim approaches me. "We're still rechecking hot spots, and we've inspected his rig but it's looking like we got everything."

"Good. Thanks Jim."

He shrugs. "Of course, McNeill." He nods toward Betty. "Joe's in there with Alberto. There's water damage. They're trying to salvage what they can."

I head to the back to see the state of things for myself. Just as I approach the door, Alberto steps out with what appears to be a kitchen drawer piled high with books and other random items. I step out of the way so he has a clear path.

"The backdoor to the house is open, Alberto. Can you take it in there?"

"Sure."

I climb into the rig, trying to ignore the smell and lingering smoke. There's another filled drawer on the counter and I lift it and put it on the top step so Alberto can carry it in next. I go back in and approach Joe, whose back is turned to me as he drags a mop along the floor.

"What can I do?"

He turns and looks over at his shoulder at me. Then closes his eyes for a moment before opening them again. "I'm trying to get some of this water up before everything warps. Not that it may matter at this point."

I hold out my hand. "It will matter. Let me."

He huffs and leans the handle toward me. Once I take it, he moves to the back and grabs a towel and starts wiping down the wet, soot-stained wood.

"There's good insurance on this place," I tell him.

"Not sure it'll cover this," he replies, his face twisted in anger. "I just hope it can be repaired."

"I'm sure it can," I say with a false confidence.

"Yeah? Don't make me empty promises, Trisha." He balls up the wet towel and throws it hard against the back wall.

I look down and keep pushing the puddles toward the front door, and I'm halfway there when he steps over me, and storms out.

As much as I want to follow him I complete my task. It's the least I can do. The interior is still a wreck, but the floor is no longer a wading pool.

I find him out front as the guys load up the truck. He's talking to Jim with his shoulders hunched over and his arms crossed. Jim is nodding with a grave expression on his face.

I glance over at Paul with a worried look. His gaze moves to Joe and then back to me. He shrugs and then shakes his head as if he's not sure if I should approach Joe or not. I hesitate and then figure I've got to be strong and at least try.

I approach them just as Scott calls to Jim, "We're set."

I speak to Jim first. "Thank you, Jim. You guys are the best."

He nods in acknowledgement. "Is that your family?" he asks, gesturing toward Paul and the group.

"Yes."

"So you'll stay with them tonight? As you know, it's

safer for you not to be here, never mind the smell of smoke."

"Yes," I reply, glancing over at Joe but he has no reaction.

Jim turns to him. "You coming back to the station?"

"Yeah."

I walk up to the truck and one by one thank the guys. They have that 'tired, but relieved that the job is done' look. I know that feeling well. Jim gets up on the rig as the engines fire and Joe and I stand at attention and watch them pull away.

"Joe—" I start.

He cuts me off. "I'm heading back, too."

"Can we talk for a minute?" I'm trying to appear calm but I'm trembling inside my skin.

He gives me a harsh glare. "It would be better not to talk tonight. I can't control what I'd say."

"Maybe I should hear it." I challenge him.

He stares up at the night sky as his tense muscles flex in his folded arms. A long weighted pause follows until he clears his throat.

"The thing is I've had this feeling ever since you cornered me in the yard at the station and offered the space for my rig."

Cornered? I chew on the corner of my lip. "What kind of feeling?"

"I wasn't sure at first, but then when you brought your unstable husband back here after he went off the rails, it all clicked for me."

My stomach sinks. Maybe he's right. Maybe I can't handle this right now. But from the way it looks like he's gearing up, I think I've realized this too late.

"Your suicidal husband, and me, the broken firefighter—are we like stray pets that you took in because you felt sorry for us?"

"What?" I gasp, my eyes growing wide as I fight back instant tears.

"'Cause yeah, you're tough and strong, T. Rex, and like every man at the station you want to save people. But let me tell you, you sure as hell haven't saved me . . . you've just thrown me in the middle of your three-ring circus and turned my life upside down."

"You're wrong. I never saw you like that, Joe."

"Say what you want, but it's time you realize that I'm not your stray pet . . . or your damn project. I don't need anyone or anything but my job and my rig, to keep moving on."

I don't even try to hide the stream of tears now running down my face. I square my shoulders back, fighting the instinct to curl over and protect my heart that's taking a beating. "Joe, please . . ."

He gives me one more harsh look before turning and walking away. He doesn't acknowledge me or my family with a good-bye, just climbs on his bike and roars off, leaving me and my spirits shattered.

Elle reaches me first as I start to sob. It's all just too much and I fall into her arms.

"Baby, baby," she whispers. "He was speaking in anger, don't let it break you. He'll calm down and see reason."

"He won't," I respond in between gasps.

"Yeah, he will," says Paul as steps close.

Patrick and Skye approach us.

"This is a karmic split," Skye states. "We need to smudge the house and property for peace to be restored."

I look over at Patrick with wild crazy eyes and shake my head.

He glances over at Paul and then back at me. "Maybe it's time for us to leave. Skye has a really early yoga class tomorrow."

I give him a frantic nod.

"It's okay," Skye says. "We need to be here for Trish."

"No. Thanks, but please go," I say.

"We're taking Trish home now anyway," Paul points out. "If you Ubered home that would be great, since we live so close and you're over the hill."

Patrick pulls out his phone and orders the ride.

Elle steps away from the group and holds out her hand to me. "Come on, Trish. Let's go get what you need while you're at our place."

"I'll stay with them until their ride shows up," Paul says.

I say good-bye to Patrick and Skye before heading inside with Elle. I hand her my overnight bag and she follows me silently, carefully placing my change of clothes, p.j.'s and toiletries inside the bag as I pass them to her. We then turn off the lights and lock the doors.

The silence lingers as we pull away from my property. I left it earlier tonight in fine shape and now leave it just hours later with my property scarred and battered.

We get to their place quickly and I help getting my room set up.

"Drink? A shot of whiskey may help you sleep," Paul says as Elle brings me fresh towels.

"No. Just water."

Elle brings me a glass, and I hug and thank them both before heading to bed. I know it will be a sleepless night, but only in the privacy of my room can I face the agony of what seems lost tonight.

Chapter 22: The Rulebook of Joe

Love is a fire. But whether it is going to warm your hearth or burn down your house, you can never tell.

~*Joan Crawford*

Come dawn, the guest room windows filling with light feel like fire, the brightness burning my sleepless eyes. I curse the new day and desperate for a distraction, I reach over for my phone so I can look for cute animal videos on Facebook. As I watch the frolicking pups, the fluffy panda playing in the snow, and that otter video with the baby cuddling on the mama's chest, I know these distractions are the only things keeping me sane at this point.

Just past seven I hear noise from what sounds like the kitchen so I wander in and find Paul loading the coffeemaker and yawning.

"Hey you. Tired?"

He pulls another mug out of the cupboard. "Yeah, how about you?"

I shrug. "I didn't sleep at all. Sorry I kept you guys up so late."

"Don't be, we're always up late."

Oh yeah. How could I forget?

"So what happens next?" he asks.

I groan and pull up my chair to the kitchen table, then prop my head in my hands. "Hopefully the insurance inspection this morning, and then maybe Joe has calmed down a bit. I'm hoping he's shifted into just disliking me, not hating my guts."

"Yeah, progress would be good. Maybe he'll even do better than that."

"I'm not counting on it."

"Just know, Trish, that it's going to take some time to sort out."

Paul fills my mug with coffee and sets it in front of me before filling his tumbler. "I've got to be in early today, so I'm going to hop in the shower and head out. Will you let me know how it goes, and if you need anything?"

"Yeah, I will. Thanks."

Mike calls to tell me that our agent, his friend Monika, and the insurance investigator will meet me at the house at ten.

I text Joe and ask if he can come for the investigation and bring the fire report.

He replies back with a single word.

Yes.

The air is tense as we all meet on the front porch. Joe is the last to arrive. It's a couple minutes past ten when he parks across the street instead of in our driveway. As we step through the gate and into the yard, the inspector starts taking pictures.

"So where was the point of ignition?" he asks.

I walk to the patio, my gaze running over the mess until I see the patch of melted wax and remnants of the torch base burned into the grass. I point down. "Here. It was one of those citronella torch candles to ward off mosquitoes."

Joe rolls his eyes with a look of disgust.

The inspector shakes his head and takes pictures of the mess, and then keeps at it as he moves around the yard with his thousand-and-one questions. He spends a lot of time on Betty with Joe close behind him asking questions back.

I'm completely drained by the time the insurance guy

leaves, and Monika stays back for a minute and tries to assure us that quick action will be taken to make things right. I'm grateful for her being the one person in this group who seems to care about the feelings behind all of this, not just the physical damage.

I almost expect Joe to leave when she does but he stays behind, his eyes darting from his bike to the open gate where we've just left his scarred rig.

After an awkward moment I walk over to the chair on the porch and sink down in defeat. He stares at me with a resigned expression, but steps a few feet closer.

"Do you want to talk?" I ask.

His gaze trails back to his bike like he's still considering escaping.

I let out a deep breath as I watch him. "Are you okay?"

He gives me a look that's a cross between frustration and disappointment. I can take anything from him but disappointment.

I rub my hands over my tired face and will myself not to cry again.

"I had a lot of time to think last night," he finally says.

"Yeah?" I ask warily.

"The thing is, Trisha, all of this is too much for me. I made a vow to myself after Sharon that I'd never allow relationship drama in my life again. And honestly, you're drama with a capital D."

"Is that so?" I ask. I resent his accusation yet can't deny it with the way things have gone lately. How can I argue with him like it's been no big deal?

"Yeah . . . you're an out-of-control wildfire, burning hot and I never know what to expect next."

I squint up at him. "Some people would find that exciting, you know?"

He shakes his head firmly. "Not me."

"Well, my life wasn't like this before, and I don't want it to continue like this now. I want the same thing, Joe. No drama. Surely you can see that most of what's happened has been out of my control."

"Maybe. I don't know. I'll have to think about it."

"As you pointed out, you've had big drama in your life that was out of your control," I say.

He shrugs and doesn't deny my accusation but instead agrees. "Another reason I don't want yours."

"Life isn't flawless. Even if you get everything lined up like dominoes, in perfect order, I can guarantee that something unexpected will come your way and the tiles will start to fall."

"*Dominoes?* What I do know is that I've risked my job and my home to be with you. After last night I've realized I can't afford that kind of risk when you're still figuring things out with your husband."

I feel my blood pressure soar. "I've been clear with you that Mike and I are over. So you're saying that I'm not a sure thing to you. Not someone you think you can depend on?"

"I'm saying I'm not sure."

"I see. And where does love fall in the rulebook of Joe? Last on your list of requirements? A quiet, calm life is more important than love?"

He doesn't say yes or no, just gazes off in the distance, his arms folded over his chest.

I feel the small cracks in my heart expand to fissures, and then full pieces start breaking away inside my hollow chest.

"So is this it?" I ask, my voice barely a whisper.

"I don't know. I need to process all of this. My rage right now isn't logical. I hate your husband, and I'm angry at you for giving him the opportunity to screw up what we had together."

"It's only screwed up if we let it be that way. I'm going to get Betty fixed up as good as new—no matter what it takes, Joe."

He gives me a wary look. "Like it's that simple."

"Why are you assuming it's going to be too complicated? As for my divorce, I'm going to get it finished up, no matter what it takes. If that isn't enough to make you willing to take a chance on me, on love . . . then what more can I do?"

"I don't know. Like I said, I need some time to get this sorted in my head. Last night was one fucked up situation."

He walks from one end of the porch to the other, and back again. Those damn long legs. It suddenly hits me that I may never be in his arms again, us stretched across his bed, my legs draped over his, skin against skin. The idea takes my breath away and fuels my fire. I stand up and face him, moving closer, a challenge to see if he'll back away. He stands tall, unyielding.

He lets out a huff. "What?"

"Okay. I get it. I may have already lost you. Sounds like you've decided we're not worth fighting for. But before you go you need to know one thing."

He arches a brow at me, like he's waiting for another one of my crazy proclamations.

"You were never my stray rescue. *Never.* You were anything but that. It all goes back to the time you called me to the office to check and see if I was okay after my marriage blowing apart. I'd always been a faithful wife, never looked sideways at any of you guys. That just wasn't me. But that day the kindness you showed me, set you apart."

He turns his gaze away, maybe my intensity is too much, but at least he's still listening.

"From that moment on I watched you, and I liked what

I saw. I'm not going to deny my intense attraction to you. You're a handsome devil, you know that . . . but it was more than that. You were the kind of man I began to want, and the very man I knew I needed."

He looks back at me, his gaze intense like he's feeling my words.

"So yeah . . . that day in the yard when I *cornered* you and offered you my land . . . *I* was the stray who needed rescuing. Even the strongest people need help sometimes. Why can't you see that? You saved me at my lowest point, damn it! Not the other way around."

He shakes his head, as if he doesn't accept what I'm saying.

"Believe me, after what happened to me, I could easily have just crawled into a hole. My brother and Elle were the ones who pointed out that I hadn't really been living even before I found out the truth about Mike, and maybe it was time that I did."

His brows knit together. "What the hell does that mean?"

"It means, that know it or not, you inspired me to feel alive again. I believed we were becoming a team, better together than when apart. You challenged me, and loved me with passion, in your bed, and in your heart. And God, I've loved you back . . . so big, so fiercely . . . like you were the fuel to my fire. Surely you know how real this thing is between us."

He nods, but looks like it hurts to do so.

"You've read all those books about fascinating people . . . people who took chances at love and life, people who lived big. I want to be like one of those people, Joe. And I want to be that person with you by my side."

He holds up his hands, like I'm driving too fast and need to slow down. "Please," he whispers.

"What?"

"Believe me, I'm taking all this in but I can't hear anymore. I need time, Trisha . . . and space. Give that to me so I can figure this all out."

Right now in my emotional and physical exhaustion I'm tired of being patient. I put my hands on my hips. "How long are we talking about?"

"Trisha," he moans.

"Okay, okay . . . get out of here. Just don't forget me."

"Like that's possible," he says with a huff.

"I'll wait for you as long as this passion burns, Joe. But I'm telling you—if things grow stagnant while I wait for you, and this thing starts to die, I'm out. Okay?"

He visibly wilts. "God damn woman, you exhaust me."

"Shut up." Stepping closer to him, I gesture back and forth between us. "You like me. You like this. Us together . . . we're alive."

He gives me a look like I've had too much to drink or something. "Is that a haiku?" he asks before pressing his lips shut. I'd like to think he's fighting back a smile.

There's a long pause as I realize there's a crack in his suit of armor and I could either flip him off or widen the crack to crawl inside. I opt for the later.

"It *is* a haiku that I just started writing, and I'll be waiting for you to finish it."

The next few weeks are a clusterfuck of weirdness.

The day I leave Elle and Paul's place again to move back home, I see that Betty is gone. All that's left are the grooves left from her tires. For a blurry moment I wonder if Betty was ever really there. It's not that I'm surprised he cleared out, but it feels lousy nonetheless.

The day I return to work I learn that Joe changed the

schedules so we're now on opposite shifts. He wasn't joking around about needing some space. Also, apparently Chief threw the rule book away since he let Joe park Betty at the far end of the station's lot while he gets estimates for the fire damage repair. He's also letting him stay at the firehouse until he gets things figured out.

Jim shares with me one afternoon that he's worried about Murphy—that he's been so on edge lately. I nod and keep quiet.

I know Joe asked me for time and space to "figure things out," but I can't help but start wondering if that was some bullshit line just to get me off his back.

In my quiet moments, I succumb to my weakness when the fears start to add up. I just miss him so damn much, but I need to prove to myself, and him, that I'm strong and I can be okay with him or without.

Three days later Mike calls me and asks if I want to reconsider keeping some of our old furniture, including his prized Regency pieces. I almost drop my cell phone out of shock.

"But you love that stuff, and I don't," I say.

He lets out a long sigh. "I finally realized that it's time for a change. Stanley's loft downtown in the old brewery building is industrial with that raw, edgy look. It's growing on me. We're talking about doing something Steampunkish with the decor."

"Really? So farewell to the Regency period and hello Steampunk? Will you be turning the elevator lift into a time machine?" I tease. "Sounds like you're staying there permanently."

"Yeah," he admits sheepishly. "He asked if I would. Are you okay with that?"

"Sure. It's good to know at least one of us is getting their shit together."

"What about you and Joe?" he asks. I can hear the concern in his tone and his sympathy makes my heart hurt.

"Not so much. I think I was more than he could handle. Or more accurately, I was more than he wanted to handle."

"His loss," says Mike. "Maybe he'll come around. He better, if he knows what's good for him."

I smile, picturing Mike shaking his finger in the air, his lips drawn together in a straight line.

"By the way, I have a carpenter friend that owes me favors who could do wonders with his trailer repairs."

"Another one of these mysterious friends?" I ask.

He guffaws. "Never you mind, he did the carpentry rebuild at the front of the shop last year. Do you think Joe would allow him to look at his trailer?"

"Maybe you should have the friend call him directly . . ."

"Bruno," Mike says. "That's his name."

"Seriously?" I chuckle. "Bruno?"

"Yes indeed. He looks like a Bruno too."

"Okay, have Bruno call Joe and tell him that he's a friend of mine and wants to bid on the job."

"That could work," Mike says.

"Okay, I'll email the contact info for Joe."

"Good."

"And just so you know I've talked to Paul about designing something with this goddamned drought situation in mind for the backyard. I want to get this shit done so we can put this place on the market."

"He's going to do Xeriscape?"

"Wow! Our fancy florist supports Xeriscape?"

"Of course I do. It's all the rage, what with the DWP chipping in to cover the costs. I think it's a great idea."

I don't have to employ my rocket-scientist skills to know that the busier I am the less time I have to fixate on how much I miss Joe. So on Saturday when Paul and Elle come by the house to go over his design for the backyard, and we talk about the schedule, I ask them when they think I'll be able to put the house on the market. I'm anxious to keep moving ahead with the divorce and all it entails.

"Do you have a real estate agent you like?" Elle asks. "I know a dynamo agent from this area I put an event on for. Why don't you meet with her and see what she thinks? If you like her she'd be great to represent the house."

"Shouldn't I wait until the yard is done?" I ask.

"I wouldn't. She'll have suggestions for both inside and outside the house so you guys can get top dollar for this place."

Paul nods in agreement.

So now it feels like my life is moving backwards and forwards at the same time. The backwards is when we move all of Mike's furniture back in the house, pictures, lamps and all. It was like the furniture took a long vacation and now was back. All of this is because Jada the agent, who has a great eye, said that "staging" a house with Mike's high-end stuff will help sell it.

Besides, houses sell fast in this area so I figure that I won't be living with his pretentious stuff much longer.

So long, farewell, to Ikea-land, and hello to fancy pants Regency and velvet pillows. Mike said that we could offer the house furnished, or sell the furniture on Craig's List once we'd accepted an offer.

The moving forward part is that Mike and I have come to agreement on all the key points of the divorce so now it's just the technicalities of getting the house sold to wrap things up. Jeanine is very pleased, and has offered to let me stay in her guesthouse until I figure out what kind of place I want to move to. I really appreciate not having to rush into that decision. There's enough crazy going on right now as it is.

So in this spirit of moving forward I've gotten very involved in the re-landscaping of the fire-scarred backyard. Despite Paul's protests that we use his people to turn the soil in preparation for re-planting, I insist that I take a shot at rototilling the backyard.

Kellie, the woman I usually buy my plants and stuff from at Armstrong's Nursery is anti-rototilling . . . something about terrorizing the worms and tiny creatures which keep the soil alive. But when I explain about the fire and ash she agrees to an exception and points out that as long as I used the shallow setting the replanting would benefit from the ash being worked into the soil.

Despite her encouragement, it was a clue that I may be in over my head when Joaquin, the equipment guy, gives me a nervous look as he loads the rental rototiller into my truck.

"You know how to use this?" he asks.

I shrug. "I watched a YouTube video."

He purses his lips as he looks down at my flip-flops. "Don't stick your feet too close when you're working. It'll cut off your toes."

I make a face at him but he remains serious and that unnerves me.

"I'll wear my steel-toe boots just in case," I say.

He nods with no reaction like every woman he knows has a pair of steel-toe work boots.

Okay then. Maybe I better watch those YouTube videos a few more times. But seriously, it's about the size of a lawn mower. How hard can it be?

Sometimes I get off on doing hard stuff that prissy women wouldn't even consider. Believe me when the zombie apocalypse comes I'll still be standing long after those high-heeled gals are down for the count.

But today for all my bravado I have to admit this might be a bit much. When I get the rototiller fired up and grab those handles and squeeze, the thing starts shaking me like a maraca. *Holy hell.* It takes all my strength just to keep the thing on my intended path, and my arms feel like jelly after one pass across the yard. I shut the thing off, brush my hair off my sweaty forehead, and then turn the monster to do another row. I get it going again and I'm a few feet in when I see something out of the corner of my eye.

I pause and look over to see Joe standing near the porch with his hands jammed in his pockets, looking even more handsome than I remember him. He watches me for a moment and then pushes his sunglasses up on top of this head.

After turning the monster off, I stand with a blank expression waiting to hear what Mr. Murphy has to say for himself. Part of me wants to show him how happy I am that he's here . . . the other part of me that's mad for being ignored, not so much.

"Looks like you've got a wildcat by the tail," he says, one corner of his mouth turned up and a bemused look in his eyes.

"Yeah? I can handle it," I say, narrowing my eyes at him.

"I'm sure you can."

I wait a few seconds but he doesn't say anything else and it irritates me, so I lean over to turn the monster back on. I'm not going to make conversation when he's the one who showed up here. He's going to have to work a lot harder than this.

I'm about to start rototilling the next row when he calls

out, "Hey, can you take a break for a minute so we can talk?"

"I suppose." I wipe my sweaty hands on my jeans as I slowly walk over to him. "What's up?"

"I saw the 'coming soon' sign in your front yard. What's that about?"

"I told you I was selling the house. I have an agent and it's going on the market as soon as this damn yard is done."

He nods and turns his head so that his gaze scans the property. He points at the rototiller. "Need help?"

"No."

His eyebrows knit together. I don't think he was expecting a flat-out rejection.

"Anything else? I'm going to get back to work."

He shifts from one foot to the other. "I was thinking . . . well, I was hoping that you could come with me to get something to eat."

I glance down at my watch. "It's four o'clock. Eat what?"

He seems flustered. "What ever you want. I thought we could talk."

"So does this mean you're done avoiding me, or is this get-together an exception?"

"Please, Trisha . . ." he says.

I bite my bottom lip and look over at the sharp-toothed rototill monster then back at Joe. "Well I could be persuaded to go for a hot fudge sundae. But you'd have to wait for me to jump in the shower. I can't go in this state." I brush some loose dirt off my arm. "I look like Pig Pen from the Peanuts cartoons."

He smiles and it takes my breath away. I'd almost forgotten how my insides spark when this man smiles. "Sure, I'll wait."

I make showering a quick business, and while I dry

myself off something occurs to me. Maybe it'd be okay if I were a little bit nice. I grin as I pull on my blue sleeveless sundress instead of my new jeans. He manned up and came by here to talk, I'll woman up a bit to show my appreciation.

When I step onto the front porch his gaze softens.

"You're wearing a dress."

I swish the skirt around my legs. "I know. Awesome, right?"

He nods with a concerned expression. "But this isn't a date."

I pretend pout. "No? I thought it was."

He looks gobsmacked. "I mean it could be a date, but I was thinking it'd be good to just talk."

I want to keep things light so I push him in the shoulder. "I'm teasing you. As long as I get my hot fudge sundae I'm fine with just talking."

About fifteen minutes later we're at a table at Bob's Big Boy in Toluca Lake. It's totally retro cool with a drive-in set-up and a massive fiberglass Big Boy sculpted figure in front of the restaurant with his hand up in a wave to passers-by.

The Warner Bros. Studio is just down the street and so you might expect a studio crowd, but these are regular folk like us tucked into the booths surrounding where we sit.

"Are the sundae's good here?" he asks after I've ordered the most elaborate one on the menu.

I shrug. "I don't know. I guess we'll find out."

I don't eat hot fudge sundaes often but today I'm feeling like I've earned one.

He orders coffee.

We talk about goings on at the station while we wait for our order, and once the mountain of ice cream, fudge sauce, bananas, whipped cream, and what-not arrives, he's amused as I tackle it with my long silver spoon.

"Hungry?" he asks.

"Have you ever rototilled? It was a workout just getting that thing unloaded from my car, let alone wrangling the damn thing."

He arches his brow. "I offered to help. You turned me down."

"Hmmm, I wasn't sure your offer was earnest."

He casts his gaze down to the printed placemat. "I guess I deserve that."

We remain quiet while I take several bites of my sundae. He watches as I methodically dip my spoon in the pool of fudge sauce, scoop up some ice cream and then drag the spoonful through the whipped cream and nuts. In between each bite I lick the spoon clean. He's observing me intently and I can't read why.

"Want a bite?"

He shakes his head and takes a sip of his coffee.

"I wish this wasn't so awkward." Lifting my spoon up, I point it at him. "Maybe you should just say what's on your mind."

"Sorry," he replies, snapping out of his haze. "You were distracting me."

"Are you planning on saying more mean things to me, like after the fire? If so I'd appreciate a heads up so I can prepare for it."

He frowns. "No, I was going to tell you that I'm sorry at how harsh I was with you after the fire. Now that I've calmed down I feel bad about it."

"Yeah, you were pretty pissed off about far more than just the fire, but I'd be lying if I said I didn't understand why."

His gaze is shadowed with melancholy. "I've missed you, Trisha."

My heart thumps so hard I wonder if he can hear it. "I've missed you, too."

I blink back a tear. His forgiveness is a small miracle in this wildfire season of my life.

I chew on my lip as I study his warm expression. "Does this mean you're done avoiding me?"

The corners of his mouth curve up into a quiet smile. "Well, I thought we could try things again . . . but this time take things slow."

"Sloooow," I say with a long drawl. "I'm not sure if that works for me."

He twists his hands together. "I realized as I sat with it that it really bothers me that I'm messing around with you and you're still married and regularly dealing with your husband."

"Seriously?" I scrunch up my nose.

"I guess I'm an old-fashioned guy."

"But I'm practically divorced from my gay husband, you know."

"Yes, I can see that you've made progress."

"Speaking of Mike, I owe you an apology about the situation with him."

Joe raises his brows as he waits to hear what I'm going to say.

"You know the night in the hospital when Paul came to sit with me while we waited for word after Mike's suicide attempt? Well, Paul warned me to be mindful of you and pay attention to how the resulting attention I was giving Mike would affect you. He said you are my future and Mike is my past."

Joe's eyes widen before he looks down at his cup of coffee and straightens it on its saucer.

"I regret that in the drama of it all that I didn't put myself in your shoes. What I know is that if it had been Sharon, I wouldn't have been happy about her moving back in with you and all that went along with it."

He nods knowingly.

"I'm really sorry for that."

"Thank you," he says.

I nod. But as I watch him I get the feeling he's not done with his reasons to tap the brakes on our relationship. "So what else?"

"I have to be honest. I hate that we have to pretend at work that we aren't more than friends. It feels fake—like a lie."

"But what choice do we have?" I ask, and then a thought occurs to me. "So are you really saying you want to be friends for now, and you don't want me to put my sexy on?"

To give the question more flair I grab the stem of my sundae's maraschino cherry, close my lips around the glossy red ball of sweetness and pull the stem out with a pop.

He looks at my lips and sighs. "No. I just think it would be good to figure things out slowly. What's the rush?"

I shrug, but I'm not feeling excited at the prospect. It all sounds so complicated when all I want to do is sit with him on his side of the booth with one hand wrapped possessively around the top of his thigh, and the other feeding him bites of whipped cream and fudge sauce in between my bites.

When I've polished off my dessert Joe drives me home. I kind of figure that he's going to just drop me off, but he parks and walks me up to my front door.

"Thanks for the sundae," I say with a bright smile.

"You're welcome." He stares at me unabashedly. "I like this dress on you. Actually what I mean to say is that *you* make this dress look great."

"Thank you," I reply with a coy smile. I swear he looks like he wants to butter my biscuit. "Do you want to come in?" I ask, leaning into him just slightly.

"I shouldn't," he answers with a stoic expression.

"That's not what I asked. I asked if you want to?"

He swallows hard, his Adam's apple bobbing. "Yes."

I turn slowly to the door and slide my key in the lock. Meanwhile he leans into me close enough that I can feel the heat radiating off his skin.

Once in the door I walk over to the couch, sit down, and smooth my skirt across my lap, waiting for him to decide what he wants to do.

He takes a few steps into the living room and then stops as his gaze moves from one end of the room to the other. "What's this about?"

I realize that he never saw my house before Mike and his furniture were extricated from my life. "It's called staging," I reply. "The realtor insisted on it. Supposedly it can really help a sale."

He shrugs. "It looks different—fancy, not my thing. I prefer less showy stuff."

"I like that about you." I pat the cushion next to me. "Would you like to sit down?"

He slowly walks over and joins me, but he sits with his back straight and his arms rigid.

I turn toward him. "I've got to tell you something and I know you won't like it but I'll always be honest with you."

"What's that?"

"This furniture is Mike's. He's moved into his boyfriend's place and so he's decided to sell it, but meanwhile it saves money to use it for staging while trying to sell the house."

Joe lets out a long sigh.

"It's going on the market in two weeks . . . as soon as the backyard's done. And then I'm out of here."

"Where are you going?"

"Jeanine said I could stay in her guest house until I decide what to do. But if me being here with his stuff bothers you I'll move into Jeanine's guest house tonight."

He shakes his head. I know he doesn't like any of this, but he has to know the whole picture. I'm a package deal.

"She lives pretty far from the station," he says.

And you, I think to myself.

"I know."

His gaze moves over the room again before he looks back at me. "Thanks for offering, but it's okay with you being here. Everything is heading in a clear direction now."

"It is," I say while thinking that I wish it was a little more clear about our future. I guess time will tell.

We sit silently but the longer he's next to me the harder it is to resist him. My attraction to this man is even more powerful since our time apart. I study the stubble on his sharp jawline, his broad shoulders, and the way a wavy dark strand of his hair curls onto his forehead like Superman.

My Superman.

My fingers start to tingle and I can't help myself, I reach over and place my hand on his thigh.

He glances down to where I'm touching him. I can feel his muscles flex so I tighten my fingers over him. I wish his legs were bare and not clad in jeans. He has the most perfect, manly legs.

"I wish you weren't wearing your jeans," I say, and then immediately realize that I'm saying this out of context of our discussion. "So I could see your thighs," I throw in hoping I sound less lewd. Of course then I realize that I just sound crazy.

"You want to see my thighs?" he asks, his expression confused.

"Well, and the rest of you too."

Laughing, he shakes his head. "You sure speak your mind, don't you?"

I shrug. "I don't see any reason not to. You'll always know what I'm about."

He smiles kindly, yet there's a glimpse of desire in his dark eyes as he places his hand on my lap. "As long as we're confessing . . . I'd like to see your thighs too." He reaches lower and then skims his fingertips up under my skirt and rubs tiny circles above my knee. It feels flirty and encouraging, and suddenly hope wraps around us, lifting my spirit and strengthening my resolve.

It's promising that we're moving away from our initial awkwardness, and I fall into the circle of his arms knowing everything about this feels right.

"There now," he whispers, his lips pressed against the bare skin of my shoulder.

My whole body relaxes with his attention and I lean back into the cushions of the couch. "I've missed you so much, Joe."

His gaze is intense. "*That* much?"

I nod and swallow, then press my eyes shut feeling glad that he's here and touching me. This is something . . . it's progress, when yesterday things were just steps away from hopeless.

Even with my eyes closed I can sense him coming closer and I can feel my cheeks warm. He cups my face in his hand, and I sigh.

"I missed you too, Trisha . . . something fierce."

When his lips press against mine, I welcome his attention. He tastes like mint gum and longing, and in this moment they're the two best flavors in the world. It's a slow, soulful kiss, but it's also the kind of kiss you only get from a man who wants more, and means business.

His tenderness reminds me that in this epic battle

between practical intentions versus pure desire, his love is worth fighting for.

"You still love me," I whisper.

He nods. "I do. Too damn much."

"Maybe too damn much is just the right amount."

Pressing my face into his warm neck, I feel his pulse against my cheek, so strong and sure.

"I love you like crazy," I whisper before I pull back and look up at him. "This is a big love," I say with conviction letting him know that I mean business.

Reaching over, I grab a handful of his T-shirt and pull him close again until his weight is on me. I kiss him like he's my Mr. Everything—the answer to all my questions—as I wrap one hand around the nape of his neck, and tug his hair with the other.

Our kisses tumble over each other, fevered and near desperate. I end up flat on my back against the velvet pillows with Joe lying on top of me, with my skirt pushed up and one of his large hands in my panties. His other hand is holding my breast as his fingers tease my nipple. The way he edges my legs apart and rocks his hips into me reminds me that we're alive, glowing like a hot neon sign.

His touch stirs me up as his gaze grows more heated. I run my hand over where he's hard. He looks down and watches my movements before his gaze moves back up and our eyes meet.

"Let's go to the bedroom, sweetheart."

Smiling, I nod. *Sweetheart.* He gets up and lifts me off the couch.

Once in the bedroom he stands facing me with his hands on my shoulders. "Is this too soon? Are you sure?" he asks like he's remembering our talk about the pain in my past.

Maybe this isn't his idea of *going slow,* or maybe he's

not sure about anything when it comes to us, but I sure as hell am. We hit a low point in the previous week, but I still believe in him completely.

Doesn't he understand that in this moment he's all I want in the world?

I start unbuttoning his shirt and when I pull it open, I trail kisses down his neck and across his chest. His grip tightens as I trace my tongue over his nipple. I move to the other as my hands reach down and undo his belt, and then his jeans.

"Trisha," he moans when I slip my hand inside to grasp him. He feels so incredibly good in my hand.

As he drags his shirt off, my fingers tighten over the waistline of his jeans, and when I pull them down, I sink to my knees, slowly stroking him as he watches with hooded eyes.

Leaning in closer, I circle my tongue around the head of his cock, then trail down his length and back again. I look up at him with wide eyes as I take him fully in my warm mouth, my lips tightening over him. The low groan in his chest gives me chills. He gently runs his hand through my hair as I pull him in deeper, loving his reaction . . . imagining I can feel the thundering of his heart.

"Jesus, Trisha," he groans. "What are you doing to me?"

"Loving you," I say before taking him in deep again.

I take my sweet time paying attention to what stirs him up the most. I'm lost in the rhythm of giving him pleasure when suddenly he loops his hands under my arms and lifts me off my knees.

"What?" I ask. I'm not done but if he has other things in mind I won't complain.

"I want to love you back." Pulling me tightly against him, he kisses me along the nape of my neck. He turns me around slowly and undoes the zipper of my dress, pushing the straps off my shoulders while I squirm impatiently, until it falls to the floor. He glides his hands down my back and caresses my hips and butt with a sigh of appreciation. "Beautiful," he whispers.

He gets on the bed, and pulls me along with him before leaning back into the pillows. "Come here, sweetheart."

I edge closer and then lift up to straddle him. As I settle onto his thighs, I whisper, "I want you so much."

He nods, closes his eyes for a moment and takes a deep breath. "I want you too," he murmurs, his fingertips circling my breasts, as he watches me arc toward him with pleasure.

I place a hand on either side of his face and pull him close. This time I'm the one kissing him, putting my heart and soul into this kiss, my lips consuming his breath, his heartbeat . . . his heat.

His hands cup my ass, as he presses his fingers into my flesh. I moan long and deep as he slides me down over where he's hard for me.

I kiss him again and again as I rock against him. His chest is cut and solid, perfect to press my bare breasts against. I run my fingers over his hardness, smooth skin sheathing steel.

His gaze studies my every move. "Do you know how much I love watching you like this?"

"No," I whisper.

"Let me show you how much." Leaning over, he takes one of my nipples between his lips. I moan as he holds me, his hands everywhere I need them to be.

I'm stunned. I've never felt this desired before, and suddenly I can see the sense in slowing *this* down, right here, right now . . . because I don't want this feeling to ever end.

I lift myself off of his lap and slide back toward his knees as he watches, his jaw slack and his desire fighting to keep me in place. With narrowed eyes, he holds out his hands toward me.

"Where are you going? Come back here," he demands, his voice rough and sexy.

"I'm slowing us down."

"Really? You sure about that?"

One look at his determined gaze confirms what I know in my heart . . . forget slowing down.

"Not really," I say with a smile.

I want all of this man. I don't care about being careful, taking things slow, or anything that's sane. I climb closer and rise up, taking his cock in my hand so I can rub it against me.

"Trisha," he moans, and with that I take him. I start out slow but then take him all the way inside of me, and deep as I can. I rise up, and sink down again and again as his hands grip my hips to guide me, us both looking down and watching with wonder how our bodies seem made for each other, the glory of his thick cock sliding in and out of me.

When we reach our rhythm, he takes me in his arms and kisses me as deep as he loves me. I surrender to his lips and cock, and hold on for dear life as he powerfully thrusts. There's a raw thrill coursing from every place he's touched until I'm completely undone.

When this man comes it's like thunder and fireworks, sirens of ecstasy and the hushed whispers of prayer. I ride into my own climax as he holds me tight, filling me . . . loving me. I cry out from somewhere deep and gasp for air.

Once again . . . I am reborn.

Chapter 23: Wrangling Wildfires

Life shrinks or expands in proportion with one's courage.
~Anaïs Nin

From the star-scattered hills of Hollywood to the stretch of beach paradise where the sea meets the sky, Los Angeles feels like the place where anything can happen. People come here to chase their dreams, and sometimes they come true.

Unfortunately *anything happening* also includes earthquakes, riots, and brush fires. After a dry rain season the house-stacked hills become parched and colorless. They're a precarious place to live, especially with Mother Nature being prone to wrath. But some people will do anything for a great view.

On this unusually hot day, it's a given that the dry Santa Ana winds will put the whole station on edge. We leave the TV in the day room on the news with stories of brush fires on alert. One wildfire started in the hills above Santa Barbara a few hours ago, but thank God it's quickly contained.

Only hours later word comes that Malibu is burning and in this case, it's not looking good as the hot winds have picked up intensity. We all gather around the TV and eat to fill up knowing we could be called to action any time. They've already called in all the stations in the nearby areas from Oxnard to Santa Monica and Venice Beach.

As I watch the news and caffeine up, I think about all the brushfire training we've had. The vastness of a wildfire, and the possibility that flames will move faster than we can keep up with, fills us with adrenalin and a healthy dose of fear.

When the call comes, we pile into the trucks with our wildland gear, and quickly pull out of our station's bay. I know to many civilians this loud blur of speeding trucks and flashing lights is high drama, like something from a movie. But as we rush off to battle the fire-spitting beast and save lives, the reality is that most of us will end up on a smoky hill with our Pulaski ax's, trenching firebreaks in strategic spots to hold the line of fire as it rages toward us.

The truth is when the winds have cursed us and flames are almost a hundred feet high and moving at breakneck speed, our usual methods of firefighting are useless. I've heard stories of firefighters facing a five-mile wall of flames with little more to do than run to save their lives.

We end up on the 101 Freeway with the Studio City station right behind us, creating a powerful chain of howling trucks, so that even the worst of those asshat commuters have to move over to make room for us to pass.

Many long minutes later we exit at Malibu Canyon road, and as we head toward the canyon we hear the roar of water-dropping, and fire-retardant copters overhead.

Bobo is checking the TMAC app on his iPhone for conditions. "How can a beach community have such damn low humidity? The winds are picking up even more, and it's way hotter than usual. This is fucked up."

Charlie shakes his head with a somber expression. "It's why Malibu is the wildfire capital of North America. I guess money can't buy everything."

Scott nods. "This one could be bad. My dad was on the line for the Agoura-Malibu Firestorm of 1978. I grew up hearing those stories, crazy shit . . . birds exploded in the sky, homes imploded, while horses caught on fire and had to be shot. Dad said it was hell on Earth."

The truck falls quiet. Joe checks his watch and then glances over at me. It's going to be a long call—maybe my longest ever.

The Studio City force ends up being directed to the camp at the edge of the canyon, while we get orders to continue onto PCH. When we reach the base camp, Chief and Joe check in with Site Command overseeing all the adjoining forces.

While we quickly suit up with our coats, wildland packs and helmets, Jim starts going on about the latest in satellite imagery and infrared technology. By the time he's babbling about slope aspects and elevation I sorely want to tell him to cut it, but I don't since each of us have different ways of dealing with nerves.

Regardless, I tune him out since I don't want to hear about that crap. I leave that stuff to the experts. I just want to be told what I need to do, so I can get it done.

My blood starts pumping when word comes that we're assigned to the break line just north of Malibu High School, a campus on a hill facing the Pacific Ocean. We move to position, making note of the designated escape route.

It's tedious work, slinging the ax to break up the soil and rake away the brush, but I do my best to keep up with all the guys. With the group effort our containment line quickly expands until it runs all the way down to the highway.

We get a radio call that the winds have changed direction, and we're reassigned. Before we load up, I turn and look back up the hill. The sky is electric orange with washes of red edged with black smoke. Sparks are shooting up hundreds of feet, lighting up the sky like an afternoon fireworks show. Anxiety bubbles up my chest, growing so big that I can barely breathe, but I will myself to calm the hell down. I won't be any good to anyone if I don't get a grip.

Word is there's concern of the firestorm jumping the Pacific Coast Highway, and if it does, those densely layered multi-million dollar homes make easy tinder for the roaring beast.

A group of us are assigned ocean side, to check every house for stragglers along Broad Beach just past Zuma. Apparently there are still people convinced they can some-how save their house if they stay behind. As Charlie said earlier, money can't buy everything and that also includes brains for these nutbags with their fire extinguishers and big ideas.

We recheck our radios with instructions to call in every ten minutes and be back at base camp within the half-hour. I'm assigned to the road three streets in, and I pass through the security gate off the highway that's been rigged open.

I start at the house closest to the beach, banging on the front door and walking the perimeter while looking in ev-ery window. All clear. I repeat the process, house to house, zig-zagging across the shared road and back. I'm only two houses away from PCH when I get a radio call.

"McNeill, evacuate immediately . . . firestorm has jumped PCH and is moving our way fast."

From the tone of the command, I don't have to be told twice. I can feel the heat approaching and I sprint up the street and back to the truck. One by one the guys load in, until only Charlie and Joe are missing. As I down a bottle of water and wait for our next directive, my foot is tapping until my whole leg shakes. Where the hell is Joe?

Charlie loads in looking flustered. He shakes his head. "He went back down, something about a bunch of animals, and now he's not responding."

"Joe?" I ask, as panic edges up my spine.

"He was having trouble with his radio right before we

broke," Jim states with his brows knit together and the corners of his mouth turned down.

"Where was he? You were the road after me, right?"

Charlie nods. "And Joe was the one following. It was that crazy castle with the turrets and shit. I heard their horses were loose on the beach, but the dogs and cats were trapped inside."

I glance at Charlie and see a shadow casting down over his features, like he feels guilty for not turning around and going back after Joe despite being ordered to evacuate. He starts to stand up, but I beat him to it and nod toward the spot outside where the Chief is. "You've got a wife and kid, Charlie. This is mine."

My heart is thundering as I approach Chief. "Any word from Joe?"

He shakes his head looking pissed off. "Damn radio. I'm not even getting a signal."

"Can I—" I start to ask before Chief cuts me off.

"The Battalion Commander gave orders to pull out completely. He's ordered that for good reason. I don't like it either but don't worry, McNeill, Murphy's the smartest one in this squad. He's got his shelter and he knows the ocean is an option. This isn't his first rodeo."

"Right," I say, trying my best to sound like I agree. "But what if he got hurt or something?"

"That street is a no-zone that's already burning and you think I'm going to put your life at risk to test the commander's order? How do you think Joe would feel about me allowing you to do that knowing the risk? I know you mean well, McNeill, but go get back in the truck. I've put out directives with air and ground control to locate him. Meanwhile, you guys need to be moved to safety."

I sulk back slowly to the truck, and when I'm just feet away I turn to see Chief has moved out of sight. An adrenaline rush blasts through me with a rhythm not unlike a surging firestorm. Before I can believe I have the balls to defy Chief and risk everything, I skitter across the highway and head south, sprinting as close to the towering shrubs and stately driveways as I can. What kind of a fool am I to run toward the fire instead of away from it?

The answer is simple—I'm a fool in love.

I'm breathless before I turn and storm down the road toward the castle-shaped mansion, a miniature Hogwarts rising out of the sand, instead of English moors. As I dash across the yard and circle the house screaming Joe's name, I note a French door busted open but there are no signs of animals or Joe. I head to the back, bile rising in my throat to realize the area's already burning hot.

"Joe!" I scream into the thick smoke. "Joe!"

The yard closer to the highway looks like a war zone, the edging shrubs already on fire and a towering palm tree has crashed into a massive pergola, obliterating the table and chairs it towered over.

The roar of the fire is getting louder by the second and just before I scream his name again, I freeze. *Was that a moan I just heard?*

As my gaze frantically scans the scene for signs, I look at the potting shed on fire and then back at the downed patio and gasp. There's a body trapped under all the wood and debris, and it's not moving.

Joe!

I run over and drop to my knees, then place my hand on his head. He blinks, as if he wants me to know he's alive, and so I lean in closer and start chanting, "I'm here, I'm here," so he knows I'm truly with him and not just a hallucination.

Ironically as soon as he becomes more lucid he starts arguing with me, commanding me to run for my life, and save my own skin. *Really?* Does he have any idea how much that's pissing me off? He has a lot of nerve telling me to leave him so he can die alone. *Not on my watch.* If he's going up in flames, I'm going up with him.

I pull out my radio and report in quickly before Chief can yell at me, then get to work pulling debris and planks of wood off him, trying to set my man free.

You know how sometimes days and weeks go by where you keep disappointing yourself, not getting enough done, eating crappy food and not taking care of yourself, being a bitch to strangers or even your friends? I have plenty of those days, but if there was ever a day where I needed to rise up high, and be my best self . . . or even be a level of epic-self I could only imagine, today needs to be that day.

And thank fuck it is.

So while delirious Joe is still trying to tell me what to do, and I'm ignoring him, my mind is calculating every possible way to get through this so I can save his life.

I look up toward the highway and see this beast of a firestorm rising higher than I've ever seen flames burn. I'd be lying if I said I wasn't completely terrified. And at that very moment it hits me that our time is up. We're about to become a couple of flaming s'mores with our gooey insides charred to a crisp. What can we do when Joe is too broken to stand up, let alone flee the firestorm with me? I stand frozen for several long seconds with my mouth hanging open, almost tasting our impending demise.

And that's when the beast inside of me rises up just as high as those goddamn flames. "Fuck you!" I yell into the smoky air as I frantically set forth to save us. In that moment the obvious smacks me in the face: we're feet from a swimming pool full of water. It's our only hope.

I start dragging Joe across the cement like a sack of potatoes, yelling at him like a crazy track coach to help me by moving faster. But instead of a finish line, Joe claws and drags himself toward the line between life and death, and I'm determined to get him to the right side.

We take a graceless flop off the pool's ledge, but when we hit the water it's a sort of baptism, hope for life in whatever shape God wants it to take.

I can't tell you much about the span of time that follows. It could be minutes or hours. All I know and care about is that Joe stays conscious and keeps breathing.

There are low points where it's so hot that I start to lose faith, but then my epic-ness kicks back in and I deal with it. Finally things start to cool, and we realize that it's quieter outside our bubble, so I make the decision to lift away from the pool's surface the protective little tent I made of my wet coat, and assess the situation.

There's a side of me nervous to see if we'd outsmarted the beast. It's the same side that is frayed around every edge and wants to cry like a baby, but I know me crying would freak out Joe. As it is I can tell how weak he is, the stress and pain of his injuries wearing down whatever spirit he has left.

After I let my gaze scan the yard beyond the pool, I lean in close so he can feel how excited I am.

"Joe, we're not dead!"

He winces again, like he's a little sad about that. Damn this man needs some morphine. "Apparently not," he whispers.

"It's not just that we're not dead inside, we're not dead outside either. We're completely alive."

"It sure seems that way," he agrees with a small smile.

"We're so fierce! We did it!" I cry out.

He grimaces in pain but then looks me in the eye.

"Thanks to *you* we're *not* dead."

Smiling, I bounce excitedly in the water, making waves that are alive too.

"When we get out of this hell-hole, what do you say that we keep this *alive* thing going?" I ask, my head spinning with ideas.

"Sounds like a plan."

"That's right!" I cry out.

He's placating me, and would probably like me to shut up and be quiet for a while. But despite that I love him more than ever.

I grin at him and throw my arms straight up in the air. "So kiss my ass you stupid, fucking firestorm . . . *we're alive!*"

Epilogue: Alive

"This is Hell, dude . . . I'm expecting to see Satan come out at anytime now."
~ *A Malibu Canyon resident fleeing his home torched by the historic 1993 Malibu wildfires*

Two Months Later ~ Joe

I've always had a fascination with wildfires, and I've read a number of articles and books about them. One in particular is by John Maclean, called *Fire and Ashes: On the Front Lines of American Wildfire*. A line from the book really stuck with me: "As long as no one is standing in its way, a wildfire is a natural event. Put people in front of it, and it becomes the stuff of tragedy."

Firefighters know that better than anyone, and of course as a firefighter I've done a lot of training for how to fight them.

I just never thought I'd die in one.

As I was lying on that Malibu pool deck pinned under a massive collapsed pergola, and delirious from pain, I thought about my family and how I wished I hadn't let my brother's sin create a chasm between me and my parents. I desperately wanted to talk to them one last time.

But most of all I thought about my brave girlfriend, Trisha, and I prayed to God that she was safe and that in her strength she could rise out of this hell and go on for the two of us.

I looked up and saw the wall of flames, a brilliant burst of hot reds and oranges, licking the sky, and I'd never felt so small. Closing my eyes, I prepared for my flesh to burn, willing myself to be brave and accept death with dignity.

It all sounds ridiculously dramatic now, but in that moment I really believed I didn't have a chance to survive. And I didn't really, except I had underestimated the determination of one woman's spirit. There isn't a superpower or a firestorm that can touch the fierceness that is Patricia McNeill.

At the point that she appeared before me as a vision, I was delirious, falling in-and-out of consciousness from the smoke and searing pain. She cried out, rushed over and fell to her knees, placing her hands on my face as she called my name, and I mumbled back incoherently.

"I'm here," she said over and over, her voice breaking.

For a moment I forgot that I was trapped under a cage of fallen wooden beams, but I was quickly reminded by the look of terror in Trisha's eyes as her gaze scanned over me. She pulled out her radio and reported in for back-up.

I wasn't even sure the bottom half of my leg was still there, but there was the pain, the howling horrific pain telling me that I was still alive.

I had a moment of clarity, when I realized that with the firestorm jumping the highway, it was more than my life at stake. Trisha was frantically pulling debris away from me and testing my responses to determine if my back was broken. I lifted my head off the cement and yelled at her to evacuate and save herself. I was aware of the inferno of flames enveloping us, the circle of survival closing up as every second passed. She was going to die if she didn't run for her life, and my rage became another inferno when instead of choosing survival she continued pulling the debris and wood beams off of me, and wasting the last precious seconds of her life.

I lost it and summoned up my full breath to yell at her,

"Get the hell out of here, you're going to die!"

"I'm not leaving without you, so back off!" she screamed as I felt more weight lift off my back, freeing my shoulder, which had been pinned down.

As I drifted in and out I could hear her cursing. I found out later that the weight of the largest beam that shattered my leg was beyond her strength, but when the back end of the beam sparked she had an idea and gathered her determination for one last Herculean effort.

"Crawl, crawl!" she screamed while the metal pool sweeper handle, she'd wedged under the beam to jimmy it up, was starting to bend.

Somehow I dragged myself forward just far enough to clear the beam before it fell one final time, shaking the earth beneath us.

Our eyes met and I could see the fear in hers, telling me we didn't have a prayer in hell of surviving this. Her eyes started darting around as she pounded her fists against her thighs. With one final glance up to the highway, black smoke obliterating any sight that would bring us comfort, her head dropped. My heart fell in my chest but then I noticed her eyes widen and dart from me, splayed out on the deck like a beached monk seal, and then toward the swimming pool.

She waved her arm dramatically at the pool, then grabbed the collar of my coat and pulled. Bewildered I stared at her. *Crawl?*

"Crawl, damnit!" she screamed again. I didn't have the energy to tell her she should stop yelling at me, so instead I clawed forward, dragging my useless bum leg as she yanked me along the rough cement and right off the ledge.

When we hit the water I thought, *This is it.* It must have been the shock because I was sure I'd died and was floating away from the living world. I was eerily calm—I think I felt at peace because I was with Trisha, and we'd move toward the bright light of death together.

But then my smoke-seared nostrils filled with chlorinated water and I realized that I wasn't on my way to heaven, but sinking in a goddamned swimming pool, lame leg, heavy firefighting garb and all.

I was suddenly very lucid, aware of Trisha pulling off her coat to create a wet bubble over our heads as the flashover blasted the firestorm across the landscape, surely taking everything in its path.

Under her wet coat, which she'd pushed up and tented above the surface with her flashlight, we took tiny breaths. Her arm wrapped around me holding me close. We sunk down, fully emerged in the pool with only our lips exposed, as our bubble got hotter and hotter. We were being cooked alive for what felt like forever, until suddenly we weren't, and the heat subsided and the water and air grew lighter.

When Trisha lifted the edge of the coat enough to check the conditions, she whispered, "Thank God," and I knew we had survived.

Trisha radioed our status in again, and settled me on the pool steps until help arrived. I blacked out with pain when the guys slid down into the pool water and maneuvered my body to strap me to the spine board. Despite my delirium I still had a sense of Trisha chanting words to me while she held my face out of the water protectively until they hoisted me out to the pool deck so I could be airlifted out.

The next thing I remember clearly was waking up in a hospital bed with Trisha's fingers intertwined with mine. I squeezed her hand gently and blinked repeatedly as my vision slowly cleared. When I finally got a good look at her I realized that she'd passed out asleep, her chair pulled close, and her head resting on the bed right next to my good leg.

"Trisha, baby," I said, wiggling her hand. Her hair was matted and from what I could see her uniform was filthy. She looked like she'd been through hell and back, and since she had, it would've be good for me to let her sleep but I needed to see those blue eyes and know she was okay.

I heard a sob and I glanced up to see my parents stoically sitting in chairs across from my bed, my mother crying. I was shocked, and with so many emotions hitting me at once, I hardly knew what to say. Just then Trisha stirred and lifted up her head.

"You're awake," she said, stumbling upright. She ran her hand over my forehead, her gaze softening as she smoothed my hair back. "Oh Joe. Thank God you're so strong. You're going to be okay."

Another whimper and cry grabbed our attention and we both turned to my parents. Trisha straightened up and froze.

It may have been an awkward way for her to meet my parents, but Chief had told them how Trisha had saved my life, and they embraced her like family.

As they hugged, Trisha looked back at me, and I nodded and smiled.

I found out later that Mom and Dad jumped on the first plane they could after Chief's call, and I was grateful to have this chance to right things between us.

Trisha and I looked death in the face and lived to tell about it. Seemed like a good time to put the past behind us for good.

I'm not going to lie, the next few weeks were rough. It wasn't just the surgery on my leg, I was jacked up from head to toe: cracked ribs, a dislocated shoulder, my back sprained. Just getting up and dealing with crutches to use the bathroom was a bitch, but I had to move if I wanted to heal right. So I pushed myself, first rolling round and round the hospital ward on my one legged scooter, trying to ignore the nurses flirting with me. Then later, when Trisha brought me from the hospital to Jeanine's guest-house, we'd roll around the block or I'd see how far I could make it on crutches. The doctors were impressed with my progress.

I'd expected Trisha's bedside manner to be tough love, and I was ready for it, but then she threw me a loop by babying me, catering to my every need. My mom teased her about it, but I could tell that Trisha won a lot of points with my parents. In their eyes, she could do no wrong.

Dad had to fly home for work after a few days, but then Jeanine offered her guest room so Mom could stay on longer and look out for me on the days Trisha was at the station. Now, including Jeanine, I had three women doting on me and it was fine by me.

One morning about two weeks after my surgery I had overslept and when I finally rose, and hobbled into the kitchen I found Trisha and Mom talking away. They were sitting at the table with mugs of coffee going over my medications, my physical therapy sessions and what I might like for dinner that night. I stayed back and watched them, going on about me like they'd known each other for years.

It gave me a powerful feeling, a warmth unfurling inside, and I realized that in two weeks Trisha had bonded with my mother in a way Sharon never could.

The night before Mom left, I was finally strong enough for us to accept the McNeill's dinner invitation. It was a little tight in the front of Trisha's truck with the three of us, but Mom was delighted when Trisha took the scenic route pointing out celebrity homes, Warner Brothers and stuff that interested mom far more than it ever did me.

She especially loved it when Trisha went out of our way

to drive by Disney, and then later stop near the Hollywood sign to take pictures. I was embarrassed when mom insisted on asking another tourist to take a shot of the three of us so she could show all her friends, but Trisha went along with it with a smile.

At dinner we sat Mom next to Patrick, since she had an appreciation for a man who worked with numbers. Sure enough they hit it off, despite Skye occasionally setting the conversation off course with her weird ramblings.

"Did you hear that Patrick and I are going to Ireland in the fall?" Skye announced just after the trifle dessert had been passed around.

All eyes turn to Skye, and then Patrick, just in time to see his cheeks turn red.

"What happened to Morocco?" Paul asked.

"Oh, we're doing Ireland first," Patrick said.

"Morocco isn't in the right alignment right now for a visit, instead we are going to the thin places."

Trisha let out a long-suffering sigh and I had to look away from her rolling her eyes or I'd laugh.

"The thin places?" Mom asked.

Skye's eyes grew wide and she sat up taller on the edge of her chair. "Yes, it's from a Celtic belief in rare locales where the distance between heaven and earth collapses. We're hoping to catch a glimpse of the divine."

Paul narrowed his eyes at his brother and Patrick shrugged.

"What collapses exactly?" Trisha's dad asked. "I've never heard of distance collapsing. What kind of nonsense is this?"

"If you see the divine, will you make sure and say hey for me?" Trisha said. When Mom looked over at her and giggled, Trisha winked at her with that *I warned you* look. I leaned back in my chair and enjoyed that my idea of family had expanded beyond what I'd ever imagined.

Later Paul moved to the living room with his dad and Patrick, while the girls tackled their turn at the dishes. Meanwhile I stayed with the moms who remained in the dining room chatting away about the stress of having children in public service.

When Trisha returned to the table to check for stray dishes Mom took her hand.

"Your girl saved my son, Millie. I owe her everything."

"Oh stop now," Trisha said, wiggling out of her grasp.

Millie sniffed and then looked over at me with a gentle gaze and then back at Mom. "She hasn't told me any details. Just that Joe was at death's door."

"Indeed," said Mom as she poured Millie another glass of wine. "Did you know he was buried under a collapsed patio and she got him free and then dragged him into the pool just before the flames took over the yard?"

"My God! Is this true, Patricia?"

She shrugged. "I guess so."

"It's true," I said. "I owe your daughter my life, Millie."

Millie leaned back, fanning her face with her napkin. "This is too much. I'm beside myself."

Mom nodded. "I understand. I was the same."

Millie held up her wine glass. "You know my dear, I'm counting on these two getting married one day, and when they do we could host it here. We have a lovely backyard and the most understanding neighbors that will pay us no mind."

Trisha put her hands on her hips. "Hey, hey, hey . . . enough with the wedding talk. Do you see a ring on my finger?" She waved her hand at both of them. "Nope. So calm yourselves down."

"Would you like a ring?" I surprised myself by asking.

She turned to me with an alarmed look and then

narrowed her eyes as she slowly nodded her head. "Sure Murphy, two carats or nothing. I don't come cheap."

We were on a roll and it felt great. "Okay, two carats it is. Nothing's too good for my sweetheart."

She was close enough that I reached over and grabbed her by the hips, and pulled her to my lap. "You're mine, woman. Go big or go home."

I imagine the guys could hear the roar of laughter from the living room.

That night was the first time we made love since the firestorm. I'd been fighting my raw need for her from the day we left the hospital, but I think we were both afraid to even try since I was such a physical mess. But once we were kissing and naked under the sheets, we figured out that being tender and slow could be satisfying too. Besides there was plenty of time later for wild stuff, this was about love.

After, I pulled her into my arms and she rested her head on my chest as she settled down.

"Do you remember that time at the station that I told you that I'd paid attention to you longer than you realized?"

She nodded and then snuggled further into me.

"Do you want to know what I meant?"

She paused and then nodded slowly. "If you want to tell me."

I chuckled, it all sounded funny in the moment, when it wasn't funny at all at the time.

"It was your first day at the station. From the moment I met you I knew."

She lifted up and looked at me, her brow arched. "Really?"

"Yes, really."

"I had no idea," she said.

"Of course, I made sure you had no idea about how I felt. You were married, so it was impossible. After Sharon and all the game playing with other women I'd been with before her, I needed someone who'd be straight with me and always have my back. I realized you were exactly the kind of woman I'd always wanted, yet never had. You were right in front of me, but you couldn't be mine. It was torture. I asked Chief if we could fix the schedules so I'd never be working with you."

She looked up at me, recognition lighting up her face. "So after my marriage imploded . . ."

I nodded. "I knew this was my chance."

"But I chased you," she argued. "I offered my land to you."

"And I accepted," I said. "I knew you needed time, and that was the one thing I had on my side. I'm a patient man."

"Wow," she said.

"Wow?" I asked.

"Well, remind me not to play cards with you because I bet you're masterful at not showing your hand."

So the weeks passed and good things were happening. Trisha's house sold above asking price after only two days on the market, despite or perhaps because of, all that fancy furniture inside.

And I had to hand it to her ex, Mike—his friend Bruno was a craftsman and artist and he fixed Betty up beyond what I'd hoped for. Mike also insisted on paying for the work that insurance didn't cover from his part of the house proceeds.

I respected him for that, stepping up like a man and following up with Bruno and sending me pictures of the progress when I couldn't physically get there. Through the process of my healing and Betty's repair, we found our peace.

It took a while to get Trisha to agree to our plot of land in the hills of Burbank. After Malibu she didn't want to live anywhere near wild brush. But I convinced her saying what were the odds that we'd be trapped in a wildfire again. As I figure it, we have a free pass for life.

Yesterday we went to see the progress on the KitHaus that Trisha wanted in our "compound" as she calls it. The modular home that she calls Burt, is bigger than Betty and not on wheels, but all stream-lined and modern. Jeanine had told her about the L.A. company that designs and builds them.

The best part is that now I get to tease her that it's *kind-of* a tiny house. She teases me back that she needed a back-up place to sleep when I piss her off. But based on the full kitchen that's the focal point of the space I suspect she was angling to get me cooking again. I think I might be ready to do just that.

We went for the whole thing—the hot-tub, the outdoor shower, and a wide deck between Betty and Burt. It should all be done right before I return to work at the station. I've really appreciated Jeanine putting us up, but I'm ready for Trisha and I to be in our own place so we can start our new life together.

So now as Trisha sits across from me on the deck attached to Jeanine's guesthouse, I'm sure you aren't surprised to know that there's nothing about this woman that I'll ever take for granted. Trisha gave me life, not just that day in Malibu, but the day she let me into her heart and gave me a reason to take a chance on love again.

Every day, one way or another, I thank her for saving

me. She normally tells me to shut up, or rolls her eyes and says that I would've done it for her or any of the guys. But today she falls quiet instead.

Reaching over, she takes my hand, and squeezes it gently.

"So now we're even," she says.

"How's that?" I ask, and wait for her snarky reply.

"We saved each other, Joe."

God I love this woman.

My breath catches as our eyes meet. She nods. There's an intensity in her gaze that can't be denied. I hold my arms open. "Come here, sweetheart."

She gives me a lazy smile and navigates her way onto my lap carefully. She doesn't need to be so tentative. I keep telling her not to worry. I'm healed and strong as ever, albeit with a metal rod in my leg.

When I pull her close, she nuzzles her face against my neck.

"This is nice," she whispers

"Hmm," I hum. "I love you, T. Rex."

I can feel her lips spread into a smile, and I swear I sense her heart fluttering as she lets out a contented sigh.

"Ditto, Murphy. Now shut up and give me a kiss."

And I do.

Also by Ruth Clampett

Wet~L.A. Untamed Series Book 1

Animate Me

Mr. 365

Work of Art~Book 1 The Inspiration

Work of Art~Book 2 The Unveiling

Work of Art~Book 3 The Masterpiece

Wok of Art~The Collection

Many thanks to those of you that
take a moment to leave a review
~ it's much appreciated.

Acknowledgements

The experience of writing this book made my admiration for firefighters and their families grow tenfold. I have so much appreciation and respect for the brave women and men that put their own safety on the line to help others.

Thank you to my wonderful friends who have held my hand through the creation of this story: Erika, Susi, Dawn, Kellie, Suzie, Lisa, Glorya and DJ. And a big shout out to my #1 girl, my daughter Alex, who always inspires me and lets me know she's proud of my efforts. It was such fun working with her on the BURN trailer.

I love our community of indie bloggers, authors, and readers and I'm so grateful for their support of my work. Thank you!

Huge thanks to my wonderful content editor, Angela Borda, who with great humor and grace pointed me back to the correct path with this story every time I veered off course. Her many talents and kindness make me look forward to the editing process.

My cover designer, Jada D'Lee is the yin to my bookcover yang. She puts up with my nit picky ways and outlandish suggestions. The requirements for the BURN cover had all the potential to create a hot mess and yet once again Jada made magic. Thank you so so much, my friend.

It's been a delight working on promoting BURN with Jenn Watson from Social Butterfly PR. She has an astounding ability to calmly talk me through my anxious musings, and make me laugh at all the crazy. Our friendship is the icing on the cake.

Thank you Flavia Viotti and Meire Dias of Bookcase Agency for believing in me, and my stories. I appreciate your support so much.

Many thanks to Melissa, of There For You Editing, for cleaning up the error of my ways...and to Christine of Perfectly Publishable for doing a terrific job formatting.

Love and thanks also to smart friends Elli, Helena, Marla and Angie who all contributed to the book's final polish. And a special second shout out to Elli Reid for her amazing and inspiring Pinterest board for BURN.

Finally, a heartfelt thanks to you, dear reader. Writing is my passion and I love my characters like old friends. The fact that you read my work and share your enthusiasm for it completes the circle of joy for me in a profound way. I am very grateful.

About the Author

Ruth Clampett is a 21st century woman aspiring to be Wonder Woman . . . now if she could only find her cape and magic lasso. Meanwhile she's juggling motherhood, a full-time job running her own art business, and writing romance late at night. Travel is her second obsession after writing, and it's enabled her to meet reader and writer friends all over the world. She's happily frazzled, and wouldn't change a thing about her crazy life.

The rooms in her home are all painted different colors and her books are equally varied, infusing humor, drama, and passion into the romantic lives of strong heroines and their worthy and determined counterparts.

Ruth has published seven books: *Animate Me, Mr. 365,* the *Work of Art Trilogy, WET and BURN.* She grew up and still happily resides in Los Angeles, and is heavily supervised by her teenage daughter, lovingly referred to as Snarky, who loves traveling with her mom with a sketchbook in hand.

Connect with Ruth:

RuthClampettWrites.com
https://twitter.com/RuthyWrites

For book stuff:
https://www.facebook.com/RuthClampettWrites

For a more general stuff:
https://www.facebook.com/RuthClampett
http://instagram.com/Ruth_Clampett